Praise for the Novels of
Anna J. Evans

"Anna J. Evans weaves a tale full of passion, intrigue, betrayal, and friendship that will leave readers in awe of the raw power behind the words."   —Romance Junkies

"Enough sexual heat to create an avalanche."
—Fallen Angel Reviews

"Arousing, amorous . . . pulled me right into their sexual encounters. . . . Ms. Evans's storytelling ability was amazing, without a single flaw."   —The Romance Studio

"A powerful story about the deep and undeniable connection between soul mates. . . . The love scenes were so primal and raw that you're going to want to keep a spare pair of dry panties, a bucket of ice, and extra batteries nearby."   —TwoLips Review

"Extraordinary. . . . I didn't put this down until it was read all the way through."   —Romance Divas

Skin Deep

ANNA J. EVANS

HEAT

HEAT

Published by New American Library,
a division of Penguin Group (USA) Inc.,
375 Hudson Street, New York, New York 10014, USA
Penguin Group (Canada), 90 Eglinton Avenue East, Suite 700, Toronto,
Ontario M4P 2Y3, Canada (a division of Pearson Penguin Canada Inc.)
Penguin Books Ltd., 80 Strand, London WC2R 0RL, England
Penguin Ireland, 25 St. Stephen's Green, Dublin 2,
Ireland (a division of Penguin Books Ltd.)
Penguin Group (Australia), 250 Camberwell Road, Camberwell, Victoria 3124,
Australia (a division of Pearson Australia Group Pty. Ltd.)
Penguin Books India Pvt. Ltd., 11 Community Centre,
Panchsheel Park, New Delhi - 110 017, India
Penguin Group (NZ), 67 Apollo Drive, Rosedale, North Shore 0632,
New Zealand (a division of Pearson New Zealand Ltd.)
Penguin Books (South Africa) (Pty.) Ltd., 24 Sturdee Avenue,
Rosebank, Johannesburg 2196, South Africa

Penguin Books Ltd., Registered Offices:
80 Strand, London WC2R 0RL, England

First published by Heat, an imprint of New American Library,
a division of Penguin Group (USA) Inc.

First Printing, July 2009
3   5   7   9   10   8   6   4   2

Copyright © Stacey Iglesias Fedele, 2009
All rights reserved

HEAT is a trademark of Penguin Group (USA) Inc.

LIBRARY OF CONGRESS CATALOGING-IN-PUBLICATION DATA:

Evans, Anna J.
Skin deep/Anna J. Evans.
p. cm.
ISBN 978-0-451-22697-6
I. Sexual dominance and submission—Fiction.   I. Title.
PS3605.V363S57 2009
813'.6—dc22   2009003253

Printed in the United States of America

For Mike, my husband, love, and friend.

Acknowledgments

Thanks so much to Kerry Donovan, who I'm pretty sure is one of the best editors in the world, and to the entire team at NAL. You have made this process a complete joy. Thank you so much for all your hard work, commitment to excellence, and professionalism. Also a big thanks to Caren Johnson, my fabulous agent, and, as always, to my family. I treasure you all so much. Thanks for your love and support.

Skin Deep

She was nearly naked again, wearing nothing but tiny black panties, and his hands were everywhere but where she needed them to be. Calloused fingertips traced the column of her spine down to the small of her back, then deliberately avoided the aching place between her legs as he gripped her thighs and pulled them apart.

Wider. Wider. Strong hands moving to grip her ankles with a careless ownership that made a soft moan escape her lips.

"See there, Nicky. Aren't you glad I caught you in time?" His voice was as rough as the rope he used to secure first one ankle and then the other to the bedpost behind her. As he worked, Nicky could feel her mind softening, sinking into a pool of cool, clear water even as her entire body caught fire.

Descending into submissive space, into that place in her mind where nothing mattered but one man and what he would command her to do, had always reminded Nicky of floating. Drifting into a delicious dream where pleasure and pain fused together, where mind and body finally made peace with each other, where

1

her consciousness focused to a knifepoint and she finally felt completely alive.

Subbing was a better high than any drug and three times as addictive. It was like flying without any fear of the fall.

At least not any fear until it was all over . . . and it was too late to take back those parts of herself she'd given away.

"Tell me, Nicky." He'd finished with her ankles and was now hovering above her prone form, braced on the hands he'd placed at either side of her shoulders, close enough she could feel his heat but not the comforting weight of his body. His breath was warm against the back of her neck, his lips brushing lightly against the sensitive skin as he spoke. "Tell me what you want."

Nicky shivered, but not because of the cold. She'd grown accustomed to the chill in the cabin. Too bad she couldn't grow accustomed to what this man did to her, couldn't seem to control her body's instinctive response to the dominant he'd become.

Of course, even if he hadn't grown into just the kind of man her twisted libido craved like a fat man craves cake, just the fact that he was Jack would have probably been enough. The familiar smell of his skin made her wetter than she'd been in years, the feel of his large hands moving to her wrists had her nipples drawn into tight, aching points, and the way he said "want" was nearly enough to make her come. Right then, without as much as a fingertip between her legs.

And he knew exactly what he was doing to her. The bastard.

"Fuck you," she whispered, the defiant words kicking her arousal into overdrive. Unfortunately for her, the only thing more arousing than being a good girl was being a bad one. That's why she didn't fight him as he rechecked the cuffs securing her to the headboard. Fighting only fueled the fire.

"I don't think so. No more distractions. We're going to finish this," he said, the surety in his voice underscored by the buzzing of the tattoo machine beside the bed. Her pulse pounded unhealthily in her ears and a cold sweat broke out between her shoulder blades as she realized a needle could be only a few inches away from her skin. "Tell me what you want, Nicky. This is your last chance."

But she didn't say a word, only pressed her face into the cool quilt and waited for the familiar sting. Waited for Jack to mark her flesh the way he'd already marked her heart.

Chapter One

Did it still count as a kidnapping if she went with him willingly? What if she wanted out of the car once she realized they weren't stopping anywhere inside the Los Angeles city limits? If he simply refused to stop, would that decision automatically make him a felon?

Even at sixteen, Nicky hadn't been easily intimidated. He couldn't imagine her sitting quietly beside him as he headed off into the middle of Bumfuck mountain country, no matter how physically intimidating most of the population found giant Jackson Bledsoe of *Sin City Ink*. Nicky would remember good old Jack from when they were kids, when he'd been a six-foot-two-inch beanpole with elbows bigger than his biceps who had his ass beat by their foster father on a weekly basis.

She would try to run and he'd have to use the rope he'd packed in his trunk if he didn't want her leaping out of a moving vehicle to gain her freedom. Because she would do something like that. She'd always been wild, and from what he'd observed in the bar earlier tonight, she'd only gotten bat-shit crazier with age.

Not that he was in a position to throw stones. . . .

What he was planning was more than crazy. It was stupid, criminal, and could completely ruin the life he'd worked so hard to build. He should start up his truck and get the hell out of here right now. Do not pass go, do not kidnap the only girl he'd ever loved, do not collect multiple felony charges.

"This is crazy. You realize that, right?" His best friend and business partner, Christian, echoed Jackson's thoughts as he took a pull on his flask. There was whiskey in there tonight, if Jack wasn't mistaken. Jack had decided to stick with a Coke while they staked out the staff parking lot of the bar. No need to risk a DUI as well as abduction charges. "You haven't seen her in how long? Six years?"

"Eight."

"And she didn't respond to any of your letters?"

Jack's teeth ground together. "Nope." Not with words anyway. Instead, she had ripped every letter into tiny pieces and mailed them back to his address in Vegas. So she *had* responded, just not in a way that made Jack think she would be accommodating to what he had in mind.

"But you still think it's a good idea to just show up where she works and ask her to go away for a long weekend so you can work on her tat?"

"Yep."

His friend laughed as he clapped Jack on the shoulder. "You've lost it, man. You really are crazy."

If he only knew.

But Jack hadn't told Christian his real plans. No need to make him an accessory to a felony and ruin two lives instead of one.

"Hell, who knows? She might enjoy a little vacation," Jack

said, not believing the words even as he spoke them. "Or maybe I'll be able to change her mind about the money. Fifteen grand isn't chump change and she must need cash. Why else would she be working here?"

"Maybe she's slumming." Christian shrugged as his dark eyes scanned the parking lot of the bar where they'd finally found Nicky.

It wasn't in a bad part of the greater Los Angeles area, but it was by far the raunchiest place still serving drinks in Pasadena. Most of the town had been converted into one big outdoor mall, purely PG stuff, but the Hard Way had managed to stay open. Probably because it was the one place in the sleepy suburb where a man could still hope to see some skin while he slammed back a few beers.

The oversize bar doubled as a stage for drunk college girls looking to add their bras to the collection hanging from the ceiling and the bartenders were scantily clad ex–porn stars from the Valley. They took turns dancing on nights when the coeds were hitting the books instead of the bars.

Except Nicky, of course. She was a lingerie model for the biggest fetish store in Los Angeles. Or had been at one time. Jack hadn't seen any new pictures of the stunning natural blonde with the big hazel eyes for nearly two years. Not that he was a glutton for punishment who checked the Good and Trashy Lingerie Web site on a weekly basis or anything. . . .

God, what was he doing here? Obsessing over Nicky's picture on a Web site or writing her letters was one thing. But tracking her down in person with every intention of forcing her to take a little trip up to the San Bernardino Mountains was certifiably insane.

Exactly. So get out of here. Now. Before this woman ruins your life a second time.

"I don't know, man," Christian said, his tone revealing his obvious appreciation of Nicole "Angel" Remington. "If she looks anything like she used to, it's hard to believe this girl can't get modeling work anymore. I checked out the Web site this morning. I've never seen real tits like that. No wonder you're still hung up on—"

Jack silenced Christian with a look. No one talked about Nicky that way, even his best friend. It didn't matter that she'd betrayed Jackson and broken his heart back when he was a stupid kid. He wouldn't tolerate anyone treating her like a piece of meat, even if he *was* planning to do nearly the same thing himself.

But then, he'd earned the right to teach Nicole a thing or two about payback.

"Listen, Jackson." Christian looked completely serious for one of the first times in their five-year friendship. "I know you're a big boy and can take care of yourself, but—"

"Exactly, so get lost already. Before you get too drunk to drive yourself back to the hotel," Jack said. It was twenty minutes until closing time. He had to get rid of Christian before then.

Christian sighed. "Well, if you ask me, you shouldn't be wasting your time or your money on shit from the past."

"I didn't ask you. For your opinion, or your company," Jackson snapped. In fact, he'd done his best to ditch his friend, but the other man had insisted on accompanying him to L.A.

"Easy, killer. All I'm saying is that we could be in Miami getting pussy right now instead of wasting time with a bunch of Los Angeles bitches," Christian said, his Puerto Rican accent coloring the city's name so it sounded like some exotic mecca. Which it was, in a way. At least for the two of them.

After three years as stars of the reality show *Sin City Ink*, they had quit the entertainment biz to go national with a string of tattoo parlors. The Sin City Ink locations in Reno and Vegas would stay open and be joined by new locations in Memphis, New Orleans, and Miami. Jackson and Christian were going to cash in on their celebrity status and cement their reputations as the best of the best, *the* people to trust when you were looking for more than your average ink, when you wanted certified body *art*.

"You've got a matching tattoo with the chick, Jackson, and she managed to cash in on it. That doesn't mean she's got a piece of you." Christian barreled on, despite the warning look Jackson shot in his direction. "You were young. You made a mistake and got burned. Who cares if—"

"I care." Jack took another swig of his own drink, the warm, sickeningly sweet Coke as foul as his mood. If he hadn't already been determined to go through with his plan, what he'd observed tonight would have more than done the job. He'd only stepped into the bar for a few minutes, but it had been enough to see everything he needed to see.

Nicky still had the tattoo he'd given her the night before his eighteenth birthday, not that it was any surprise. She'd used the tat to make a name for herself and obviously hadn't been impressed by Jack's letters asking her to have the thing modified. After all, his work had been as responsible for her nickname as her angelic good looks.

The five-inch figure on her shoulder was the first of the angel tattoos Jackson had later become famous for, an exact match to the wide-eyed fallen angel on his own forearm. It was the only one of his tattoos he hadn't sketched himself and the last remaining example of his father's work. Adrian Bledsoe had never made a living or a name for himself before his death, but he'd been a real talent, a more gifted artist than Jackson could ever dream of being.

More than anything in the world, Jackson wished he could go back to that night when he was ten years old and grab more than one of his father's sketches before he ran from their burning apartment. Maybe then he'd have more of his dad, the only real family he'd ever had, to hold on to and wouldn't be so damned obsessed with this one tattoo. Or with the girl he'd once loved enough to share a piece of his soul with her.

Your soul? It's just skin. You should know that better than anyone.

Ah, but there was the kicker. He *should* know a lot of things. But right now, all he knew was that he had to convince Nicky to let him cover the tattoo, to rework it into something no longer recognizable as the same angel on his own arm.

It tore him apart knowing she still sported the profession of his adolescent love on her shoulder. Once the evidence of his foolish belief in soul mates and happily ever after was erased, Jackson was certain he'd finally be able to let go of his obsession with his former flame and move on.

Cultures across the world recognized the mystical power of working permanent ink into human flesh. Jackson had never been one to believe art was anything more than art, but he couldn't deny the connection he felt with the only person in the world with whom he shared the exact same ink. A connection that had haunted him for eight long years as he tried to forget about the last night they'd shared and the promises they'd made. Promises Nicky had broken as easily as she'd broken his heart.

Your soul, your broken heart. God. You're right. You need to do whatever it takes to get this girl out of your system so you can stop being such a fucking pussy.

"Are you laughing?" Christian asked, obviously as surprised by the phenomenon as Jackson himself.

"Yeah." He smiled and downed the last of his soda. "I was thinking about Delilah and her pussy lecture."

"The one about the power of the pussy to give life and pleasure and how we shouldn't use the sacred name of her holy vajay-jay as an insult?" Christian asked, his contempt for their Vegas office manager's feminist rants clear in his voice, though his expression softened perceptibly.

No matter how often his partner insisted his decision to transfer Delilah to the new Miami location with them was purely good business, Jackson suspected Christian had a thing for Dee and would gladly cut off a finger or two to get into her holy vajay-jay. Too bad Delilah couldn't see through Christian's machismo bullshit to the extremely decent guy inside.

She actually seemed to have a thing for Jackson, and had asked him for drinks on more than one occasion. He'd always declined. Jackson didn't mix business with pleasure. And even if he did, he didn't feel anything but friendship for the magenta-haired manager. He'd never felt anything but friendship, or lust, for any woman . . . but one.

And it was high time he did whatever it took to get *her* out of his system. He was nearly thirty, for god's sake. It was time to get the hell over his high school crush, and that wasn't going to happen while they still shared the same ink. He'd tried everything he could think of to stop thinking about Nicky and their matching tattoos—hell, he'd even gone to see a therapist a few times—but nothing helped. Something had to be done. He was on the fast track to having everything he'd ever wanted and he wasn't going to waste another eight years of his life fixated on the one that got away.

"Yep. That's the one. Speaking of the power of the pussy, I think it's time for me to head back to the hotel, see if I can snag a starlet or two at the bar," Christian said. The two men got out of the truck, slamming the doors behind them. "You sure you won't come back with me?"

"Nope. See you in a few days."

"Or a few minutes, if she turns you down." Christian paused at the door to his BMW roadster. "You know what, I think I'll come in and watch this go down. See what she has to say—"

"No, you can't come in. I don't want to be recognized."

"Are you kidding me? You're giant Jack Bledsoe. People are going to—"

"You think people at a bar like this watch Brava?" Jackson asked, happier than ever that their reality show hadn't been on one of the major networks. A certain degree of celebrity he could contend with, but being recognized everywhere he went would have driven him insane. "Besides, I'm undercover." He pulled his hat lower on his face and tugged down the arms of his black sweater, concealing his full-sleeve tattoos.

Without them, he was a fairly average-looking guy with short dark brown hair, dark brown eyes, and unremarkable features. Not ugly by any means, but his wasn't the face that had kept female viewers glued to the screen for the three seasons of *Sin City Ink.* Christian was the pretty boy. If anyone was going to be recognized, it would be him. Jack doubted even Nicky would be able to guess his own identity, at least not right away. He'd shot up three more inches and gained about sixty pounds of pure muscle since the last time she'd seen him. Unless, of course, she watched the show . . . and had seen the kind of man he'd grown into.

Jack hadn't allowed himself to think much about that, to imagine she might be sufficiently interested to follow his life. Thinking like that was a great way to let this situation get out of hand. He wasn't here to make nice with an old friend—he was here to right a wrong and move on with his life. End of story.

"I'll have my cell if you need me," Jackson said, a grim smile on his face as he stood and shoved his wallet in his pocket.

"I'll be in Miami by tomorrow afternoon, man. I won't need anything." Christian slammed the door to his roadster and rolled down the window. "Call me if you come to your senses and want to be on the flight tomorrow morning."

Jack waited until Christian's car was out of sight before walking around to the front entrance of the Hard Way. There was no longer a doorman on duty and the crowd inside had thinned considerably since ten o'clock. As he strode across the plank floors, the bartender with long black hair announced last call, but the clutch of men surrounding the bar looked far from ready to call it a night.

But then why would they, when Nicky was holding court on top of the bar and kept getting more and more daring with her dancing? No matter that state regulations expressly forbid the bartenders from stripping, Jack expected clothes to start coming off any second, an expectation obviously shared by the men surrounding her like a pack of dogs.

His hands tightened into fists on their own accord, his body itching to defend Nick the way he had when they were kids. Back then she'd been an innocent fourteen-year-old attracting the wrong kind of attention from the senior boys at school. They'd known she was a foster kid and had no one to look out for her. She'd been cornered behind the gym within three days of transferring to Carson City High.

Jackson had earned himself two weeks of detention for beating the shit out of the three football players who had decided it would be fun to pass around the new girl, but it had been worth it. No one messed with his foster sister again. He wouldn't even allow himself to touch her until she turned sixteen, though she'd made her interest abundantly clear. But Jack had been nearly two years older and hadn't wanted to take advantage, no matter how many nights he had lain awake with a raging hard-on, fantasizing about the girl sleeping in the next room.

Apparently she still had the power to inspire a similar reaction in him and just about any other member of the penis-possessing segment of the population. Jackson was going to have to watch his step. Pulling Nicky away from her pack of horny and delusional admirers was likely to make tempers flare. He couldn't afford to attract that kind of attention. He needed to get Nicky out of here without anyone taking notice.

That meant he'd have to stay back in the shadows and watch, bide his time until she was finished with her performance, no matter how torturous a part of him found it to see Nicky bumping and grinding for a bunch of horny drunks.

Or how arousing the other part of him found it.

Damn, but she was even sexier than he remembered. The way she tossed her long hair over her shoulder, flashing those big eyes in a way that seemed to promise untold pleasure to every man in the room, made his entire body ache. It was going to be hellish to be trapped in a cabin with her for three days without being able to touch her, kiss her, be buried deep inside the only woman who had ever—

Who ever ruined your life. Focus, Bledsoe.

His inner voice was right. He had to focus because there was no turning back now. Soon he would be leaving Pasadena with Nicky by his side, either as his passenger or his captive. At least *that* choice would be hers.

Five more bucks from her regular Carl, three from the thirty-something Latino guy, and two from his girlfriend. Combined with the twenty she'd lifted from the frat boy too drunk to see what he was fishing from his wallet, the money she'd made in the past ten minutes brought Nicky up to an even four hundred for the night. It made it worth the anxiety she felt every time she took her turn on top of the bar. And it was more than enough to pay for an entire hour of very expensive attorney time . . . if she ever got the guts to hire the woman she'd met with last week.

She knew Derrick expected her to sign the divorce decree as it stood without a word of protest. He would probably bust a blood vessel if he learned she was even considering hiring representation to fight him in court. Her soon-to-be ex-husband was *that* certain of his ability to scare her absolutely shitless. But then, he had every reason to be sure of himself. She had rarely dared to stand up to him during their three-year relationship. Back in the beginning, however, there hadn't been so very much at stake. . . .

But she couldn't think about that now. Right now she had to concentrate on raking it in, doing whatever it took to part the men surrounding her from the last of their cash before her shift ended. And if that included getting a little creative, so be it. She didn't particularly enjoy having some stranger suck a body shot out of her belly button, but what she enjoyed didn't matter. Nothing mattered anymore except reclaiming her life from the man who held it hostage.

"Time for a shot!" Nicky forced a naughty smile onto her face as she pulled her shirt a little higher, baring more of her midriff. The little white schoolgirl top tied at the waist, combined with the shortest kilt she could find, was always a recipe for big tips. Cliché as it might be, dirty old men still went crazy for a schoolgirl uniform, especially if you were willing to lie down and let one of them suck alcohol off your stomach while wearing it.

"Pick me, Angel!" someone drunkenly called from the opposite end of the bar as she poured the cinnamon liqueur into the well of her navel.

"Not tonight, gentlemen," she said, winking at the Latino guy's girlfriend. "I'm in the mood for a softer touch." A new song came over the sound system and Nicky clapped along as the blushing girl sidled up to the bar.

The roar of the men cheering as the petite woman held back her dark curls and suckled the Goldschlager from Nicky's stomach was too loud for her to tell for certain, but the song sounded like vintage Rolling Stones. One of her favorite bands of all time. Hell, she might actually be enjoying herself right now if she were just getting a little wild on a Friday night, not playing the tart for a crowd.

It had been so long since she'd been able to just go dancing, to hit a club or a bar for fun with some girlfriends. Not that dancing at the Hard Way was torture. She'd never been particularly shy about her body, and her time as a celebrity lingerie model for

Good and Trashy Lingerie had made her even less so. Still, she wished she didn't have to be on display every night. At least not right now, not when she still felt so vulnerable.

Screw it. Suck it up and give the customers what they want.

Nicky hopped back to her feet and finished out the song with her usual flair, fueling just enough naughty into her moves to keep the men panting, but keeping it clean enough that the crowd didn't get out of hand. It was somewhat of an art, but one she'd perfected in the past month. She worked up and down the length of the bar one last time, collecting another twenty bucks before the closing bell sounded.

"Happy Trails to You," the bar's signature closing song, began to play. Nicky stopped dancing, drawing sounds of protest from several of the drunker patrons. "See you tomorrow, gentlemen," she said with a grin and a flutter of her fingers.

Always leave them wanting more.

"Hey, Angel, can you clean up the well?" Cassandra shouted from where she was loading the last batch of glasses into the dishwasher behind the bar. "I've got everything else ready to close."

"Sure thing," Nicky said, already feeling the familiar exhaustion that washed over her at the end of the night, once the adrenaline rush was over.

She pulled her shirt down and was preparing to leap from her perch when a large hand closed gently around her ankle. Her first instinct when customers tried to take looking at the goods to the next level was usually a slap on the wrist and then a kick somewhere more painful if they didn't wise up fast. But for some reason, the feel of this hand was different, intriguing, electric.

Then she heard the voice that went with the hand and dry panties were a thing of the past. "Nice tattoo." Damn. A voice like that, so deep it practically had its own reverb, was nearly enough to make her forget she'd sworn off men for at least the next ten years. Or twenty, depending on the day and how much time she'd had to think about Derrick.

"Thanks. It's what made me famous," she said, smiling down into the shadowed face of one of the biggest men she'd ever seen in real life.

He was six and a half feet tall, at least, and the way his arms and chest stretched out his sweater left no doubt he was strong enough to snap her in half without breaking a sweat. The very thought of something like that should have been enough to cool her rapidly heating blood, but it wasn't. She was freaking hopeless when it came to big, strong, domineering men.

Even after three years with a dom who had made her life a living hell and taken away everything that meant something to her, a part of Nicky still fantasized about finding someone man enough to take control of her the way a real dominant would. The way she'd seen some of the men at the clubs treat their subs. With respect. Like they were people to be treasured, protected, and valued, not lower life-forms as interchangeable as sheets of Kleenex.

"Doubt it. I think you've got a few other things going for you." His thumb flicked gently across the inside of her ankle, sending a sizzle of awareness racing up her leg. God, she'd never been so glad she chose heels instead of her fuck-me boots.

Though those could have been good, too. She could already see herself pulling this man into her tiny studio in South Pasadena and taking off everything but her boots. Then she'd turn around, lean over the bed, and show him how wet she was, how ready to take whatever he was packing in those black jeans. He wouldn't say a word, or maybe he'd just tell her to spread her legs a little wider. Then he'd be behind her, large hands gripping her hips, thick cock spearing inside where she was—

"Hey, we've got to close up," Nicky said, her voice betraying exactly where her thoughts had been headed. "But I know a diner not too far from here. We could get a coffee."

"I'd love a coffee. My car is in the back lot," her mystery man said, reaching a hand up to help her off the bar. "I could give you a ride."

Oh, dear, she just *bet* he could give her a ride.

She hadn't even seen his face, but he practically radiated sex. Controlling, demanding, *completely-dominating-the-woman-he-was-fucking* sex. The kind she'd been craving for nearly two years during her Derrick-imposed celibacy. Two years without even the comfort of another warm, human body, let alone the fucking she craved.

A good *fucking*—not lovemaking, not even gentle sex—that's what she wanted. What she needed. Nicky was a carnal person, always had been. She needed it rough, hot, and primal, and it was past time for her to scratch her itch. Tomorrow she would be back here, working another double shift. But tonight was for her.

Or even better yet, for him. There was nothing she enjoyed as much as bringing a big man like this to his knees with pure, unbridled lust.

Nicky smiled, wishing she had the guts to skip coffee and head straight back to her apartment with a total stranger, but even two years of celibacy hadn't made her that daring. Of course, she could at least clue this guy in on what she was hoping they would get around to doing after coffee.

Ignoring the hand he held out, she leapt straight into the big guy's arms, looping her hands around his neck and her long legs around his thick waist. Hot damn. It looked like this guy was as big below the belt as he was everywhere else. And he was hard, hot, and ready, so erect she could feel him throbbing against her even through his jeans and her damp panties.

"Looks like we're on the same page," she said, breath coming faster as she flexed the muscles in her legs, urging her clit into even tighter contact with his cock. "And I really hope you—"

Oh . . . god. Why hadn't she made sure she got a good look at his face before she started humping him like a nympho on roofies?

"Something wrong, Nick?" he asked, even as he set her down on the ground. Several seconds passed in awkward silence before she could remember how to form words.

And once she did, only one word came to mind.

Shit.

Shitshitshitshitshitshit!

Of *course* the first man she'd decided to sleep with since her breakup would be the one man she never thought she'd see again. It was Jack. And whoa if he hadn't grown up in all the right places. Back in high school he'd been sweet, lovable, and sexy, but now he was . . .

"Why don't we get out of here, Nicky? We can go for a drive, catch up. Get your things," he said, his tone revealing there would be no argument.

Trouble. That's what he was, trouble.

And damn her if that didn't make her panties even wetter.

"I don't think that's such a good idea, Jack," she said, moving slowly behind the bar and concentrating on capping the well liquor no matter how much a part of her wanted to hasten to obey him. But then, she supposed some sub tendencies died hard. "We haven't— I mean it's been years and— I've just got a lot going on right now, and I—"

"It's just a ride. And talk."

"That's not what it felt like a few seconds ago." She blushed, cursing the shot of Jack Daniel's she'd tossed back before her last turn on the bar. This was all the whiskey's fault. She never would have jumped into a stranger's arms and started rubbing herself all over him like a cat in heat without it.

She might have *wanted* to, but she wouldn't have actually *done* it.

"That was a few seconds ago." He smiled, and she caught a flash of the skinny boy who'd appointed himself her protector from the second they met, making her wonder how much he had really changed. "I came here to talk old times, not re-create them. Though I wouldn't put up a fight if you decided you wanted more than talk. Seems we've still got the same chemistry."

"Seems like it," she said, finding it easier to return his grin. She capped the last of the well drinks and eased out from behind the bar, highly conscious of Cassandra's eyes on her and Jackson. The other bartender had been giving her shit for weeks, begging Nicky to let her set her up with an eligible screw or two. Now Nicky could practically feel the "go for it" vibes surging toward her from across the room. Unfortunately, Jackson wasn't any more her idea of eligible than the ex–porn star crowd Cassandra hung with. "But that's probably not a good idea."

"Some things are better with a stranger."

"Yes." She nodded, grateful he understood. He didn't seem angry or disappointed, either. In fact, he was amazingly casual about the whole thing. If she hadn't felt how hard he'd been, she would never have guessed he was interested at all. Which was a good thing . . . though she couldn't deny a certain disappointment.

"But other things are better with an old friend." He stepped a little closer, making Nicky tilt her head back to look him in the eye. When he spoke again, his voice was soft, almost a whisper. "Come on, let's go for a ride."

"Go, Angel," Cassandra said, flashing a knowing smile as she wiped down the bar. "I'll finish closing up and Pedro's still in the break room. He'll walk me to my car."

Nicky hesitated for the barest moment more. There was still a voice inside her that urged her to forget she'd ever seen Jackson, to grab her purse and call a cab to take her back to South Pasadena alone. But it was a quiet voice, one that couldn't compete with her curiosity. Why was Jack here? Why had he tracked her down now, after all these years? She had to know.

Besides, Jackson was the most trustworthy person she'd ever known. Hell, the only trustworthy person she'd ever known. If he said he was cool with talk and nothing more, he meant it.

"Just let me grab my purse," she said, strangely exhilarated by the thought of just taking a drive with this man.

But then, some of her best memories were of being in the car with Jack, racing down the desert back roads, imagining they were on their way somewhere, anywhere but back to Carson City, Nevada.

Chapter Two

"So, tell me, what brings you to L.A.?" Nicky's bare feet were propped on his dashboard, just like in high school. Her long legs were the same shade of tan, but this time the tiny moon-shaped toenails were painted a deep black instead of cherry red.

Black like her soul, man. Don't forget it.

But it would be so easy to forget. To forget what he'd come for, what they'd been to each other, to forget the dreams she'd abandoned when she'd hauled ass out of Carson City the morning after his eighteenth birthday. From the second she'd jumped into his arms in the bar, he'd wanted to forget it all. To forget and to *fuck*. To strip away those black panties she was wearing and get balls-deep in Nicky.

She'd been more than ready for it before she'd realized who he was. Even then, she'd still agreed to go for a ride. She might very well be up for heading to the nearest hotel. They could check in for the weekend and he could have her in every filthy way he'd imagined for the past eight years. Maybe that alone would be enough to get her out of his system. Come Monday morning, he could drop her back in the parking lot of the bar and be done with his obsession forever.

"Is it business or pleasure?" she asked, reclining her chair until she was lying almost horizontal in the passenger's seat beside him.

Jack's eyes flicked to the newly bared skin at her midriff and then quickly back to the road. Jesus, who was he kidding? One weekend would never be enough. The second he felt that hot, tight little pussy encasing him, he'd be a goner. Fucking Nicky Remington had been an unparalleled pleasure and he was sure fucking Angel Remington could become a bona fide addiction. She'd had eight years to perfect what had been an amazing natural aptitude for sexing a man's soul from his body, and just the way she'd danced on the bar made it clear she'd been hard at work mastering the skill.

"I'm guessing business if I know you." Nicky let one of her knees relax outward, giving him a clear view of her panties. God. Damn. They were fairly modest as far as women's lingerie went and looked like sensible cotton, not anything lacy. But just knowing Nick's hot little cunt was beneath those granny panties was enough to get him hard enough to shatter glass.

"Something to do with that show you're in? I've never seen it, but I've heard you're great." Her legs squeezed back together, depriving him of that glimpse of black fabric.

Probably a good thing, since he should be keeping his eyes on the road. California drivers took no prisoners. You were expected to be going eighty miles an hour and tailing the driver in front of you close enough to count the dents on their bumper or it was grounds for a drive-by. Even at past midnight, Interstate 10 was hopping, packed with cars headed to Palm Springs and destinations beyond. He needed his attention on the traffic, not his passenger.

Thankfully the streetlights beside the highway would disappear in a few miles, once they were out of the city. Then it would be too dark to obsess about what Nicky was or wasn't revealing.

"So do you like being a reality television star?"

Jack shrugged and moved the car into the car-pool lane. In California, two people counted as a car pool. No wonder the traffic was so brutal.

"I thought you said we were going to talk while you drove?" she asked, a hint of amusement in her tone. "Don't tell me you've turned into a real man and can't do two things at the same time."

He smiled in spite of himself. Nicky had always been able to make him smile when no one else could. "You haven't asked where we're going."

"Maybe I don't care where we're going," she said, following the words with a sigh that sounded sadder than anything he'd ever heard out of her mouth.

It was just the tiniest exhalation of breath, but it spoke volumes. Even back in the day, when she'd been the new girl at Casa de la Hell—Jackson's nickname for his final foster home—she'd never been anything but upbeat and sassy. Nicky defined sass. She'd more than done her part to earn the occasional backhand from their foster father, Phil.

Phil. Such a fucking friendly name for such a demented bastard. Jackson wouldn't have blamed Nicky for running away from that man, if only she'd told him where she was going.

"I've got a cabin up in the mountains, not too far from Lake

Arrowhead. I figured we could have some privacy, hang out and drink a few beers and watch the snow fall," Jackson said, figuring now was as good a time as any to fill Nicky in on his plans.

Even she wasn't crazy enough to jump out of the car while going eighty on the interstate. It's when they turned off the highway that he'd have to get out the rope, assuming she wasn't any more accommodating to his in-person request than she'd been to his letters. Speaking of . . . or thinking of, anyway . . . might as well get that out in the open.

"I got the letters you sent back to me. That was a mature response."

"I'm sure it was." She laughed, but it was a short, bitter sound, not at all like the old Nicky. "Unfortunately it wasn't mine. I haven't been receiving my mail for a long time. Well, the past few weeks I've been getting mail at my new apartment, but nothing from you."

Jackson was quiet, taking in the information, knowing she would clarify if he stayed silent. Nicky always divulged information in bits and pieces. Stories burst from her like hiccups, interspersed with other random information totally unrelated to the matter at hand.

"You hungry? I'm dying for a burger. With onions. Lots of onions, the grilled kind."

He smiled again. At least some things were still the same.

She sniffed, then reached down and fiddled with the controls on her seat until she was nearly upright again. "My soon-to-be ex-husband intercepted all of my mail. He was very . . . controlling."

"That why he's going to be your ex?" Jackson asked.

"That's part of it," she said, her tone making it clear she would rather not talk about the man. Fine with Jack. He didn't

ANNA J. EVANS

like to think of any man in connection with Nicky. Part of his own set of mental glitches. "So what did the letters say?"

She sounded uncertain, and strangely . . . hopeful. Jack risked a look at her side of the car, but now it was too dark to see her expression clearly. "Just hello from an old friend."

"Bullshit."

"How do you know? You didn't read them." But he couldn't keep from grinning. This might actually work out. If Nicky hadn't been the one to rip up his letters, she could be open to having the angel tat modified.

"My bullshit meter still works fairly well. Most of the time." She laughed, a lighter sound this time. "So what else did the letters say?"

Okay. Here was the hard part. He actually kind of wished they weren't driving now that he knew Nicky hadn't read his request. This was the kind of thing more comfortably discussed if you were sitting down, looking someone in the eye, not driving down the highway at a million miles an hour.

But here is where they were.

"I was asking if you would be open to having me modify your angel tat."

"Why?"

Here was the tricky part, the part so much easier said in a letter. Good thing he wasn't the type of man who could only do things the easy way. "Obviously things didn't work out the way we planned when we decided to get identical tattoos, Nick. That's fine by me. You made your own choices. But I've come to the place in my life where I'd rather not have a matching tattoo with a woman I don't even know anymore."

"And you can't change yours because of your dad," she said. "That's a pretty sucky position to be in."

"Only if the woman in question isn't open to having me modify the tattoo." Casual, just keep it casual. "I've got all my stuff in the car, ink and—"

"This is hardly a car. It's an Expedition, for god's sake. It's like half an eighteen-wheeler. Lot different than that Impala you had in high school. Bet it doesn't die every three days."

"I'm one of the best in the business now," Jackson said, refusing to be distracted. "I was an amateur when I did that work on your shoulder. Now, I've got the skills to give you something really beautiful and unique."

"Though I did actually like that car a lot," she said, crossing her legs on the seat as she reached down to the floorboard for her purse. "It had personality."

"And don't worry. I'll do it for free."

She sucked in a deep breath and let it out through pursed lips. Even before she spoke, Jack knew he wasn't going to like what she had to say. "No, you won't. You won't do it at all. I'm sorry, Jack, but I'm not going to change the tattoo."

"Would fifteen grand change your mind?"

"You want to pay me to—" She seemed angry for a second, but when she spoke again her voice was soft, almost defeated sounding. "No, I'm sorry. It wouldn't."

"I understand it's become a big part of your professional persona, but—"

"It *is* my professional persona."

"Like I said in the bar, I think you have a few things—"

"My name is Angel now, for god's sake. Not legally, but it

might as well be." She flipped down the visor and opened the mirror, causing light to spill across her face, showing him how sincerely troubled she seemed as she dug through her purse. "That's what I'm known as and the tat is a big part of what I'm known *for*. I'm just now trying to get back in the business after two years. I can't change one of the most memorable things about me."

"That's understandable," Jack said, not losing hope just yet. "What if I reworked it so that you still had an angel? I could lengthen the wings, change up the colors, maybe even add some darker hair on one side so it looks like she's facing—"

"I can't," Nicky said, as she smoothed on a coat of berry-colored lipstick. No, gloss, that's what they called the stuff that made a woman's lips shine like she'd just been kissed, or just had her mouth smeared with—

Nope, not going to let his mind go there. Nicky was going to be pissed when she realized he didn't plan to take no for an answer. There was no chance she'd still want to go to bed with him, and he wasn't the type to take what wasn't freely offered.

Except control over what she's going to have tattooed on her skin for the rest of her life. Isn't that just as bad? How can you do that to someone, even someone who—

"You can, Nick, and you will. I'm going to modify your ink this weekend." He forced the words out through his clenched jaw, refusing to listen to the voice of reason. "If you decide what you want by Sunday afternoon, I'll do my best to accommodate your request. If not . . ."

"You wouldn't." But the way she flung her lipstick back into her purse with enough force to make it bounce back out again revealed she thought he would.

"This is something I feel very strongly about."

"Yeah? Well, I feel very strongly about getting the hell away from—"

His hand whipped out, closing tight around her upper arm, not hard enough to bruise, but firm enough to let her know he meant business. "Don't touch that door handle. You'll kill yourself if you jump out of a car going seventy. Do you understand me?"

"Yes." She shivered lightly in his grasp and then Jack felt the tension suddenly leave her body. She slumped slightly in her seat, her lips parting and her eyes sliding closed.

Goddamn, but she looked almost . . . aroused. Like she'd gotten off on . . . like she enjoyed the feel of . . .

Oh, no, no way. It wasn't possible. Nicky was one of the toughest girls he'd ever known, pure steel beneath the sass. She was a fighter, a scrapper, not a submissive, and there had been nothing in their early relationship to hint she wanted to be dominated.

But then . . . she'd said her ex-husband was "controlling," and there was no denying how her entire body language had changed when he'd pulled out the scary voice, the one the girls around the Vegas parlor jokingly called his "Yes, Daddy" tone. It was also the one he'd used in the Vegas bondage clubs when he needed to indulge that part of his personality, the part of him that needed to command another's pleasure to fully experience his own.

Could Nicky . . .

There was one way to find out.

"Put your purse on the floor," he said in the same firm voice. She obeyed immediately, making his cock twitch with excitement inside his pants.

Down, boy. She might just be scared. It might have nothing to do with sex.

It was true. She might just be intimidated. Sometimes he forgot his mere size alone was enough to frighten people, even without the scary voice. He'd never been the kind of person to use his bulk as a tool to get what he wanted. Still, it was something he had to consider.

He loosened his grip on her arm slightly and softened his tone. "I have some questions. Will you answer me honestly?"

"Yes," she whispered, her voice ripe with feelings that certainly didn't sound like fear.

"Are you turned on right now?"

She shivered again and her breath caught, but she didn't speak.

"Answer me, Nicky. Are you turned on? Tell me the truth."

One beat, two, and then the word he didn't realize he'd been afraid to hear until she said it. "Yes."

Oh. Fuck. This wasn't good. He'd been right about what Nick wanted, but it would be so wrong to act on what he'd learned. A dominant and sub relationship should be based on trust. He would never enter into even a casual scene with a sub with an agenda other than shared mutual pleasure. To use this to control Nicky, to persuade her to let him alter her tat, would be way beyond wrong.

But then . . . he didn't have to abuse the knowledge. Once they arrived at the cabin, he could go back to treating her like an old friend and keep all persuasive efforts aboveboard. Or at least above the waist.

Right now, however, he had at least thirty more miles before he'd be out of urban areas and onto the dark mountain road leading to his cabin. He couldn't afford to have Nicky jumping to her freedom or risk the chance someone might notice a girl tied up with rope in the back of his car as he drove through downtown San Bernardino. And he could think of the perfect way to occupy her busy little hands, to keep those fingers so focused on their work she wouldn't even think about going for the door handle.

"Is your pussy wet?" he asked, before he had the opportunity to talk himself out of his decision.

"Yes." Nicky moaned softly and Jack saw her hands clench into fists on her lap. Oh, yeah. She was more than ready for what he had in mind. It was clear in every tense line of her body.

"In a few seconds I'm going to tell you to touch yourself, Nicky. When I do, I want you to slide your fingers in and out of your cunt. Play with yourself, make your pussy hotter, wetter. Can you do that for me?"

"Yes." She spread her legs wider and Jack had to fight the urge to turn off at the next exit and find the nearest motel.

His cock was already ridiculously hard, his balls aching like he'd been sucker punched between the legs. He was going to walk like he'd been riding bareback by the time they made it to the cabin. But then, that was only fair. He deserved to suffer, especially considering what he had in mind for Nick.

"I want you to touch yourself everywhere and anywhere it feels good." He paused for a moment, his own desire spiraling even higher when Nicky stayed perfectly still, waiting for his command before she moved a muscle. She was obviously no newbie to the scene, and understood the kind of pleasure that came with bending her will to another's. "But don't touch your clit. That part of you is mine for the next hour. If you come without touching it, that's fine. But if you disobey me, if you run even a pinkie finger over that nub, I'll know. And you'll be punished. Do you understand?"

"I didn't agree to punishments and we don't have a safe word," she said, her voice breathy with excitement.

"No, you didn't, and no, we don't. If that bothers you, we can stop this right now." He sounded surprisingly calm considering how desperately a part of him wanted to know Nicky was willing to obey him, to let him guide her to her pleasure. He could already picture her with her head thrown back, her eyes closed as she drew closer and closer to coming on her own hand, could practically hear the sound of her eager fingers delving in and out of her slick cunt. "Is that what you want?"

Only the briefest of pauses before she sighed, relaxing back into her seat. "No ... sir."

The addition of the typical sub term of respect sent another jolt of need surging down to his already aching cock. "Thank you. I appreciate your trust. Now put your hand down the front of your panties. I want to be able to smell how wet you are by the time we hit the San Bernardino exit."

Nicky spread her knees even wider and lifted her skirt, giving him a clear view as she slowly slid her hand beneath the black fabric and over her mound. She moaned as she pressed her fingers deep inside her channel, the sound so thick with need he had no doubt it had been awhile since Nicky had indulged this side of herself.

Was that because of her ex? Had he been one of those sadistic types who got off on making their sub's life a living hell? Jackson had seen his share of doms like that, cowards who needed to walk all over another person to make themselves feel like men. They were the kind of assholes who gave genuine dominants a bad name. Jack had never entered into a full-time commitment with a submissive female, but he knew if he ever did his girl would be treated with nothing but kindness.

True, sometimes "kindness" could take on unconventional forms in the BDSM world, where even punishments and pain could be considered kind if they were what the sub needed to get off, to feel safe and cared for. Jack had played with a number of women who needed to be spanked, told they were dirty little whores, or even bound and gagged and fucked with what most people would say was a decided lack of gentleness in order to experience their greatest pleasure.

But he'd never hurt a woman. He'd never left his lovers with emotional or physical scars.

Not like the kind Nicky had acquired if the tears streaming silently down her face were any indication. Even as she played with her pussy, obviously aroused by what she was doing, she wept. He could practically feel the pain inside of her fighting her pleasure, and it was enough to make his heart wrench uncomfortably in his chest. She'd been through something, something bad, and she was still suffering from the side effects.

Could he add to that pain? Even if she had betrayed his trust? Was he *that* mentally screwed by the almost mystical connection he felt to the only person with whom he shared identical ink?

Unfortunately, the answer to all three questions was yes.

"You're safe, Nick. Nothing's going to happen that you don't want to happen. At least not until Sunday afternoon," he said, ignoring the flash of conscience the last words inspired. "So relax. Concentrate on your pleasure, on getting my pussy as wet as you can make it."

Damn, he'd staked a claim without meaning to. But then, it was hard not to think of her pussy as *his*, especially when he knew exactly how he was going to reward her obedience, with his face between her legs, eating that pussy until she came so hard she couldn't remember her own name.

Nicky had always been his, a part of him ingrained so deeply he worried that not even eliminating their matching tattoos would force her out. Or that, even more disturbingly, he even *wanted* her out. Maybe they could move forward together, forget the past, forget that they'd gone eight years without—

Get it together, Jackson. This weekend is about taking back your life, not getting even more obsessed with a woman who couldn't care less about you.

It was true, even though a part of him wanted to believe Nick had loved him back when they were kids. But if she had cared that much she wouldn't have acted the way she did, wouldn't have promised him forever and then run as fast and as far as she was able the very next day. He had to follow through with what he had planned, no matter how tempting it would be to play power-exchange games with Nicky all weekend and forget why they were shacked up in a cabin in the middle of nowhere.

He'd picked the location because he didn't want anyone to see or hear if she wasn't cooperative, but it would also be the perfect place to stage a private scene. No one would be able to hear her scream when she came, again and again, on his face, his hands, his cock, his—

"God, Jack. I'm so wet," she said, squirming restlessly on the seat beside him. "Are you going to fuck me?"

"Would you want me to fuck you?"

"Fuck, yes." She moaned again, and her hand moved faster between her legs, driving in and out of her slick heat, but not touching her clit. She was being completely obedient, doing her best to earn his approval. "I want you to fuck your pussy. Hard."

Holy. Shit.

Hard. That was exactly what it was going to be to resist losing himself in Nicky. As hard as the erection pressing so fiercely against his fly, Jack swore he could feel the metal teeth of his zipper through his boxer briefs.

Chapter Three

She was going to die. Right here, right now. Spontaneously combust from the force of her sexual frustration. On her headstone they would write, "If only she could have gotten off before it was too late."

"Please . . . please," Nicky moaned, moving her hand even faster, driving fingers into the aching, bruised place her pussy had become. She'd never been so hot or so wet, never been poised on the verge of shattering orgasm for so long without being able to come. It was torture. Pure, horrible, *wonderful* torture.

"Just a few more minutes. There's a place to turn off the road and park in about half a mile." His voice was maddeningly calm as he steered through the almost complete blackness of the mountain road.

She wanted to slap him. And then fuck him. She wanted to rip open his pants and straddle him, ride his cock while she sank her teeth into the thick muscles of his shoulders. She wanted to feel his strong hands digging into the flesh of her hips, highlighting her pleasure with just a little pain. And then she wanted him to punish her for biting him without permission, have him turn her over his knee and redden her ass until—

"God. Please! Now!" She couldn't take much more, and her lurid thoughts certainly weren't helping any. Her breath was coming in swift, shallow pants, and her entire body felt like one screaming exposed nerve. She needed to come. Now. Not in a few more minutes.

"Lower your voice. If you use that tone with me again, you will lose the privilege of speech." And then he slowed down, until it felt like they were crawling up the side of the mountain in a freaking horse-drawn wagon. There was no one else on the road at nearly two in the morning. He could drive ten miles an hour if he wanted, make sure they didn't reach that turnoff until morning if she wasn't obedient.

God. Damn. Him.

Nicky pressed her lips together, the part of her that wanted to tell him to go fuck himself warring with the part of her that was willing to do *anything* it took to win Jack's approval. From the second he'd used that deep, silky dom voice on her, she'd been a goner. No matter how freaked out she'd been that the sweet boy she'd once known had turned into the kind of man who would tattoo another person against their will, that shock had faded to the back of her awareness once she'd realized what else he'd become.

Dominant. Wonderfully, perfectly dominant. In the past forty minutes he'd controlled her more completely, more skillfully than Derrick had managed in three long years. It was more than the tone of his voice, or the way he kept his cool no matter how she'd tried to tempt him into putting an end to her torture with a quickie in the back of the Expedition—and she had tried every dirty trick she could think of that didn't expressly violate Jack's order not to touch her clit.

It was something else, something she couldn't quite put her finger on, that made her want to please Jack, to be a good sub in a way she never had been before. It was like he emitted an aura of dominance, one that reached out and surrounded her in bliss when she was pleasing him and froze her blood in her veins when she was not. The odd sensation made her feel incredibly connected to the man. It was like they'd already made love even though he hadn't so much as breathed on her skin.

Whoa. No way. She was *not* going to go there.

She would submit to Jack, she would fuck Jack, but there would be no *lovemaking*. She didn't need the complication of that particular emotion at the moment. Even if she did, Jack would never want to make love to her. She'd broken his heart and her promises, two things she'd known even the eighteen-year-old Jack would never forgive, let alone the hardened man he'd become.

The realization was enough to cool her lust a few degrees until he spoke again.

"Take off your shirt. I want to see you play with your nipples."

Oh. God. He knew how sensitive her breasts were, how she'd been ready to head for a home run the first time she'd let him get to second base in the back of his Impala. Just a few minutes of playing with her nipples and she'd been wet and ready, practically dying to feel Jack inside her, no matter how lousy her first few sexual experiences had been.

"Now, Nick. Make them hard for me." He reached out with one hand and gently undid the top button on her shirt. "I want your nipples tight when I take them in my mouth."

She couldn't get the damn shirt off fast enough. Her bra

followed a second later, and then her hands were on her already aching tips, squeezing, caressing, rolling her nipples between her fingers and thumbs until they stung. The slippery wet heat from the fingers she'd had in her pussy smeared across the pebbled flesh, adding to her pleasure until she was squirming in her seat.

"Jack. Please, Jack," she whispered, squeezing her thighs together, seeking some little relief from the erotic torture he was forcing her to inflict upon herself.

His eyes flicked from her breasts to the road and his breath finally began to speed. He wanted her. So, god, why wouldn't he take her? If she had to wait a second longer to feel his cock in her, she was going to scream.

Or take matters into her own hands. Every sub had a breaking point and she was reaching hers.

"Don't do it, Nick. We're almost there. Keep your hands on your tits."

"I hate the word 'tits,'" she snapped, her tone a cross between a whine and a growl. How had he known? She hadn't made any sign she was planning to move her hands.

"Really? You're not a tit girl?"

"Oh, fuck you. You know I am." For a split second, she wondered if Jack would revoke her ability to speak for her rebellious words, but the bastard only laughed.

"That's a shame. I like the word 'tits.'" She could imagine the shit-eating grin he had on his face, though she couldn't see more than his profile in the dim moonlight. "I'd especially like it if I were fucking your mouth, pumping between those pretty lips. I'd like to tell you I was going to pull out and come on your tits."

Oh. My.

"Then I would, hot and thick all over your soft skin. I'd rub my cock all over your chest, spread my cum on your nipples, play with you until I was hard again and then push those breasts together and fuck your tits. Would you like that, Nicky? To have me fuck your tits while you played with yourself?"

She almost came right then. The man knew how to talk just her perfect idea of dirty. Before she could remember the words she needed to tell him just how hot the idea of him fucking her tits made her, he spoke again.

"Take off your panties, but leave on your shoes," Jack said as they rounded a curve in the road and a lookout point came into view. "We're here."

Nicky had never been so thrilled to see a parking lot in her life. Or so scared.

Damn, what was wrong with her? This is what she'd been dying for since the second Jack told her to put her hand down the front of her panties. Why was she suddenly scared of what was going to go down between them? She wanted this, needed him more than she'd ever needed...Hell...more than she'd needed almost anything.

There's your problem. And that's after less than two hours with the man. What state are you going to be in after two days?

But there was no time to listen to the cautious part of her mind. Jack had already pulled into a space near the guardrail at the edge of the lot. "Get out of the car. Put your hands on the hood and spread your legs," he said as he pocketed the keys.

"But I'm not wearing a shirt."

"Get out of the car. Put your hands on the hood."

"And it's freezing outside," she said, even as her hand reached for the handle of the door.

She was stalling. She didn't really care about the cold or the threat of being caught half naked. Hell, she found the idea she might be seen incredibly arousing. But it was as if the knowledge that they were *really* going to have sex had finally penetrated her lust-fogged mind.

She was going to have sex. For the first time in *two years*. With Jack.

Her Jack, one of the only people she'd ever let inside her heart, and one of the many people she'd let down in her relatively short life. What if he secretly hated her for it? What if he'd never forgiven her for leaving Carson City without telling him? Was she risking getting even more mentally screwed up than she was already by allowing him to dominate her, to trust him with her well-being while she was in such a vulnerable place? What if he—

"Don't worry," he said, reaching out, running his knuckles softly down the curve of her jaw. She still couldn't see his eyes, but the gentle tone of his voice spoke to every last one of her doubts. It was as if he'd known, once again, what was going through her mind almost before she did. "I'll keep you warm. Now get out of the car. I'm ready to fuck my pussy."

Nicky stumbled out of the car, the cold wind taking her breath away for a second. There was a big difference between mountain temperatures and Los Angeles temperatures in the winter months. They were less than three hours from the city, but there was already at least a thirty-degree drop and it was bound to get colder as they drove higher.

She didn't even have a pair of jeans to cover her legs, let alone a coat or the kind of shoes she would need if she were to try to run from Jackson. Of course, that was probably part of the reason he'd chosen the San Bernardino Mountains. They were sparsely populated in the winter months and her inappropriate clothing would keep her bound to him, ensure that she remained his captive.

That realization should have scared her, but instead it only intensified the aching between her legs. The idea of being held against her will, at least by Jackson, was painfully arousing. Which just went to show her libido was even more twisted than she'd assumed.

"Hands on the hood, sweetheart, let me feel how wet my pussy is." Jack's large, warm body was behind her then, blocking the wind, enveloping her in his energy, banishing thoughts of anything but him.

Nicky placed her hands on the engine-warmed hood. No sooner had her fingertips made contact with the Expedition than Jack's fingers were between her legs, making her cry out with relief. Just his touch was enough to banish some of her desperation, to take her that much closer to completion.

He groaned softly as he played through her folds, feeling how her slickness ran down the insides of her thighs, how her lips were plumped and swollen with the force of her need. Down one side of her pussy, and up the other, he traced every inch of her aching flesh until finally his finger brushed lightly across her clit, making her knees buckle.

"Jack," she cried out, knowing she would have fallen if his strong arm weren't around her waist, catching her, holding her upright as he continued to tease her nub with a gentle, insistent pressure.

"God, you're so wet," he murmured, his hand moving away from her pussy, an action she was about to protest before she felt him working at his pants behind her. "Do you still want my cock inside you?"

"Yes, please, yes." Tears of relief rolled down her cheeks and her entire body began to shake with anticipation. Finally! It felt like she'd been waiting for years for him, for his touch, for the feel of his cock falling, hot and heavy, out of his pants, pressing between the cheeks of her ass.

"I'm going to fuck my pussy now, Nick." Jack's breath was warm against her cheek as he whispered through her hair. Nicky heard the sound of foil tearing and then, seconds later, felt the blunt head of Jack's cock at her opening. "Tilt your hips."

Nicky obeyed and then, thank god, he shoved inside her. His thick cock stretched her inner walls to the limit, filling her completely, owning every inch of her pussy with just one swift thrust. Nicky moaned with the pleasure of it, dizzy from the familiar feel of him, the smell of him, the rightness of being bared to Jack. The cold air, his warm body, and the molten heat of his cock were nearly enough to take her over the edge. Then he moved his fingers over her clit, and she was falling.

She screamed as she came, her knees bending, feet coming off the ground as her orgasm ripped through her body with a force unlike anything she'd ever known. Her channel pulsed and clutched at where Jack lay, still buried deep within her. Her nails clawed into the metal beneath her hands, and her nipples practically burned with raw sensation. Every inch of her skin was on fire, consumed by the bliss of the release so long denied her.

Things low in her belly contracted, tighter and tighter, until it was almost painful. Her clit pulsed and throbbed beneath Jack's firm touch, making her gasp for breath. In seconds her head was spinning, lights dancing behind her closed eyes as she rode the waves of the orgasm that had taken control of her, body and soul.

No, not the orgasm. Jack. Jack was the one in control. In perfect, restrained, dominant control, a fact he made clear as he pinched her clit between his fingers and whispered in her ear, "Come again, Nicky. Right now. Come on my cock."

And she did. Oh, god, she did, another blinding release even more powerful than the first. Tears were running down her face by the time she came back into her skin, feeling her soul had become too big for her body and yet too small at the same time. She didn't fit inside her flesh the way she had before and it was frightening for a moment, but then Jack took care of that, too.

"Put your feet on the ground." As soon as she obeyed, wobbling slightly, still unsteady on her feet in her heels, he started to fuck her.

Not make love, not have sex. Fuck. He rammed into her cunt without mercy, slamming forward with such force that she had to brace herself on the hood and push back against him to keep from being glued to the side of the truck. It wasn't romantic, it wasn't emotional. It was hard, fast, brutal. In a word—perfect, exactly what she needed to ground herself back on earth. And to come near the edge of completion for a third time.

Nicky spread her legs a little wider and shoved back against Jack as he thrust forward, intensifying the penetration until she could feel the head of his cock making bruising contact with the end of her pussy. The hint of pain made another rush of wet heat flow between her thighs and Jack groan behind her. His hands flipped up her skirt and took hold of her hips, digging his fingers into the full flesh of her ass.

"Harder, harder!" Nicky begged, gasping for breath as the tension within her built to a level she'd never dreamed possible. She was either going to come again or shatter into a million pieces, and she didn't really care which. So long as Jack kept fucking her, touching her, *taking* her.

"Don't come. Not yet. Wait for me. Wait," Jack demanded, even as he obliged her by squeezing her ass even tighter.

"Oh, god. Oh, god." Nicky struggled to obey, but oh, god, it was hard.

She was so close, so terribly close, and he felt so amazing. His cock actually seemed to be getting thicker as he neared his own release, stretching her pussy even further, making her feel so full of him that there was room for nothing else. Nothing but Jack. And it was perfect, better than anything she could remember, even the other times she had been with him.

"Now. I want my pussy to come now." He punctuated his words by jerking her hips back toward him, forcing himself so deep inside her the hint of pain as he met the end of her became enough to make her wince.

Fortunately for her, she could wince and come like the world was ending in a big burst of fire at the same time.

"Fuck! Jack!" She screamed those words and a few other things she couldn't remember as her mind spun inside her skull like she'd slammed back half a bottle of Jack Daniel's and her pussy did its best to squeeze Jack's cock in half.

She moaned as his penis jerked inside her, each tiny movement enough to take her even higher. She'd never felt so connected to a lover, as if his pleasure was her own, as if every wave of his release triggered a ripple of bliss inside her. It was more than she'd ever expected, more than she knew what to do with as she finally drifted down from the high of her first triple orgasm.

Triple orgasm. She'd come *three* times and Jack hadn't even seemed like he was trying that hard. What would he be capable of if they became regular lovers, if they had the time to learn the little things that—

What the fuck are you thinking? He doesn't want to become lovers; he despises you so much he can't stand the idea that you share a matching tattoo and is willing to permanently alter the damn thing without your consent. Get your head on straight and figure a way out of here before it's too late.

"Get back in the car and warm up. We're still about twenty minutes from the cabin," Jack said as he pulled out of her, the loss of contact between them as depressing as her inner monologue. "Thank you . . . for your trust."

He kissed her softly on the top of her head as he smoothed down her skirt, but the affectionate gesture did nothing to stop the anger slowly flowing into her veins, replacing the euphoria of a few moments before.

Thank you for your trust. *Her trust?* That was it? No "You were amazing" or "That was the hottest fuck of my life"? Or even a "Damn, I can't wait to have you again"?

No, he just wanted to thank her for *her trust.* Wasn't he the big, bad, unavailable dom? Just like Derrick had been during the first year of their marriage, when he still made love to her but never had a kind or affectionate word. Never made her feel like anything but a sub in the worst sense of the word.

Subhuman. That's what she'd been to Derrick, and what she'd vowed she'd never be to any man, ever again.

The headlights came around the curve only a second later, as if some higher power had heard her thoughts and decided she deserved the chance at deliverance. Nicky ran for the road without a moment's hesitation, heedless of her nudity or of Jack's voice behind her, ordering her back to the car.

Fuck him, and his orders. She was getting the hell out of here.

In less than a few hours, he'd gotten under her skin to the point his lack of pillow talk after they'd had sex had hurt her. What kind of damage would he be able to inflict in a few days?

Nicky was not sticking around to find out. Her heels clicked madly on the pavement as she dashed for the road, racing the heavy footfalls behind her for salvation.

Chapter Four

Jackson watched the ancient pickup pull off onto the gravel at the road's edge and ran even faster, determined to catch Nicky before she got inside. Before she took her life in her hands trying to get away from him.

It could be anyone in that truck. Some mountain man who hadn't seen a naked woman in years, a couple of drunk teenagers who would take turns raping the woman they picked up on the side of the road before dropping her off on the streets of San Bernardino. Or even worse, there could be a bona fide psychopath driving that vehicle, a man who would have his fun with Nicky and then kill her, dumping her body in the surrounding wilderness where it might never be found.

Or maybe the driver is a nice grandmotherly type who will buy her some clothes before taking her to the police station to file a report against the man who kidnapped her.

Nicky skidded to a stop as the driver's door to the truck whipped open. "Help, I . . ." Her voice trailed off and she backed away as an obese man in tattered overalls leveraged himself out of the vehicle.

"You need help, darlin'?" the man asked, weaving a bit as he lurched forward. "I'd be happy to help."

Despite the chances of being convicted of a felony, a part of Jackson wished it *had* been a sweet granny in the truck. Now he was probably going to have to get into a brawl with a man who looked like an extra from *Deliverance* to keep Nicky safe. *And* he had a witness who might report what he'd seen to the authorities.

Not that it really mattered. If Nicky decided she wanted to press charges, it wasn't as if he'd do anything to stop her. Despite what the voices in his head had been telling him lately, Jackson wasn't a psychopath.

At least not yet. If this drunk did anything to Nick, however, Jack was sure he'd lose what was left of his sanity in a fairly memorable fashion.

"No one needs help." Jackson's teeth ground together hard enough to make something in his jaw pop as he watched one of the other man's large, meaty hands reach toward Nicky's chest. "Get back in your truck."

"I don't think I was talking to——"

"Get back in your truck," Jack repeated as his fingers closed around Nicky's elbow and pulled her behind him, shielding her nakedness with his body.

"Why don't you fuck off? The lady asked for my help."

Jackson cursed himself. Why the hell had he demanded Nicky take off her shirt? She was irresistible enough clothed. Of course he hadn't thought anyone would see. It was the middle of the night, for god's sake, and most people knew better than to try to navigate the treacherous mountain roads at night, especially after hitting the bottle. God, he could smell the whiskey on this character from three feet away, which gave him an idea. . . .

"All right, don't get back in your truck. I can smell the alcohol on your breath from here. Call me crazy, but I doubt this will be your first DUI. Put your hands on the hood." Jack heard Nicky suck in a breath behind him as she caught on to what he was doing. "I'm taking this one in for attempted prostitution, it will be no trouble to haul you into the station at the same time. I'll just go lock her in the backseat and come back with some cuffs for you, Mr. . . ."

"Uh . . . ca . . . um . . . Beam. Walter Beam," he said, already backing toward the door to the battered pickup. "But I haven't been drinking, Officer. I swear."

"We'll see about that when I get back with the Breathalyzer." Jack turned around and urged Nicky in front of him across the street, whispering as he went, "Get in the backseat."

"Prostitution?" She hissed the word over her shoulder, obviously angry but relieved to have escaped "Mr. Beam's" attentions. Mr. Beam . . . riiight. It didn't take much imagination to guess Beam was the brand of whiskey he'd been drinking, not the name on his license. "Do I look like a prostitute?"

"I don't know. What does a prostitute look like?" Jackson asked, not surprised to hear the pickup roar to life behind him and tires squeal as old Walter took off down the mountain like a bat out of hell.

"I don't know. You're the one who lives in Vegas. I heard it's legal out there," she said, shivering as he opened the Expedition's door and urged her inside. "That was a pretty lame cop act, by the way. I thought you had your own television show. I expected better than 'haul you into the station.'"

"It was a reality show. I just had to be myself, not act like anyone else." Jackson reached into the front for Nicky's bra and shirt and tossed them into her lap. "Put those on and don't run away from me like that again. You could have been seriously hurt."

"You've got to be kidding me." The car's overhead light illuminated Nicky's face, revealing the flush that heated her cheeks. "I could have been hurt?"

"What do you think Walter would have done to you?"

"I don't know. Taken me back to town?"

"Doubtful. And even if he did, not before he took advantage."

"Took advantage?" She laughed as she finished up with her bra, but her hands were shaking as she reached for her shirt. "He might have copped a feel. At most."

"He might have raped you," Jack said, anger making his voice even deeper.

"No, he wouldn't have," she said, returning his glare, making it clear she wasn't scared of his angry voice. "I can take care of myself, Jack. In case you don't remember."

"Then why didn't you get in the truck with him? If you were so sure he was a safe bet?"

"I guess I didn't want to see what you'd do to the poor guy if I did," she said, her eyes glittering in the dim light. "I mean, you're the psycho who's kidnapping a woman so he can make permanent alterations to her body. And you used to love *me*. Who knows what you might have done to some fat old man you don't even know?"

The bravado in her tone made him positive she was simply saying what she knew would hurt the most, but the words still cut him. Just like she'd known they would. She wasn't stupid, his Nick. Volatile, emotional, and oftentimes too impulsive for her own good, but never stupid.

"I did love you. Enough to believe everything you said to me the night before you ran away," Jack said, careful to keep the emotion out of his voice. "And I don't hate you now, Nicky. I hope you know that. I don't want to hurt you."

"Tattooing someone against their will is bound to hurt," she said, her voice still hard, though he'd seen the flash of guilt on her face when he'd mentioned the night she'd fled Carson City. "Literally hurt, and probably do a pretty decent job of destroying a person's trust."

"Trust," he said, letting the word linger between them. "Is that what this is about? You regret letting me dominate you?"

Nicky's eyes dropped to her fingers and she suddenly seemed very interested in the workings of the buttons on her shirt.

"Answer me. Do you regret what we did?"

She sucked in a deep breath and let it out on a sigh. "No," she mumbled, still not looking him in the eye.

"Then why did you run right after we finished?" he asked, certain he was onto something. This wasn't about her trying to get away from him because she was afraid or didn't want her tat modified. It was about the power games they'd begun to play, the amount of trust she'd given him so readily.

The trust that had floored him, aroused him, and come closer to softening the walls he'd built around his heart than anything had. Anything or anyone ... even Nicky herself eight years ago. If he was a smart man, he'd turn the truck around and take her back to Los Angeles right now. No amount of ink modification was going to give him peace if he let Nicky get under his skin again.

Too bad he was an absolute idiot where this woman was concerned.

"Finished? That's a really nice way to put it," she said, hurt obvious in her tone.

"I'm sorry. What do you want me to say?" Jack asked, ignoring the strange tightness that gripped his throat. "After we had sex?"

"Fucked would be fine. That's all it was, right? A little fucking between friends?"

She was hurting, that was obvious, but how much of that pain had to do with what he'd done and how much was the result of her obviously troubled recent past, he couldn't say. But he could at least apologize, try to make things as right between them as he could before they were holed up alone together for forty-eight hours.

"It was more than that. You know it, and so do I," he said. "I'm sorry if what we shared left you feeling confused, but you can't tell me you didn't enjoy it. Or that you didn't need it."

"What do you know about what I need?"

Jackson sighed, recognizing her defiance for what it was, a mask for the fear many submissives felt when starting a relationship with someone new. He certainly hadn't meant to "start" anything or inspire those kinds of feelings in Nick, but now he had no choice but to deal with them.

"Listen, it's natural to be anxious about giving yourself over to another person, even if that person is someone you used to know very well," he said, keeping his tone soft and reassuring. He wanted her to know she was safe, that he wouldn't abuse her trust, that all his cards were on the table. "Especially if you've been in a relationship where your trust has been abused."

Jackson was willing to bet money her ex was the cause of her emotional trauma. He knew better than anyone the pain an ex-lover could cause.

Nicky tilted her head back, lifting her face to his, staring deep into his eyes without a trace of fear or deference. In that moment, she was the least submissive woman he'd ever seen. If he hadn't experienced dominating her himself and seen how she reveled in being controlled, he never would have believed she was the type who enjoyed the lifestyle.

"You don't know anything about my former relationship, and you don't know anything about me," she said, every word clipped and deliberate. "Not anymore. So don't pretend you do. Just because we had sex, it doesn't give you the right to psychoanalyze me. I'm not some pathetic subbie who needs a big bad dom to show me the way."

Jackson just looked at her for a minute, not saying anything, staring into those big greenish brown eyes, seeing so much more than Nicky realized. "Is that what he taught you? That to submit is weak and contemptible?"

Without meaning to, Jack found himself cupping her cheek in his hand, then sliding his fingers into her impossibly soft hair. God, how many times had he dreamed of feeling that hair falling around his face as he kissed this woman again? And here she was, so close, but still so incredibly far away.

Her lips parted and her breath came faster, but she didn't say a word. She only watched him, like he was a circus performer about to do some fascinating trick. In that second, Jackson prayed he could live up to the expectation in his woman's eyes.

His woman. There was that thought again, that sense of ownership that felt completely natural and would never be anything but wrong.

"In a real dominant and submissive relationship, the submissive is an incredibly strong person," he said, hoping she could tell how strong he'd always believed her to be. "Sometimes even stronger than her master, depending on the dom and how much experience he has."

"Really?" she asked, doubt and sarcasm warring with the genuine curiosity in her tone.

"Just think about it. What requires more discipline, giving someone else orders or giving up control?" He leaned a little closer to her lips, unable to resist. "Trusting someone else to guide you, exploring the boundaries of your capacity for pleasure and pain, giving the gift of your faith, of *yourself* to another person . . . that's pretty amazing stuff. I don't know that I could do it."

"Call me crazy, but for some reason I don't think you'd want to." She smiled, a tiny, genuine twist of her lips that made him inexplicably happy.

"Are you calling me a big bad dom again?" He laughed and she joined in, the puff of her breath against his lips reviving the desire that had haunted him since the second he saw her dancing on that bar in Pasadena.

"I call 'em like I see 'em," she said. "Though I have to admit, I was . . . surprised."

"You and me both. I never thought . . . certainly never expected . . ." Jack took a deep breath and forced himself to pull away. He couldn't stay like this, hand buried in her hair, lips inches from hers, and not take this encounter to the next level.

He stepped back, crossing his arms at his chest, concentrating on the feel of the cold wind cutting through the fabric of his sweater. "I want you to know I never planned for there to be anything sexual about this meeting. I expected we'd come up here, maybe have a few beers and a few laughs, I'd modify your tat, and we'd part as friends."

"Or that I would say no to having the tat modified, you'd

hold me captive and modify it whether I liked it or not, and we'd part as enemies," she said, a hint of humor in her tone that made this entire journey seem even more surreal.

And here he hadn't thought it possible.

"Yeah, I admit that option crossed my mind, too," he said, the hint of a smile twitching at the edge of his lips. "But either way, there wasn't any sex involved. I can promise you that."

"But there definitely is now. So . . ." She let her words trail off as she stared at him, an unspoken dare in her eyes that Jackson knew he couldn't take her up on. Not if he wanted to keep what was left of his head.

"Don't think I'm not tempted. I'd love to show you what you've been missing," he said, his own breath coming faster as he watched her nipples bead tightly beneath her shirt. Damn, how he wanted to get those tits in his mouth, suck them until she writhed beneath him, begging him to take her, fuck her, possess her. But he couldn't. Not now, not ever again. The first time had been a mistake. "But I don't think that would be healthy for either one of us. We've got a lot of history, Nick. You should have a dominant who can provide for your unique needs and I've got too many of my own."

"Like the driving desire to modify my tattoo," she said, a hint of sadness in her eyes.

"Like that," he said, swallowing the bitter taste of regret that rose in his throat. "And the fact that I've never had a full-time sub and don't plan on getting into something like that anytime soon. Especially not with a woman who doesn't seem committed to being a submissive."

"Doesn't seem committed? You don't know how committed I was, I—"

"You're a pushy bottom, Nick."

"What?" she asked, a ragged laugh bursting from her lips. "Me? A pushy bottom?"

"From the second we started this, it seemed to me like you wanted to take the control. You questioned and resisted a lot, even for a woman with a new partner," he said, making it clear he wasn't criticizing her, just sharing his honest opinion. "You try to top from the bottom, and in a real scene, I wouldn't tolerate that. If the woman I'm with wants to be dominated, then that's what I'm going to do. That's who I am. I can't turn it on and off and I wouldn't want to."

She pressed her lips together, a frown bunching the skin between her eyebrows before she suddenly relaxed. "You know what? Maybe you're right."

"Three words a man doesn't hear very often from a woman."

"Even a dominant man? I'd think you'd get that all the time." She sighed and wrapped her arms around herself, shivering slightly as a gust of cold wind blew in the open car door. "But yeah, I'm not sure I'm ready to sub right now. I don't think I'm prepared to make that kind of commitment, even one of the 'fun for a weekend' variety. Especially with a man who cares so little about me, he won't take no for an answer."

"Ouch," he whispered, flinching at the pain in her voice. So he'd upset her? So what? She'd done her share to upset him in the past. He shouldn't let her emotions affect him so deeply. But he did—he couldn't seem to help himself.

"Let me try to explain this again," he said, hoping she'd be able to understand if he opened up and gave her the real reason he needed to banish their matching ink from her skin. "I'll be honest, Nick. I was pretty fucked up when you left."

He took a deep breath, wishing it didn't turn him inside out to talk to her this way. But it did, so he'd just have to suck it up and get it out as quickly as possible, show he was a true dom, one as in touch with his own feelings as those of his submissive. "And I've stayed a little fucked up. I loved you like . . . like I'd never loved anyone. It hurt to lose you, and looking at this tattoo every day hasn't gotten any easier, especially not when you've used yours as a hook to get modeling work."

"Believe me, Jack, I understand," Nicky said, reaching out and taking his hand, her grip strong, though her hand looked almost child-sized compared to his own. "And if I didn't really believe I *needed* this tattoo to get work, I would do what you're asking me to do. But I do believe it, and there are other people depending on me and . . . I just can't."

"What other people?" he asked, the muscle in his jaw clench-ing up again. "A boyfriend? Your ex-husband? Is he after you for money?"

"People I don't want to talk about right now," she said, mak-ing it clear that was the end of it. "So are you going to take me home or are we going up to this cabin?"

"We're going to the cabin."

"Fine," she said, the tightness in her voice making it clear she understood he meant to do exactly as he'd planned. That he'd modify her tat, whether she liked it or not. Still, she took his de-cision like more of a true submissive than he'd given her credit for. "Then let's get going, I'm cold."

She released his hand and half stood up, climbing over into the passenger's seat as he opened the driver's door. Neither of them said a word as he started up the truck and moved it back onto the road, but Jack made a promise to himself. He was going to treat Nicky with the utmost respect and care, making sure she had nothing to complain about until Sunday afternoon.

Maybe, if he showed her not all men were pigs and not all doms bastards who couldn't command their cock down one side of their pants with any authority, let alone another's life or pleasure, she would change her mind. Maybe they could get through this together without either of them being hurt.

Of course, that would be much more easily accomplished if he kept his dick in his pants and far away from the woman next to him.

Yeah. Good luck with that, buddy.

Jackson gritted his teeth and swore to himself he'd get control and keep control for the rest of the weekend. He was a man who prided himself on the ability to restrain himself and command others.

Surely he could resist giving in to temptation. Especially if he suspected that temptation was just the thing to get him in even hotter water than he was in already.

Chapter Five

Nicky watched Jackson turn onto the narrow road leading up to his cabin with a strange mix of anticipation and dread.

The anticipation part, of course, was pretty easy to understand. No matter what Jack said about a continued sexual relationship being a bad idea, she had no doubt she'd be able to change his mind. He wanted her—badly. It was clear in every heated glance he shot her way, in the tense lines of his body as he guided the truck down the twisting mountain roads. A quickie against the side of his truck wasn't going to be enough.

He was going to start jonesing for more than some friendly chat over a few beers and, when that happened, she would be ready to take advantage of the situation. She hadn't had sex in two years and she'd never experienced anything close to the pleasure Jackson had given her. But that wasn't why she had to risk the emotional fallout that could result from getting too close to this man who still had the ability to affect her like no other.

She had to get close to Jackson for one reason and one reason only—to gain her freedom. The man still cared about her, that had been obvious when he'd tried to explain why he needed to modify her tattoo. And that care was going to be her ticket out of this cabin with her angel looking exactly the way it had since she was sixteen years old. A little sex, a little submission, and a little conversation between two old friends, and Jackson would be convinced he had to let her go. He wouldn't be able to force her to do anything if he was falling in love with her again.

And that was where the dread came in. She'd already hurt him once. What would he do when he found out she'd been faking some lovey-dovey act to gain her freedom?

Nothing. Because you'll tell him you'll go to the police.

"We'll be there in a few minutes. You'll want to put your shoes on," Jack said, his voice nearly a whisper, as if he was loath to break the comfortable silence that had fallen between them.

Nicky leaned over and began strapping herself into her heels, ignoring the little thrill obeying even his smallest request gave her. Jackson was wrong. She wasn't a pushy bottom. She lived for the freedom of giving herself to a man who could handle her, and never had any urge to dominate. She wasn't a switch, she was a sub, through and through. But now wasn't the time or the place and Jackson certainly wasn't the man.

It wasn't just her history with Derrick that made it hard to let go. Knowing what Jack had in mind for this weekend didn't help matters any. She couldn't afford to abandon herself to him completely, not when the one thing he truly wanted to demand of her was something she couldn't give.

The tattoo had to stay looking exactly as it always had if she wanted to get back into modeling for Good and Trashy Lingerie. And she *had* to get back into modeling. Tending bar at the Hard

Way was never going to make her enough money to fight Derrick in court, let alone provide for the future. Being a single mother was hard enough, but being a single mother in a city like L.A. was even harder. Everything cost more than it had when she was growing up in a small town, and she was going to need a sizable income to make sure Abby never wanted for anything.

And Nicky didn't want to be dependent on Derrick for a dime. She wanted sole custody of their daughter and preferably a restraining order keeping him at least ten miles away from them both at all times. Her ex had never hit her or the baby, but he was an emotionally abusive sociopath and the last man who should be entrusted with the care of a child. Especially an infant.

It was enough to make her physically ill every time she thought about Abby going to sleep in the same house as that bastard. She had to get her daughter back, even if it meant fighting the man who had made two years of her life a living hell. Even if it meant risking Derrick following through with his threats that he would kill their baby girl before letting her be raised by "a whore like you, Nicole."

Nicky closed her eyes and swallowed hard, forcing away the memory of her ex's voice screaming those words as he'd taken Abby away. She still didn't know how he'd found them. She'd paid the rent for her new apartment in cash, and even given the landlord fake names for her and Abby. But still, Derrick had somehow tracked her and their eleven-month-old down and made it very clear the lengths he would go to in order to maintain control over at least one of the women in his life.

"This is it. It's not big, but it's well insulated so we won't freeze our asses off," Jackson said as they turned the last corner and a small cabin came into view.

He was right, it wasn't big, but even with nothing more than headlights and the porch light to view it by, Nicky could see it was gorgeous. Beautiful redwood planks were accented with white trim, making the cabin look like something out of a fairy tale.

"I don't know about that. My ass is already half frozen," Nicky said, affecting a light tone, knowing she had to stop thinking about Derrick or Abby and focus on the immediate problem of getting away from Jackson with her tattoo intact. "It would have been nice to know ahead of time I'd be doing the whole winter climate thing. I could have brought my flannel pajamas."

"Hmmm, flannel pajamas. Sounds sexy."

"You have no idea. They're bright red with pirates and parrots and buried treasure on them," Nicky said, amazed at the tingle of awareness that swept over her skin just from hearing Jack say the word "sexy." A weekend spent seducing this man certainly wasn't going to be a hardship. "I think they're technically supposed to be for little boys, but as soon as I saw them, I knew they had to be mine."

"Well, I didn't have the creativity to think of something that fascismashing, but I did bring a few things for you to wear."

"Fascismashing?" She laughed, a real laugh that surprised her more than it should have. Jackson had always been funny in his own, rather dry, way.

"I think it's a cross between fascinating and smashing." He laughed, too, though a little self-consciously. "It's something my office manager says all the time. It was added to my vocabulary against my will, I promise."

"I don't know what's more disturbing, hearing you say a word like 'fascismashing' or learning you brought me clothes." Nicky watched Jackson closely as he parked the truck. "You really thought this whole kidnapping thing through, didn't you?"

He was silent, but Nicky deliberately refused to take the hint.

"How long have you been planning to do this?"

"A few weeks," he said, all traces of humor vanishing from his tone. He was embarrassed, she could tell. He knew what he was doing was crazy. Hopefully that meant getting him to give up on this whacked plan would be relatively easy.

"Should I be freaked out? I mean, have you turned homicidal maniac on me in the past eight years?" she asked, a part of her thrilling to see Jackson's expression grow stormy.

He was wrong about the pushy bottom thing. She didn't want to have control, but she did like to test the man who thought he could top her. When she and Derrick had first gotten together, it had been one of the things that he'd loved about her, that she didn't make it easy for him and would only be a good little sub if he was in top dom form.

But oh, how quickly he'd stopped finding anything lovable about her once she'd gotten pregnant. She'd gone from being an object of fascination to a thing of revulsion in less than a few weeks. Long before she'd begun to show, Derrick confessed how revolting he found pregnant women, and that he doubted he'd ever be attracted to Nicky again. It was ironic in the extreme, as Nicky herself had never felt sexier than when she first found out she was going to have a baby. She'd spent those first few months both unbearably aroused and horribly hurt as she realized her husband no longer wanted anything to do with her—in the bedroom or out.

"If you want to press charges against me when we leave here," Jackson said, "I won't do anything to stop you. If that's what you're wondering."

"So you won't kill me and bury my body in the woods?" Nicky tried to laugh, but she suddenly wasn't finding the situation funny.

No matter how well she had once known Jack, she didn't know shit about him now. After all, she'd once believed Derrick was her dom in shining black leather, the man she'd be with for the rest of her life. When they'd first married, she wouldn't have imagined anything could tear them apart, or that the man she worshipped could so quickly become a monster she despised.

Even if she was right and Jackson did still love her, who was to say he didn't have the same capacity for cruelty? If so, it would certainly prove that she should *never* date again. Her taste in men was decidedly lethal.

"Look at me," Jackson said, waiting patiently until she did so. "I would never hurt you. Do you believe I'm telling the truth?"

Nicky looked deep into those dark brown eyes, the eyes of the first boy she had ever loved, of the best friend she'd regretted losing for eight years. And for a second, she was fourteen again—lost and afraid, putting on her best tough-girl act while inside she felt she was going to shatter into a million pieces at any moment. Those eyes, and the kind, loving boy they belonged to, were the only things that had gotten her through the day.

No matter what madness had made him formulate this plan to alter her tattoo, Jack was still that boy deep down. He would still die before he hurt her, still risk the fists of their foster father or worse to keep her safe.

"I know you are," Nicky whispered, willing the tears she felt pricking at the backs of her eyes not to fall. She wasn't going to cry over old memories. The past was the past, and she had to concentrate on the future and her little girl. Nothing else mattered.

"Good." Jackson held her gaze, for a second looking near to tears himself, but then a friendly smile spread across his face, making her think she had imagined that moment of vulnerability. "Then let's get inside and I'll find something to cover that frozen ass of yours."

As he exited the vehicle Nicky did her best to pull herself together and figure out the first step in her plan. She believed Jackson didn't want to harm her, but he was still dead set on finishing the mission he'd set for himself. And Jack was nothing if not stubborn. It was going to take a good deal of persuasion to convince him to change his mind, and she didn't have a lot of time. It was already nearly Saturday morning and she only had until Sunday afternoon. She was going to have to launch operation Sex Jackson Into Forgetting He Even Owns a Tattoo Gun as soon as possible.

Hmmm . . . well, there was no time like the present.

Nicky watched Jack walk around and grab a large suitcase from the back before she opened her own door and stepped out into the cold night.

"Shheeeeiiiit!" she squealed and ran as fast as her high-heeled feet could carry her to the door of the cabin. It was freezing cold up here on the mountaintop. The wind cut through what few clothes she was wearing, making her feel like she was naked in a snowstorm.

She dashed inside as soon as Jackson opened the door, grateful that the cabin's heat had already been running.

Thank god it hadn't been as cold when she and Jackson had pulled over for their quickie, or even two years without sex wouldn't have been enough to convince her to bang out in the elements. And it was for the best that they had that first encounter out of the way. He'd already let his guard down and done something he freely admitted he hadn't intended to do. Now it would only take a little push to get them back in bed together . . . if the cabin *had* a bed.

"This is gorgeous," Nicky said, covertly scanning the small space as Jackson went around turning on lights and cranking up the heat.

Just inside the entrance there was a small kitchen to her left that opened out into a cozy living room area. A comfy-looking sectional filled nearly every inch of the carpet, angled so that it faced both the fireplace in the corner and the floor-to-ceiling windows that looked out across a valley and the dark face of another mountain. It seemed the cabin was built right on the side of a cliff, which usually would have been enough to give her a case of the shakes. She wasn't a big fan of heights, but for some reason she felt safe here.

It was Jackson. He'd always had a way of making her feel safe, apparently even when he was the thing she had to worry about.

"Thanks. I designed it, with the help of a friend of mine." He finished with the lights and came back to fetch the suitcase he'd left by the door. "The bedrooms are upstairs."

Nicky followed him, finally noticing the circular staircase that was hidden behind the bathroom to their right. Jackson had no trouble navigating the narrow stair, even with his bulk and carrying a massive suitcase, but Nicky stumbled twice in her heels. She told herself it was just her normal klutziness coming through, but the truth was, she was nervous.

Touching herself in a dark car or succumbing to maddening lust and leaping out for a quickie on the side of the road was one thing. But starting something from nothing, especially with a man who suddenly seemed all business, was something else entirely.

"Hope you don't mind, but I'm going to give you the smaller room. It has a great view of the gorge, and you'll have to come through my room if you decide to make a break for it in the middle of the night," he said, tossing a friendly smile over his shoulder.

"And I suppose you still sleep light," she said, finding the entire situation oddly amusing again. But then, if given the choice between fear and funny, she knew which one she preferred.

"I wake up if a pinecone drops outside," he said, tramping through a decidedly masculine master bedroom, into a bathroom, and through a door to another bedroom decorated in deep pinks and bright greens. Those had been her favorite colors in high school, and for a second Nicky wondered if Jack had remembered.

"My interior decorator made all the decisions for the furniture and fabrics." He set the suitcase down on the floral bedspread and opened it. "Hope this isn't too girly for you. I know you're not a big fan of flowers."

"No, it's beautiful. Much nicer than what I've got on my bed at my apartment. Watch out or I might steal the bedspread when we leave."

"You can have it," he said, turning to her with a dead-serious expression on his face. "Hell, you can have the entire cabin and the fifteen grand I've got in the cupboard downstairs. All I want to do is work on that tat."

Nicky sighed, tempted for a moment. Fifteen grand would pay for a lot of legal advice and jump-start her and Abby's new life, but for some reason she couldn't bring herself to take Jackson up on his offer. She'd meant what she'd said in the car—she believed the tattoo was vital to resuscitating her flagging career—but there was something more to her reluctance. The tattoo meant a lot to her, always had and always would. It reminded her of a time when she'd felt truly loved, like the most important thing in the world to one boy.

"Come on, Nick," Jackson urged, as if he sensed her hesitation. "Don't make me use force."

"But you're a dom, right? Don't you enjoy using force?" It was now or never, time to get Jackson thinking about her skin in a way that had nothing to do with ink. Holding his dark eyes, she moved her hands to her shirt, undoing the buttons one by one.

"What are you doing?" His tone was casual, but his every muscle was tense as he put his hands on his hips and moved a step away from the suitcase.

"I like force, myself. If it's used properly." She slid the shirt off her shoulders, letting it fall to the floor as she began working on the front of her bra, her own excitement building so fast it made her head swim. Damn, but she was going to have to be careful or she was going to get in way over her head. "I like to be forcibly restrained."

"Nicky, stop."

"I like to be forced over a man's knee and spanked." Her hands shook as she fumbled with the button and zipper on her skirt and her pussy gushed fresh heat onto her panties. Just thinking about being turned over Jackson's knee, feeling his strong hands reddening her ass, his fingers slipping between her legs to see how wet his punishment had made her, made her entire body ache.

"I'll tell you one more time. Stop." Wow. He'd whipped out the silky dom voice, so deep and commanding, promising retribution if she continued to disobey. It was nearly enough to make her come without him laying a finger on her.

"I like to feel a hand fisting in my hair, forcing my head back as I get fucked from—"

He moved so quickly that, afterward, Nicky couldn't even remember seeing him move. He was simply across the room one minute and slamming her into the wall the next, every inch of his hard body pressed tightly against hers, his lips claiming her mouth in a bruising kiss that made her bones melt.

Oh. Hell. Yeah.

Looks like they wouldn't be making it to the bed after all, but Nicky sure wasn't going to complain. *This* was exactly the way she wanted the night to end. In Jackson's arms, getting ready for a second helping of the kind of pleasure she knew she'd never get enough of.

But you will get enough. And then you'll get the hell away from him and get your life back on track.

The voice of reason. What a pale, sad little thing that was when a man like Jackson was slipping his hand between her legs, shoving his fingers up and inside where she was already desperate for him to be.

Chapter Six

*J*ackson pushed inside Nicky's mouth, demanding entrance, claiming her with firm strokes of his tongue against hers. God, but she tasted as amazing as she always had, like spring rain and spice and something all Nicky that made him feel the kiss with his entire self—body and soul.

Kissing Nick was nearly as intimate as fucking her. She communicated things with those lips, teeth, and tongue that were beyond words. Mating his mouth with hers had always felt like they were rubbing souls, sharing dreams, devouring a little piece of each other with every press of their lips. All the things they were too young or afraid to tell each other in the old days had been said in those hours spent kissing in the backseat of his Impala. Just kissing, not taking things any further, neither of them willing to risk that the perfection of those stolen moments would be destroyed by going too far too fast.

"Jackson." She moaned his name into his mouth, her desire clear as her fingers dug into his shoulders, silently imploring him to get even closer, to shove something more serious than his fingers between her legs.

"Do you want me to fuck you again, Nick?" he asked, moving his thumb to her clit even as his other two fingers continued to drive inside her molten heat with slow, even strokes.

"Do you really have to ask?" She hooked one leg around his hips, granting him even greater access to her pussy.

"No, I don't," he said, slipping a third finger inside her, drawing another moan from the woman in his arms. The sound vibrated against his lips, making his head spin. "But I'd still like an answer."

"Yes. God, yes. Please." She bucked into his hand, sheathing his digits inside her again and again. "I want you."

"How much?" he asked, feeling how close she was to the edge by the way her cunt gripped his fingers.

She was nearly irresistible when she was like this, so abandoned, so desperate for her pleasure. But he was going to have to resist. If he couldn't manage to stay the hell away from Nicky, he'd have to do the next best thing—show her who was in control. It was what she secretly craved, any dom with the sense god gave a donut could see that. More important, it was what he had to do. He *had* to show her he meant business, in the bedroom and out, and that this weekend would be proceeding as he had planned.

What happened to being Mr. Nice Guy?

Fuck Mr. Nice Guy. He'd be Mr. Nice Dom, it was a role that suited him much better.

"Tell me, Nicky. How much do you want me to fuck you?" he asked again, finally getting an answer when he withdrew his hand from between her legs.

"More than anything." Her words came out on a moan, making it clear how much she lamented the loss of his touch.

"Show me." Jackson pulled away from her addictive lips, ignoring the slight tremor that rocked through both of them at the loss of contact. Breaking off a kiss with Nicky was like breaking off a piece of himself.

All the more reason to get them back on the right track, the track to mutual pleasure, not the one feeding his own foolish infatuation.

With his hands firmly on her shoulders, Jackson urged her down to the ground. She obeyed without saying a word, though there was a question in her eyes as she looked up at him once she knelt at his feet.

It was a question he answered by flipping open the button of his fly and drawing down the zipper. He tugged his jeans and boxer briefs a little lower on his hips, freeing his turgid length. His cock was already as hard as if they'd been at their little make-out session for hours, not simply a few minutes. All nine inches were thick and aching, the head nearly purple from the massive amounts of blood rushing to his groin. It was amazing he still had enough flowing to his brain to form words, let alone exercise the restraint it took to wait as Nicky devoured him with her eyes.

The lust clear on her face made him crazy, and the tip of her pink tongue sweeping over her top lip made him even crazier. She looked like she couldn't wait to get his cock in her mouth, to suck him between those full lips and show him what he'd been missing in those eight years away from her.

But she didn't reach out to take his length in her hands, or lean forward to take him into her mouth. She simply knelt at his feet, waiting for him to tell her what to do, showing she wasn't nearly as inexperienced with being a good submissive as he'd suspected. In fact, submissive behavior seemed to come completely naturally to Nicky. It was the other stuff that was forced, the defiance, the testing the limits of the man who would dominate her. A bad habit learned from living with a man who couldn't handle her, no doubt.

Good thing Jackson was sure he was twice the dom her ex-husband had been, or he might have been nervous himself. Nicky wasn't an easy woman to top. Of course, that's what made the experience so intoxicating. He was going to have to earn every last ounce of submission he coaxed from the woman at his feet. It was a strangely exhilarating and empowering experience. One he feared might ruin him for any other woman.

How could he go back to those silly girls who hit the BDSM clubs once a week to play when he'd had the chance to test the boundaries of a woman like Nick?

"Do you want me to take you in my mouth?" she asked, licking her lips again, the sight making a pearl of pre-cum leak from the tip of Jackson's cock.

"Yes," Jackson said, his voice deeper, rougher than he could ever remember it sounding.

"With pleasure, sir." A naughty smile flitted across Nicky's face as she leaned forward, pausing only centimeters away from his swollen tip.

Slowly she rolled her eyes up to meet his and parted her lips, letting her breath warm his eager flesh for one second, then two, before finally taking the plumped head of his cock into the wet heat of her mouth. Jackson did his best not to groan as she lingered there, suckling him, running her teeth lightly over the ridge where head became shaft. For what seemed like hours she played with him, pulling just his tip between her lips then moving away, running her tongue around and around the slit at the end of his cock until he genuinely began to leak.

But even then she didn't intensify her efforts, only moaned as she lapped away the evidence of his need, as if his cum was the best thing she'd tasted all day. If that was the case, he was certainly going to give her more of what she was craving. Very soon. But when he did so, he'd prefer it to be *after* he'd fucked that pretty mouth in earnest.

Gritting his teeth to maintain control, Jackson reached down, threading his fingers into Nicky's hair. He caressed her gently for a moment, sliding his fingers through her silky locks, marveling that anything could feel so soft. Only when he felt the muscles in her neck begin to relax did he fist his hand, claiming control of her in one swift movement.

Nicky sucked in a swift breath, surprise and lust mingling in the small sound.

Jackson looked down into her eyes, holding them as he tightened his grip in her hair, making it clear he was now calling the shots. Then, without a word of warning, without asking permission he tugged her forward. His cock disappeared between her lips and within a few seconds he hit the back of her throat. He paused there, giving her a moment to adjust, to relax the muscles barring his deeper penetration. Then he thrust even deeper. And deeper still, forcing her to take over half of his length. Once he was there, buried as deeply as he thought she could handle, he held absolutely still, watching Nicky's face.

Her eyes squeezed closed and she seemed to struggle for breath, but only for a moment. Seconds later, she was moaning around his cock, her pleasure in being filled with him obvious. So obvious he wasn't surprised when he saw her slip a hand between her legs, clearly intending to take care of herself with her fingers while his cock was busy in her mouth.

"No, Nick. Don't touch my pussy," Jackson said, accentuating his point by pulling away and then thrusting back inside her wet heat. "You can play with your tits if you want, but don't touch my pussy."

He'd done it again, but this time Jackson didn't regret claiming her pussy as his own. He wasn't going to fight the rightness of what was happening between them anymore. For the next two days, she would belong to him, every last part of her, from those hazel eyes swirling brown and green to that sweet little pussy he was going to teach another valuable lesson about delayed gratification.

But first, he was going to enjoy a little gratification of his own.

For the next few minutes, the world disappeared. There were no thoughts of Nicky's tattoo, there was no stress about what this weekend would hold for the two of them, there was no worry about the wisdom of indulging in dom-sub play with the least suitable woman he could have chosen. There was only Nicky.

Nicky's mouth, hot and eager, sucking him impossibly farther inside. Her tongue rolling against his engorged cock, her hands sliding around to cup his ass, fingernails digging into the muscled flesh until he groaned. Her little moans as he fucked her mouth, the hint of tears glistening in her eyes as his penetration grew more intense, the silent urging of her hands on his buttocks, telling him not to back off, not to stop until he was shooting himself between her lips.

Finally, the combined stimulation was too much. A deep cry ripped from his chest as he came, his cock jerking inside her mouth, cum gushing from his body in thick, hot jets.

"God, Nick," he groaned, his voice hoarse with desire as he watched her jaw work. She was swallowing him down, every last bit of fluid, milking his cock dry with a look of such bliss he knew he would have been hard again immediately if nature had allowed it.

After a few moments, she pulled away, slowly, letting his cock slip from between her lips with obvious regret. Only then did she lift her eyes back to his, a new question in their expressive depths.

"Hell, yes. It was the best blow job of my life. Bar none," Jackson said, his hand softening in her hair again, then moving down to cup her cheek. God, she was beautiful. The face of an angel and the mouth of a dirty little slut.

He laughed softly as he tucked himself back in his pants and zipped his fly. "Do you like being called names?"

"What kind of names?" she asked, her breath coming fast, her brow furrowing as she watched him put away his cock. She wasn't pleased to see it go, which pleased him far more than it should have.

"Slut. Whore. Things like that."

She blushed at his words and dropped her eyes to the ground, but a small smile twisted her lips, belying the shy expression. "It depends."

"On what?"

"No, on *who*." She lifted her eyes to his once more. All humor had vanished from her features, replaced by a look of such intensity it made him shiver. Jackson would have sworn at that moment she was seeing into his soul. "If you called me *your* dirty slut, *your* whore . . . I think I'd like it very much."

Jackson struggled to breathe past the wave of lust inspired by her words, and wasn't surprised to feel his hands tremble slightly as he moved them to his hips. "Is that so?"

"Yeah. That's so," she said, her voice pure, aural sex.

"Well, then, is my little slut horny?" he asked, his words not much more than a whisper. "Does she want to get fucked?"

"Yes." Her breasts were as flushed as her cheeks and her nipples were so tight Jackson knew they had to be aching uncomfortably. She'd been genuinely turned on by what she'd done to him, a fact that blew him away. It was a rare woman who got off on giving a blow job. But then, a true submissive got off on anything that gave her lover pleasure, as did a true dom, for that matter.

Unfortunately, what gave a submissive pleasure could be a little more complicated.

"Good. Because I'm going to fuck you," Jackson said, staring into her eyes, feeling his cock thicken slightly at the heat he saw there. "First I'll eat that wet little pussy, and then I'm going to fuck you until you scream. First your pussy, and then maybe I'll fuck your ass. Would you like to have me inside your ass, Nick?"

"I want to have you everywhere." Nicky's breath came even faster and her hands balled into fists at her sides. It was getting harder for her to wait, to keep from reaching for what she wanted. For a second it made him rethink his plan. But then, the fact that she was nearing the edge of her control was all the more reason to test it.

"I promise it will be more than worth the wait." He turned back toward the suitcase on the bed, but not before he saw the shocked expression on Nicky's face.

"Wait?" she asked, in a tone that left no doubt how little she relished the idea. It made Jackson smile, but he was careful to wipe the grin from his face before he turned back to her.

"I'm going downstairs to take a shower," he said, calmly pulling a pair of white cotton panties and a green sleep shirt from the clothes he'd packed for Nick. "You're welcome to take a shower up here at the same time. There's plenty of hot water for both of us."

"Plenty of hot water?" She laughed, a short, abrupt sound that wasn't the least bit amused. "You've got to be kidding me."

"No, I assumed you'd be wanting a shower and prepared ahead of time. There's girly soap and shampoo and conditioner in the cabinet and a new toothbrush and toothpaste in the drawer." He zipped the suitcase shut and picked it up, deciding it would be best if he didn't give Nicky access to the winter clothes he'd brought in case she decided to run. Of course, in her present state of mind, she might decide it was a good idea to run out into the snow in nothing but her nightshirt and bare feet. "We're about ten miles from the nearest cabin, so I wouldn't try to make a run for it if I were you."

"You're not going to just . . . leave me like this," she said, gesturing down at herself, as if her state of arousal should be abundantly obvious.

And it was. Damn, but it wasn't easy to resist crossing the room, kneeling down beside her to take her nipples in his mouth. He could almost feel how perfectly they would stiffen against his tongue, hear how she'd moan as he coaxed her into a state of even more powerful lust. They probably wouldn't even make it to the bed. He'd end up taking her there on the floor, her long legs wrapped around his hips, his cock buried to the hilt in—

Thankfully, Nicky spoke before the weakness of his mind could become weakness of the body. "Jackson, I swear to god, I—"

"I warned you to stop. Surely you realized there would be consequences for disobeying."

"Fuck your consequences," she said, but even with the angry look on her face, he could tell the idea of being disciplined excited her.

"I'll take care of you in the morning. Sleep well," he said, toting the suitcase with him to the door, where he stopped to look back at Nicky one more time. "And don't think about using that detachable nozzle in the shower, or your hand, or anything else. I'll know if you don't wait for me and I won't be happy."

"I don't care if you're happy," she mumbled under her breath, but he heard every word, just like she'd wanted him to.

In a matter of seconds, he'd dropped the suitcase and was by her side, pushing her back onto the carpet. Her lips met his with a soft cry and her hands shook as she looped them around his neck. He kissed her, softly, insistently, thoroughly, until she squirmed beneath him. Only then did he pull away to watch her eyes as he spoke.

"If you really don't care if I'm happy, or at least pleased with you, then we should stop this right now," he said, his voice low and firm. "A submissive takes pleasure from serving his or her dominant, it's the very definition of the word. So if pleasing me doesn't give you pleasure, if obeying my command isn't a gratifying thing in its own right, then you—"

"I'm sorry," she said, with a vulnerability in her voice that made his heart ache a bit. "Pleasing you does give me pleasure. I just . . . want you so much. It will be hard to wait."

"I know. Believe me, babe, it's not going to be easy for me, either. I've been wanting to get my mouth between your legs since the second I saw you tonight." He leaned down, pressing a soft kiss to the tip of her nose. "But I swear to you, you can trust me. I'll make it worth your while."

She took a deep breath, letting it out slowly as she dropped her arms to her sides. "Okay, go. But first thing tomorrow morning?"

"I'll have your pussy for breakfast. I swear." He kissed her one last time, relishing the feel of her moan of anticipation buzzing against his lips before he pulled himself back to his feet.

Jackson was at the door, grabbing the suitcase, and heading downstairs seconds later, without turning to look over his shoulder. If he had, and been forced to see Nicky sprawled nude on the carpet, that come-hither look in her eyes, he knew he never would have had the strength to leave.

Some dom he was.

But then, he hadn't exactly been prepared to exert the kind of control it took to top a girl like Nicky. He'd never dreamed she'd summon not only the feelings associated with what they'd shared as teenagers but also stimulate the very adult desires he'd acquired since then. He'd finally met his match, the kind of woman he could see himself playing with for the next twenty or thirty years, the strong yet entirely submissive partner he hadn't dreamed he'd find.

Too bad she was also the only woman who had broken his heart and a person who could not be trusted. He'd never guessed she would leave Carson City the very morning after they swore to spend their futures together and sealed the promise with a pair of matching tattoos. There hadn't been the slightest sign.

Hell, they'd made love right after he'd finished the work on her shoulder, sneaking into the camper behind their friend Kevin's house to do it in a bed instead of the car for a change. Even at eighteen, Jackson had known he'd never forget that night, how beautiful Nicky had looked, how excited he'd felt knowing he was going to be in control of his own life.

He'd already had a job lined up as a bouncer at a local bar and was going to be working part-time with the best tattoo artist in town. In a few months, he'd expected to have the portfolio and the money he needed to make the move to Reno, and from there to Vegas. And Nicky was going to get her GED and go with him. They'd had it all planned out.

But then she'd run away, without leaving so much as a note to tell him why. Jackson had shown up at Casa de la Hell and Phil had tried to kick his ass. He'd thought Nicky was with Jack. He'd been wrong, but that didn't stop him from giving his former foster son a black eye before Jackson landed a few punches to the older man's ribs and leveled him.

The sound of the water turning on upstairs pulled Jack back to the present, making him wonder how long he'd been standing at the bottom of the stairs with a death grip on the handle of the suitcase and bad memories souring the taste of Nicky's kiss.

"Too long," he mumbled aloud. Any time spent dwelling on those old memories was too much time. He'd already learned the lessons he needed from those days. He'd learned not to trust Nicky, no matter how much he'd loved her.

No matter how much he was beginning to think he *still* loved her.

Chapter Seven

"I'll take care of you in the morning," Nicky said, mimicking Jackson's ridiculously bossy voice as she scrubbed her skin with the loofah until it stung.

Gah! She'd never felt so dissatisfied, not even after what he'd made her do in the truck. Every nerve ending in her body screamed for relief from the unfulfilled desire still coursing through her veins, making her breath come in angry little pants. Dom or not, Jackson had no right to do this to her, especially not twice in one night. She hadn't been *that* defiant, and had sucked him off like the best little slave in the world.

Sucked him off... god help her, but even the memory of it was enough to make her pussy even wetter. Jackson had the most gorgeous cock she'd ever seen in her life—long and thick, with a bulbous head that filled her mouth like a perfectly shaped plum. And it wasn't just pretty, but made for pleasure, a woman's pleasure. The thick ridge between head and shaft rubbed all the right places as he shoved in and out of her body, stretching her, filling every empty, aching place inside of her until there was nothing but Jackson. Nothing but pure pleasure.

"Grr," Nicky growled, throwing the loofah to the shower floor in frustration.

Take care of her in the morning, her ass. She'd take care of herself. Right now.

Nicky pulled the shower nozzle from its place on the wall, a thrill of excitement shooting through her as she used it to wash the last of the soap from her body. It wasn't just the fact that she was getting ready to come that thrilled her, it was the knowledge that she was defying Jackson, disobeying a direct order. Maybe he was right, and she was a naughty little submissive who needed to be punished, but that wasn't going to stop her. She needed to take the edge off if she was going to have any hope of getting some sleep before morning.

She stuck her head out of the shower curtain for a moment, listening carefully. Thankfully, she could still hear the water running downstairs. Jackson wasn't finished with his shower, which meant he wouldn't be coming to check up on her for at least the next few minutes.

"A few minutes is all it will take," Nicky said, smiling as she lay down in the tub, propping one foot on the side, baring the needy place between her legs.

Moving one hand to her breast, she began plucking at her already erect nipples, building the simmering passion within her to near the breaking point. Then, with a sigh of anticipation, she moved the nozzle of the shower between her legs. Nicky gasped as the water streamed over her clit. God, she was so close ... so fucking close. Just a few more seconds, just a little more pressure and then ... then ...

"Shit!" Her hands shook as she pinched her nipples and squirmed beneath the nozzle between her legs.

What was wrong? She'd never had a problem bringing herself pleasure. Usually in less than sixty seconds. When you lived under the thumb of a domineering man who refused to have sex with you, but had forbidden you to pleasure yourself, you learned to get the job done as quickly as possible. If she hadn't been adept at getting herself off, she probably would have lost her mind during the past two years.

So why was her body failing her now?

And don't think about using that detachable nozzle in the shower, or your hand, or anything else. I'll know if you don't wait for me and I won't be happy.

"No. God, no." Nicky's eyes slid closed as she let the showerhead slide down to pelt water against her thigh.

No matter what the rational part of her had to say, it seemed her body had decided Jackson's happiness was essential. It wasn't going to let her come, because it didn't want to displease the man downstairs, didn't want to anger its master. God. Dammit. Her good little submissive act hadn't been an act, after all. She was going to have to do exactly as he'd told her, no matter what she wanted. Her stupid, freaking, twisted mind wouldn't allow her to do anything else.

It wasn't the first time she'd wished she'd never started exploring this side of herself, never admitted she craved the act of submission. The highs were admittedly very high, but the lows of the past two years should have taught her the danger in walking this path. *She* needed to be in control of herself right now. She had to concentrate on getting her life back on track, not on servicing another man. Even if it was only for a weekend, this wasn't smart.

Hell, if her head had already decided obeying Jackson was *necessary* in order to claim her own pleasure, this could be downright dangerous.

Tears of fear and frustration filled Nicky's eyes as she hurriedly finished her shower and dried off. She pulled on the panties and nightshirt Jackson had brought for her, but even the soft fabric felt abrasive against her sensitized skin. She brushed her hair with swift, angry strokes, and after a little searching found the toothbrush and toothpaste Jackson had purchased for her. Seconds later, footsteps sounded on the stair, making her hurry to finish brushing her teeth and escape to the relative safety of her bedroom.

If she had to see Jackson again, smell that addictive scent that was the man she loved again, she'd——

"No. No, no, no, no." Nicky chanted the mantra under her breath as she dashed to the bed, snapped off the bedside lamp, and curled into a ball beneath the covers.

She *wasn't* falling in love with Jackson again. It was impossible. They'd been together less than twenty-four hours and no amount of hot sex could make up for time spent together, getting to know each other, learning to care for each other again.

Unless, of course, she hadn't ever *stopped* loving him in the first place.

"Dammit," Nicky whispered into the ridiculously luxurious sheets Jackson's decorator had ordered for this room. Then she started to cry, though the exact reason for her tears wasn't completely clear.

Was she crying for herself, for Jackson? For what they'd lost, or for what they'd never have again? She certainly didn't know.

There were many things in her life that confused her, but love had always been the biggest and most confusing thing of all.

When she woke up, the entire room was aglow with light and an only slightly rumpled Jackson was lying beside her, propped on one elbow, watching her sleep with a tender expression on his face. Even before she'd had the chance to shake off the sleep cobwebs, that look brought all her fears from the night before rushing back with a vengeance. The anxiety was strong enough to make her scoot a few inches away, despite the fact that the heat rolling from his body made her long to snuggle against his chest and go right back to sleep.

Great, now she craved snuggling instead of sex. What a perfect example of the deep shit she was getting herself into with every second she spent with this man.

"Good morning. Did you sleep well?"

"Pretty well, considering the epic sexual frustration."

"But you still behaved yourself. I'm glad. I'd hate to have to neglect your pussy any longer," he said, ignoring her continued migration to the other side of the queen-sized bed. Maybe he thought she was worried about morning breath.

Hmm . . . *should* she be worried about morning breath? A quick run of her tongue along her teeth revealed not a shred of fuzziness. Of course, she probably hadn't been asleep more than a few hours. It was doubtful her breath had been given the time to get funky.

"What are you thinking?" A smile pulled at the corners of his full lips, making her want to smile along with him. Jackson could be a scary-looking motherfucker when he wanted to be, but when he smiled he looked like a big teddy bear.

"I was thinking about morning breath," she said with a little laugh.

"Don't worry. You're good. I kissed you before you woke up. You looked so damned sweet I couldn't help myself."

"Sweet?"

"Yeah, I was surprised, too. Amazing what being unconscious will do for a brat's looks." He grinned again as he reached out, twisting a strand of her hair around his finger. "I'd forgotten it was curly when you didn't do that thing to it."

"It's called a flattening iron. You must come into the twenty-first century." Nicky told herself she should move away from that gentle touch and the scary look in Jackson's eyes, but she couldn't. It had been too long since anyone had looked at her with such affection. Terrifying and stupid or not, she craved the warmth in his expression as much as she'd craved his body last night.

"Give me a break. I haven't lived with a girl since high school. And then you know we never spent much time getting ready at home."

"Yeah, six or more people and one bathroom was always fun." Nicky shuddered as she remembered the nasty little Pepto-Bismol–colored toilet and the tub with the cracks up the side.

She'd shared the festering little lav with Jackson; Phil and his wife, Naomi; and an endlessly shifting group of younger foster kids. Nicky had tried not to remember their names or their faces. It was easier that way. If she didn't get attached, she didn't have to freak out when they went to school with bruises on their arms or without breakfast in their bellies because Phil had gone on a bender and they didn't have money left over to buy cereal or milk.

"It was easier to get ready at school," she said, digging her fingers into her eyes, as if she could rub away the visions of the sad little faces conjured by her thoughts.

"Or in Kevin's camper."

Nicky's eyes flew open, wondering if he remembered that's where they'd spent their last night together, but he didn't seem to make the connection. Of course, Jackson hadn't known it would be their last night. She hadn't wanted to ruin it for him by telling him she couldn't wait until he raised enough money for them to move to Reno.

There was no way she could have kept living in Casa de la Hell without Jackson there, and no way Phil would have let a minor in his "care" move out to live with her boyfriend. As long as her foster father knew where she was, there was no way she'd have any peace. She'd had to get out of town, *way* out of town.

"So, you hungry?" he asked, releasing the curl he'd wrapped around his finger. "I've got the stuff to make waffles downstairs. And some bacon and eggs, or diet yogurt if you're watching your figure."

"You know me. I can take down two times my body weight a day and not gain a pound. Even when I was—" Nicky broke off, biting her lip. "Even when I stopped growing taller, I kept eating like a horse."

Shit! She'd nearly said "when I was pregnant." The last thing she wanted to talk about with Jackson was her fight for her daughter. He'd either hate her for being dumb and weak enough to let Derrick take Abby—they'd always sworn they would protect their kids if they ever had any of their own—or he'd decide to wring Derrick's neck with his own hands. As appealing as that image was, Nicky didn't want to be responsible for getting Jackson put in jail for beating another man to a pulp or be indebted to him for rushing to "rescue her."

She was going to rescue herself, thank you very much. She had an appointment with the marketing head of Good and Trashy Lingerie next Friday. Kelsey Greer had always been a big Angel fan. He'd hire her on for the spring line photo shoot for sure. Maybe not in her former position as the "it girl," but the job would earn her a few grand, easy. Then she'd be in a much better place to fight Derrick in court.

Or you could take that fifteen grand Jackson's offering and be in an even better place, even sooner.

No way. She didn't want Jackson's money, especially not for something as creepy as letting him alter her tattoo. Even if she could be convinced that a slightly different fallen angel would serve her modeling career as well as the one she had now, she didn't want to look over her shoulder in the mirror and see anything but what she saw now. It would be like losing a piece of herself to lose that tat.

"So I guess that's a yes for breakfast?" Jackson asked, the look in his eyes making Nicky wonder if he'd been reading her mind. He looked so smug and satisfied with himself, like he knew she'd just realized the damned tattoo was so much more to her than a marketing device for her modeling career. The ink had kept her connected to Jackson no matter how much time and distance separated them. But where that had given her comfort, it had obviously driven Jack crazy, made him willing to do anything to sever that connection.

"Yeah, breakfast sounds good," Nicky said, ignoring the tightness in her chest.

"What's wrong?"

"Nothing." She smiled, determined not to get her precious little feelings hurt by the fact that Jackson wanted to erase the evidence of their past. She'd known that's what he wanted to do since last night. Why should it bother her so much more this morning?

Because now you know you still love him, never stopped loving him.

"I'm starving. Let's eat." She tried to bolt from the bed, but a rock-hard arm closed around her waist and pulled her back onto the covers.

"I haven't forgotten my promise," Jackson said, his hand wandering down to her bare thigh, caressing her with a gentle insistence that had her body waking up faster than downing a double shot of espresso. "I just wanted to make sure I wasn't starving you to death. You can't live on love alone and all that."

"Lust alone, you mean." Nicky strove to make the words casual, but the joke fell flat, and if she wasn't mistaken Jackson looked a little hurt by the correction.

Could he be feeling the same way she did? Did he more than "care" for her? Could he still feel the way he had when they were so young and stupid, but so very, very in love?

The thought should have been exhilarating. Isn't that what she'd hoped for? Less than eight hours ago she'd sworn to do whatever it took to make Jackson start falling for her again, and then use his feelings to make this weekend end the way she wanted it to end. But now ... the thought of Jackson loving her just hurt. Badly.

"Babe, don't cry. What's wrong?" Jackson pulled his hand away from her thigh, moving both arms to surround her and pull her close to his chest. He was so much bigger and stronger than he'd been when they were younger, but the feeling of safety she'd always felt when he held her was the same.

God, why had she ever left him? No matter how bad things had been at her foster home, she should have stayed and found a way to wait for him. How had she ever thought she'd be okay without Jack?

Of course, at sixteen, she hadn't realized how precious he was. She'd known there weren't a lot of good guys out there, but she'd assumed she would find another, move on from her first love. But she hadn't, not even when things were still good with Derrick. She'd never loved her husband the way she loved this man. And on those nights she'd cried herself to sleep when her marriage had soured, it wasn't Derrick's arms she imagined holding her close, making her feel safe and loved.

It was Jackson. It had always been Jackson. And probably always would be.

Still, that didn't change anything. Jackson didn't want her, not really. If he did, he wouldn't have written asking her to change her tattoo. He would have written asking to see her again, to see if they could reconnect in some way. He hadn't known she was married. She'd kept her maiden name instead of taking Derrick's. Nicky Remington certainly sounded a lot more glamorous and lingerie-model-esque than Nicky Sakapatatis, and not even Derrick's wrath could convince her to take that trip down to the Social Security office.

No, what Jackson really wanted was his freedom. Whatever it was he was feeling, he wanted those feelings gone, and he thought modifying her tattoo was the way to get that accomplished. Who knew? Maybe it was. Maybe the connection between them would finally be severed when they no longer sported matching ink.

"I'm okay." She sniffed, wishing she had a Kleenex. Seconds later, Jack reached out and plucked one from the bedside table and pressed it into her hand. That small act of compassion was nearly enough to get her tears going again.

"Listen, I meant what I said, Nick. I don't want to hurt you, and I really don't want to make you cry."

"You look scared." Nicky sniffed and wiped her nose.

"Well, a crying woman is a pretty scary thing." He smiled as he tucked a stray lock of hair behind her ear. "Especially you. I can count the times I've seen you cry on one finger."

"Really? I never . . . No, I guess I never did." She laughed, remembering the tough little nut she used to be. Of course, most of it had been an act, a front to hide how scared and sad she was sometimes—well, just about all the time when she wasn't with Jackson. "It's all right. Now, I cry all the time. It's no big thing."

"Sounds like a big thing to me." His smile faded and he started to look like scary Jackson again. "What's been making you cry? Your ex? If so, I'm sure I could arrange for him to have a visit from some people who would make him think twice about—"

"Let's not talk about my ex," Nicky said, tossing her Kleenex to the floor behind her. "In fact, let's not talk at all."

Before Jack could say a word, she'd wrapped her arms around his neck, pulling him down for a kiss. And then another kiss, and another, until he moaned into her mouth and rolled on top of her, crushing her into the mattress with his weight, all concerns about who or what might have been making her cry clearly vanishing in the wake of the heat that never failed to flare between them.

Nicky wrapped her legs around his hips, a moan bursting from her own lips when she felt how hard he was beneath those blue-and-white-striped pajama bottoms. "What time is it?" she asked in between nibbles at his bottom lip.

"Nearly noon." He took his turn capturing her bottom lip, tugging it between his teeth before he let it go.

Damn, she'd never realized she enjoyed being bitten so much. But then, she enjoyed everything Jackson did to her, even the stuff she was sure she hated. Like it or not, he'd been right to make her wait. She was even more eager to have him now than she'd been last night, and knew when she finally came it was going to blow her mind. And probably her heart, too, but she wasn't going to think about that now. She wasn't going to think about anything except how amazing he made her feel.

"That's horrible. I can't believe we're still in our pajamas at noon," she said, reaching down to run her fingers under the waistband of his pants. "I think it's time we both got out of them. Don't you think?"

"I couldn't agree more." His laugh rumbled against her lips, making them tingle.

Then they were pulling at each other's clothes, laughing as shirts and pants flew, sighing as bodies came back together with nothing to separate skin from skin. And for a moment, as her breasts pressed against Jackson's hard, lightly furred chest and her lips met his—teeth bumping together as they kissed through their matching grins—Nicky was happy. As happy as she'd been in longer than she could remember.

Chapter Eight

*J*ackson pulled away from Nicky, looking down at her sprawled naked beneath him, her hair glowing gold in the light. She'd washed off the makeup she'd had on last night and looked the way she had eight years ago. Even the look in her eyes was the same, that vulnerable expression that had always made him feel like the focus of her entire world—at least for the moment.

It would have been enough to make his heart break if he'd let it. But he couldn't dwell on past losses or betrayals now, not when she looked so beautiful. Not when, strangely, he was the happiest he'd been in years.

"I want to eat my pussy," Jack said, running his hands up and down the thighs she had hooked around his hips.

"You do?" She wiggled her hips, grinding her center against his erection. "Are you sure you don't want to save that until after breakfast? You could fuck me now and have your pussy for dessert."

"I'd rather have my pussy as an appetizer." He dipped his hand down between them, capturing a bit of her wetness on his fingertips and then bringing them to his lips. She tasted as amazing as she ever had—sweet and salty, with that hint of feminine musk. To him, the taste of Nicky was the taste of pure desire.

It made him even harder, thicker. With his cock pressed tight to where she was so wet, it was tempting to forget the preliminaries and drive straight into where he'd been dying to be since he'd left her last night. But she'd proven she could keep her promises. Now he was going to prove he could keep his.

Besides, he *was* dying to eat his pussy, to see if Nicky was as responsive as she had been the last time he'd lowered his head between her legs. And, of course, to show her he'd learned a thing or two about giving a woman pleasure since his eighteenth birthday.

"Open your legs. Spread them wide for me," he commanded, his breath coming faster as he watched Nicky obey. She reached down, grabbing the inside of her thighs, pulling them apart, baring her slit to his gaze.

His cock started to leak again as he took in what was probably the most gorgeous pussy in the world. The delicate lips were a deep pink, and plumped with the force of her desire. Just above, her clit stood firm and erect, and between her folds, her entrance glistened, already dripping wet. She was hot and ready for him, and he was past ready to have another taste of his girl.

"Wider." He grunted his approval as she moved her hands behind her knees, tugging them up and out, bearing every inch of her sex from clit to ass. She concealed nothing from him. Instead she offered up everything, without hesitation or fear. It was enough to snap the last of his control.

With a groan he lowered his face between her legs, forcing himself to start slowly, to trace the swollen folds of her pussy, to tease her to an even greater state of arousal. He ran his tongue up one side of her entrance and down the other, intensifying his pressure until she moaned and arched closer to his eager mouth.

Only then did he drive slowly inside her, once, twice, her addictive flavor coating his stiff tongue, making his hands shake as he brought them to her hips. His fingers dug into the full flesh there as he began to fuck her with his mouth in earnest. In and out, in and out, he penetrated her with his swift strokes, coaxing even more cream from her body.

"God, Jackson." Nicky's breath came faster and her hands dropped to his head, her fingernails tunneling through his short hair and digging into his scalp.

Jackson moaned, humming against her swollen flesh, making her cry out as he moved his thumb to her nub. He circled her clit with a slow, insistent pressure even as the thrusts of his tongue grew faster, deeper. Nicky's pussy tightened around where he worked inside her and her thighs began to tremble. A glance up the landscape of her body showed her nipples were drawn into tight points, her head thrown back in prelude to ecstasy.

She was close, so close, but he wasn't finished with her just yet.

Without missing a beat, Jackson moved his mouth from her entrance to her clit, swirling his tongue around and around the erect bud. Two fingers took up the rhythm inside her pussy, while his thumb found the puckered ring of her ass. She was already slick from her own juices, so there was little resistance as he penetrated her, easing his thumb inside the tight hole.

"Jackson!" Nicky gasped his name and spread her thighs even wider, giving him unimpeded access to every inch of the paradise between her legs.

She obviously didn't have a problem with having his fingers fill her anywhere and everywhere. It was enough to make him wonder how she'd feel about having his cock in her ass. He'd never had anal sex before, and had never been particularly inclined to try it, but for some reason the thought of shoving his cock into Nicky's second hole made him impossibly harder. It wasn't a newly discovered kink, it was simply that he wanted to do everything to Nicky, *with* Nicky. He wanted to explore every inch of her body, claim her mouth, her pussy, her ass, make it clear her body belonged to him, would *always* belong to him.

"Oh god, oh god." Nicky panted above him, eager sounds issuing from the back of her throat. "Can I come? Jackson, can I—"

"Come for me, babe. Come on my mouth," he mumbled against her aroused flesh, then returned his attention to her clit, flicking his tongue across the hard nub as Nicky came with a wild cry.

She bucked beneath him, heels digging into the mattress, pelvis lifted into the air. Jackson moved his hands back to her hips, holding her still as he softly lapped up every last bit of her cream. Only when her breath began to slow and some of the tension left her muscles did he increase the pressure of his strokes once more, playing through her folds with his tongue, teasing her clit with the barest touches here and there.

Within a few minutes, her hands fisted in the sheets and her pussy gushed fresh cream, her arousal so great the slick heat leaked down the sides of her thighs. Finally the sight and smell of her was too much to resist.

Jackson surged over her in one swift motion, shoving his engorged length into where she was so hot, and so very wet. "Fuck, Nicky." He groaned the words into her mouth, meeting her eager lips with his own, slipping his tongue between her teeth and letting her taste her own salty heat.

"Yes, fuck Nicky. That's exactly what you should do." She wrapped her legs around his hips and squeezed, urging him even deeper insider her welcoming sheath.

The head of his cock bumped against the end of her and his balls fit snugly in the crack of her ass, but still Nicky flexed her muscles and tilted her hips, as if she could never have him deep enough. Jackson knew exactly how she felt. It wasn't physically possible to get as close as he'd like to be to her. He couldn't crawl inside her and share her skin, couldn't pull her so close their separate bodies fused into one mass of pulsing, aroused flesh.

But fucking her was pretty close.

With a sound closer to a growl than anything human, Jackson pulled back and then slammed home, burying himself to the hilt in Nicky. Slow thrusts all too quickly became swift and desperate as the last of his control vanished in the heat they generated whenever they were together. He rode her, shoving in and out of her slick sheath, setting a brutal rhythm Nicky matched with eager lifts of her hips.

"God, Jackson. Yes!" She came without warning this time, her pussy clamping down on where he moved inside her, triggering his own release so quickly he barely had time to realize he wasn't wearing a condom.

"Shit." He cursed as he pulled out of her tight heat, his cock pulsing against her belly seconds later, spilling thick, sticky cum across her stomach. He groaned as his release rocketed through him, sending waves of pure bliss flowing out to every inch of his body, the pleasure at complete odds with the voice inside his head that was screaming he was a fucking idiot for forgetting protection.

Jackson collapsed on top of Nicky a few seconds later, breath still coming faster as he pressed a soft kiss to her lips. "I'm sorry about that."

"Don't worry," she panted, a smile on her face, though she looked a little confused. "I like feeling you come on me." She kissed him again, her arms wrapping around him, fingertips tracing patterns on his sweat-dampened back. "I might even be into letting you come on my tits like you were talking about last night. After some breakfast."

He smiled. "No, I meant sorry for forgetting a condom."

"Oh," she said, comprehension dawning. "Well, I'm on the pill and clean. I . . . haven't had much sexual activity for the past few years. So you don't have to worry about my end of things."

"I'm clean, too. I was tested a couple of months ago and I *never* forget to wear a rubber," he said, not realizing how true the words were until they were out of his mouth. He had truly *never* forgotten to use protection. Not a single time in his life.

Shit, no wonder he'd come so fast. He wasn't used to the bliss of being inside a woman without a latex barrier, especially this woman. "This was the first time that has happened. Ever. I don't know what I was thinking. I guess I was just—"

"Overcome by how hot it was to eat my pussy?" she asked, a wicked gleam in her eye.

"I'd imagine that had something to do with it," he said with a laugh. "It's an extremely hot little pussy."

"Hmm, well. Some dom you are, losing control like that. I think *you* ought to be punished this time."

"I think you're right. How about I serve you waffles on my hands and knees like a good little slave?" he asked, unable to resist dropping soft kisses along her bare shoulder as he spoke. It was impossible to keep from kissing her when she was this close.

"I was thinking you could grab a towel from the bathroom and clean me up, but the hands and knees stuff sounds good, too."

"Yes, ma'am. Your wish is my command." Jackson leapt from the bed, taking a second to wash his hands and run warm water on a washcloth before returning to Nick with the cloth and a towel. "I have returned, Mistress."

Nicky laughed. "Do you switch? I mean, I can't imagine it but I have to ask."

"No, never. Do you?"

"No. I like being a submissive, no matter what you think," she said, obviously a little offended. Jackson remembered his words from the night before and felt guilty.

"You know, maybe I was a little too quick to judge with the whole pushy bottom thing. How can you really know something like that about a person unless you spend significant time together?"

"A dom admitting he was wrong?" Her eyes grew comically large. "Gasp! The world must be coming to an end."

"I don't know what kind of 'doms' you've been dealing with, but I admit I'm wrong all the time. I'm only human," he said, then added with a grin, "Though an exceptionally sexy and masterful human who should be obeyed with humble submissiveness."

"Right. Is that even a word? Submissivissism—I can't even say it." She giggled. "But yes, sir, you are totally sexy and masterful."

"And don't you forget it." He sat down on the bed and scooted close to where she still lay stretched out on her back, looking so satisfied he couldn't help but feel a surge of satisfaction for being the one to pleasure her so completely. "Now let me get this nasty cum off your gorgeous belly."

"It's not nasty cum. It's very nice cum, actually." She sighed and closed her eyes as he ran the warm rag over her skin. "It smells like green apple slices with salt on them, just like it always did."

"You never told me that," he said as he softly wiped away the last of the stickiness and began to dry her with the towel.

"Yeah, well, I was all shy and shit."

"Right."

"I was!" She laughed, belying her words. "Besides, I thought all cum smelled like that. I'd never been so up close and personal with a guy's spooge until you and me."

"Spooge? That's classy."

"You prefer jizz?"

"Even classier." He tried not to smile as he crossed the room and threw the towel and rag in the dirty-clothes basket. The decorator really had thought of everything.

This cabin was better outfitted than his house. And he loved the way Patricia had used his suggestion of Nicky's favorite colors in decorating her room, but still managed to make it look like a woman's place, not a teenager's. The little getaway was so comfy, a part of him wished he could stay forever. Forget Miami and his and Christian's tattooing empire. He could just live here in the woods with Nicky, happy as a pig in shit.

Too bad that scenario was about as impossible as they came.

Is it really? Look at her, man, she still cares about you. A lot. This weekend might have a happier ending than you thought possible.

Jackson pushed the thought away. He couldn't let himself start thinking happily-ever-after thoughts about him and Nick. That path led to nothing but heartache. He'd just have to enjoy this weekend for what it was—a fun forty-eight hours and nothing more.

"How about jism, or squirt?" Nicky asked, her head emerging

from her nightshirt as he turned back to the bed. She'd decided to get dressed. Probably a good thing or their chances of getting out of this bedroom today weren't going to be good.

"How about plain old semen? Or cum?"

"I knew a guy once who called it baby batter." She threw him his boxer briefs and pajama pants and started hunting for her underpants. Jackson saw them on the floor a few feet away, but decided to let her look for a while, enjoying the glimpses of her bare pussy as she bent over to look under the bed.

"I don't want to hear about guys you've known," he said, the idea of anyone else with Nicky making him unreasonably cranky.

"Relax, he wasn't a lover. He was a guy I worked with at this restaurant in Santa Monica." She found her panties and pulled them on as she chattered. "He had six kids. And a very sweet, though certifiably insane, wife. I mean, *six* kids. That's too much of a good thing if you ask me."

"How many kids is enough of a good thing? In your opinion?" Jackson asked, ignoring the part of him that said those kinds of questions were the dangerous breed of stupid. He and Nicky were never even going to date again, let alone shack up and start making babies together. How many kids she did or didn't want was none of his business.

"I don't know. I always thought I wanted three, but now I think two might be enough," she said, a wistful look on her face that reminded him she wasn't the girl he'd known eight years ago. That girl wouldn't get bummed out talking about making babies. Even at sixteen, Nicky had talked about wanting a big family and kids she would lavish with all the love they hadn't been given as children.

"What changed your mind?"

"I've done some babysitting for girlfriends. Newborns are a *lot* of work. Especially if you don't have any help." She ran her hand through her hair, anger replacing the sadness in her voice. "My husband didn't like to touch anything human under six months of age. So he wasn't much help on the nights I was on babysitting duty."

"Afraid he would break them?"

"No, he called them blobs. Said they weren't real people until they could do something other than sleep and shit. I think small babies disgusted him."

"He sounds like a winner," Jackson said, unable to keep the anger from his voice. What the hell had Nicky been doing with a man like that? Hadn't she learned enough self-respect to know she deserved better? She'd always despised Phil's wife for being a doormat to her abusive husband, yet it looked like she'd gotten herself into a very similar situation.

"Derrick is a piece of shit, but I didn't know that when we were married," she said, as if she'd read his thoughts. He shouldn't be surprised. They'd always been eerily connected when they were younger, finishing each other's sentences so often their friends would make fun of them for it. "There were . . . situations that developed after we were together for a while that changed things between us."

"What kind of situations?"

"Just . . . unexpected things." Nicky shuddered, as if the memories of her marriage were repulsive enough to cause a physical response. "But you know, I really don't want to talk about my stupid past decisions. Let's go get some breakfast and you can catch me up on all the dumb things you've done in the past eight years."

"Assuming I've done such things," Jackson said, trying to smile and lighten the mood, though a part of him wanted to keep pushing at Nicky, to find out what she was hiding about this Derrick character.

Of course, if he found out the man had been more than emotionally abusive, he was going to land himself in another sticky situation. If her husband had dared to hit Nicky or manipulate her with the threat of violence the way their foster father had his wife, Jackson knew he wasn't going to be able to rest until he did something about it. And unfortunately for him, he was no longer a minor who could get away with beating the shit out of any guy who hurt his girl.

His girl. God, but he wanted to be able to say those words and have them be true. He wanted Nicky to be his again. For now, and for as long as he could have her. Of all the things he'd worried about when he'd planned this weekend, begging her to come back to him and give them another chance was the very last thing he'd anticipated.

"I'm betting you've done a stupid thing or two." Nicky laughed as she took his hand and pulled him through the bathroom into the bedroom where he'd passed a restless night, knowing he was so close to her. "There's no way you went straight from law-abiding citizen to kidnapper without a few stops on the crazy train in between."

"Considering you're my kidnap victim, you really shouldn't be finding that funny."

Nicky paused at the top of the stairs and turned back to him. "I know you would never hurt me, Jackson. Not *really* hurt me."

"Even when I alter your tattoo tomorrow?" he asked, the guilt that washed over him at the idea of doing anything to Nicky against her will so strong it sickened him. The longer he spent with her—talking to her, making love to her, laughing with her—the smaller the chance he was actually going to go through with what he'd planned.

"Even if your stubborn ass insists on messing with my tat, it won't be enough to hurt me. Not really." She dropped his hand and crossed her arms, the defensive gesture making her look smaller all of a sudden. "I certainly wouldn't respect you as much as I do now, or trust you. But I'd be fine. You'd have to take a lot more than a tattoo away from me to break me."

Before he could think of what to say to those words, she'd turned and scampered down the stairs, yelling something about being ready for her slave to make waffles. But he couldn't seem to concentrate on her words, not when his head was spinning. Lose Nicky's respect and her trust. His gut reaction to the thought was another nauseating twist of his stomach. He didn't want to lose her trust. Hell, he didn't want to lose *her*, period.

Even remembering the way she'd betrayed him didn't provide any comfort anymore. He'd loved her when they were kids and meant to keep his promises. That had given him comfort no matter how shattered he'd been by her leaving. He'd at least known *he'd* acted from a good place, no matter what she'd done.

But if he betrayed her now and abused the faith she'd so readily placed in him—both in the bedroom and out—he was going to be a far more wretched example of a person than she'd ever been. She'd been sixteen, not much more than a kid, and their lives hadn't been easy back then.

Now he was a successful man with a promising career, friends, money, security—in short, everything he and Nicky had ever dreamed about. If he acted like a lunatic from that place of safety, forcing his will upon a woman who was obviously not in the best place in her life, Nicky would be right to never trust him again. He would be as much a monster as her former husband.

With those cheery thoughts swirling through his mind, Jackson headed down the stairs, no longer certain how this weekend was going to end, just wishing it didn't have to end at all.

Chapter Nine

Vicky didn't know why she was surprised that Jackson could cook with a capital C, but she was. Even after she'd consumed her half of a tomato, basil, and goat cheese frittata and polished off two gingerbread waffles with batter she'd watched Jackson make from scratch, she couldn't quite wrap her head around it. After all, just because the only other dom she'd had breakfast with couldn't fry an egg to save his life, it didn't mean all dominant men were the same.

Jackson had already demonstrated an abundance of differences between himself and her soon-to-be ex. Not the least of which was an insatiable desire for her after-baby body. He didn't seem to notice that her breasts sagged a little and had stretch marks on their sides, or that the skin on her stomach wasn't as tight as it used to be. She'd hit the gym every day in hopes of resuming her career and knew she looked good enough to model, but there were things a lover saw that a camera didn't.

But Jackson didn't see them. Or if he did, he obviously didn't find them repulsive.

"You want the last one?" he asked, pausing with his fork half-way to the last waffle on the plate between them.

"No, thank you." She sat back in her chair with a contented sigh. "I'm stuffed. I shouldn't have finished that second one, but I'm a sucker for real maple syrup. Soooo good."

"Yeah, not like that fake butter-flavored crap we used to eat in high school. Remember when we fixed the little kids pancakes for dinner?"

Nicky nodded, noticing Jackson didn't refer to the other kids by name, either. No matter how much they'd both tried to help the other minors unlucky enough to end up in Phil's house, they had kept their emotional distance. It was the only way to stay sane when you were underage and helpless to change the lives of anyone, including yourself.

"They thought it was so cool we were having breakfast for dinner," she said. "Like it was a special occasion."

"When really we just didn't have anything else to feed them except cereal."

"Yeah. Good times." Nicky crossed her legs in her chair and reached for her coffee. "But I'm more interested in hearing some new dirt. I thought you were going to give me the goods on the lifestyles of the rich and famous."

"I was on a reality show on an arts station." He shrugged, as if he really thought it was no big deal that he'd been on national television every week. Of course, knowing Jackson, he probably *didn't* think it was a big deal. He'd never wanted to be a star. Not like she had when she was younger and certain she was going to set the modeling world on fire. Now she'd settle for making a decent living for her and Abby. "I'd hardly call that famous. Probably more people know your name than mine."

"Doubtful."

"From what I hear your picture was on half the billboards in L.A."

"That was two years ago." She laughed, remembering how totally weird it had been to see herself blown up ten feet tall. "In Los Angeles time that's eons ago. I'm old news."

"You're still the featured model on the Good and Trashy Web site."

"I'm sure that's just because they've been too lazy to change the template. My body is part of the banner."

"Yeah, I've seen it. That red corset thing is ... very nice."

Nicky laughed. "Stop trying to change the subject. I want to hear about you."

"Me." He sighed as he scooted his chair back and began to gather up the breakfast dishes.

He hadn't served her on his hands and knees like he'd promised, but he had cooked, set the table, and motioned for her to stay seated as he continued cleaning up. A dominant man who didn't mind serving as well as being served. God, she'd never dreamed such a person existed. She'd be falling for Jackson even if this were the first time they'd ever met.

"Yes, you."

"Let's see. After high school, I did the part-time tattoo artist, part-time bouncer thing. I built up a nice portfolio in the first six months and started planning my move to Reno."

"Just like you said you would. Good for you."

"But then I got an offer to move to Vegas and work as a bouncer for some new club. They were looking for a certain type and I fit the bill."

"The tall, sexy, and scary type?"

"Something like that." He poured himself another cup of coffee and then refilled her cup before easing back into his chair. "So you think I'm sexy, huh?"

"No, I've been faking all those orgasms," she said with a roll of her eyes.

"You're an excellent actress."

"I'm thinking about trying my hand at movies if the whole modeling thing doesn't work out." She grinned at him over the rim of her cup.

"Really?" he asked. "I bet you'd be great."

"No, not really. Modeling is bad enough. I couldn't deal with all the actor crap."

He laughed. "So the famous thing isn't as great as you thought it would be, huh? Hate to say I told you so, but . . ."

"No, you don't. You love it. You always did." Nicky's smile faded as she narrowed her eyes in Jackson's direction. "Must have been the dom in you, dying to come out and impose his will on people in need of his guidance."

"I don't know about that. I just thought you'd be happier doing something a little more low-key. You always hated it when people paid too much attention to you at school, I couldn't imagine the attention of strangers would be any better."

"You were right. It was weird getting that much attention, especially the lingerie-model kind of attention. But by the time I got the Good and Trashy gig, I was pretty tired of working ten-hour shifts at restaurants to pay my rent. The money made up for the weirdness factor."

"Money does help. I was against the reality show idea at the beginning, but my partner, Christian, was right to push me into it. It was amazing free publicity. Quadrupled our business in the first year."

They talked for another hour and a third pot of coffee, the conversation flowing more smoothly than any in her recent history. How long had it been since she'd been able to sit and have a relaxing conversation with a good friend? It seemed like forever. And she'd never felt so homey with a man.

Derrick had been the type of man who liked to keep his dom hat on at all times. At first, twenty-one-year-old Nicky had thought that was a wonderful thing, but after six months she'd started to crave some downtime. Time when they could just be comfortable together. She'd started to wish for a dominant and submissive relationship where the different roles underscored their relationship like music, not smothered it like a wool blanket.

It would be different with Jackson. She could just feel it. Sitting across from him at the breakfast table already felt achingly familiar. They'd never had the chance to live together, just the two of them, but this is how she'd always dreamed it would be. Hell, it was even better than she'd dreamed it would be. In her younger fantasies, she hadn't known how much she craved the thrill of submitting to a dominant man or guessed that her first love would grow up to be her dream guy.

Of course, she should have known. Jackson had always been a total knight in shining armor, the kind of brave, confident, caring man who seemed extinct in modern times. Even in the BDSM club scene it was rare to find a man in possession of himself the way Jack was. A lot of crazies who lacked the personality or finesse to win a woman in the "real world" assumed they could come into a club and find a docile little submissive to put up with all their crap. A real dom was a damn hard thing to find.

"So how did you get into the scene anyway?" Nicky asked, not realizing she'd propped her toes on the edge of Jackson's chair until he took a foot in hand and began to run his thumbs along her instep. "Breakfast and a foot rub? I must have been a very good girl."

He laughed softly under his breath. "You were."

"I tried to use the shower nozzle last night. I wasn't planning on obeying that last order of yours," Nicky said, the confession spilling from her lips before she could think better of it. The compulsion to be honest with Jack was just too strong. No matter what her rational mind had to say about it, her inner sub wanted to turn over control to this man, to trust him with every thought, every secret.

He didn't pause in his massaging of her feet for a moment, but Nicky saw the muscle in his jaw get tight. "So what changed your mind?"

"My body did." He raised an eyebrow, silently urging her to continue. "I couldn't come without your permission."

"You *couldn't* come?" he asked, sounding more curious than angry.

"I physically couldn't. And I tried, believe me." She bit her lip as she set her empty coffee cup back on the table. "But a part of me wanted to please you too much."

Jackson just stared at her for a few minutes, his dark eyes unreadable. When he finally spoke, his silky dom voice was back in full effect. "I think that's one of the hottest things I've ever heard."

"Yeah?" she asked, a part of her hoping he'd prove it by tackling her to the floor of the kitchen and showing her just how hot he was.

But he only smiled, and then he turned his attention back to her feet. "Yeah."

"Well . . . I try," Nicky said, ignoring the heat pooling in her belly. She couldn't be ready for more already. It had only been a couple of hours since she'd come so hard she was sure she'd done herself damage. "So are you going to tell me how you got into the scene or not?"

"My first girlfriend after I moved to Vegas was interested in checking out this dungeon they had going at the edge of town. She said she always had fantasies about getting chained to a wall by a man wearing black leather."

"Sounds fun."

Jackson laughed. "She thought so, too, until she was all strapped in. Then she couldn't get out of her restraints or that club fast enough. Turns out the BDSM scene wasn't for her. But I liked it just fine."

"Yeah, some people just want to have the fantasy, not actually act it out." Nicky squirmed slightly in her chair, finding it damned difficult to consider Jackson's foot rub relaxing instead of arousing. "Never had that problem myself. When I first discovered the BDSM clubs in L.A., I wanted to live there all the time. Twenty-four-seven."

"I can imagine."

"Can you?" She grinned.

"You're excited right now. Aren't you? After we spent half the night and all morning playing, you still want more."

Nicky's smile faded as she nodded her head. Within seconds her breath grew faster and her pussy wet simply from watching the heat flare in Jackson's eyes.

"You just can't get enough, can you?" he asked, continuing when Nicky shook her head again. "So why don't you take that shirt off. I have something I want you to put on while we finish talking."

Nicky's hands were trembling by the time she stripped her nightshirt off and threw it to the ground, amazed that the moment had gone from comfortable to erotic so quickly. It was incredibly arousing . . . almost as arousing as the sight of what Jackson had fished from the kitchen drawer.

"I didn't think to bring my nipple clamps, but I think these will work just fine." Jackson knelt in front of her, setting the clothespins on the table before placing his hands lightly on her hips. "Would you like me to put those on your tits?"

"Yes." Her tits were already aching at the very idea, her nipples drawing into tight points despite the warmth of the room. "Very much."

"I thought you would." Jackson held her eyes as he lowered his mouth to her chest, capturing one aching tip in his mouth. He suckled her gently at first, teasing her with the tip of his tongue, swirling around and around the taut bud until Nicky's eyes slid closed on a moan.

"Open your eyes, watch me while I suck my tits," he said, his words sending a jolt of arousal sizzling along her nerves, and more heat pooling between her thighs. "And don't move until I give you permission."

Nicky met Jackson's eyes again as he plucked one of the clothespins from the table and attached it to her nipple. The pinching sensation only intensified her desire, the pain and pleasure fusing together to create an arousing sensation more powerful than either one alone.

Jackson waited until she regained a measure of control over her rapid breathing before transferring his attention to her other breast, licking, sucking, and biting, driving her mad with the need to move. It was hellish work not to squirm in her seat, not to thread her fingers through Jackson's hair and hold on for dear life. But she wanted his approval, and the pleasure—which she had no doubt he would give her as a reward for her obedience—far more than the small relief movement would afford.

"Good, so good." Jackson breathed the words against her breast, then flicked his tongue out across her nipple one last time, making her gasp. He attached the second clothespin, his own breath coming faster when she moaned. "So, what have you been doing for the past two years? Why did you quit modeling?"

"Do we really have to talk anymore?" she asked, her voice thin and strained.

"I think we should give the clamps some time, don't you?" His calm tone and the relaxed way he reclaimed his chair would have been enough to make her scream if his excitement hadn't been abundantly obvious. The front of his pajama pants were tented where his erection strained the fabric.

Nicky could see the outline of the bulbous head of his cock through the thin material and it was enough to make her mouth water. She wanted his cock back in her mouth. She wanted to suck him until he cried out in that way that made her positive no one had ever given him the kind of pleasure she had.

She wanted to swallow down every last drop of his cum and then keep sucking him until he was hard again, until he pulled his thick length from her mouth and shoved it between her legs. There wouldn't be any foreplay aside from the nipple clamps, but she knew she'd be wet. Though hopefully not wet enough to ease his passage too much. She loved the slight hint of pain as he forced himself inside her the first time. The resistance of her body, the sting as he demanded entrance, took her halfway to orgasm in the initial thrust.

"What the hell are you thinking about?" he asked, his voice thick with lust.

"How much I want to suck your cock." Nicky met his eyes, but didn't move an inch from her present position, determined to show him she could be a good little sub and a naughty one all at the same time. "I was thinking about how hot it felt to have your hand fisted in my hair, to feel you fucking my mouth."

"What about your ass? Would you like my cock in your ass?"

"We'd need lube," she said, her pussy getting even wetter despite the fact that anal had been her least favorite activity with her ex. Somehow, she knew that would be as different with Jackson as everything else. "But I want you to fuck me any way you want. I want you to use me for your pleasure in every filthy way you can imagine."

"Would that turn you on?"

"Yes." The word came out as not much more than a moan as she imagined Jackson forcing her to her hands and knees and taking her in the ass. She could practically hear him calling her his little slut, feel his large hand landing stinging slaps to her bottom as his cock stroked deep inside her. "And I'd . . . I'd like you to spank me while you fuck me."

"Spank you, and call you my dirty girl?" he asked, leaning

forward with his elbows on his knees until his lips were only inches away from her mouth. "My little whore?"

"Yes. Please, yes." Nicky swept her tongue across her lips, her entire body screaming with the need to be touched, with the need to throw her arms around Jackson and never let him go.

"Why do you like to hear those words from a man, Nicky?" he asked, his eyes drifting to her lips.

"I don't like to hear them from a man. I like to hear them from you."

"You didn't like your husband to—"

"No, I didn't," she said, the sound of the word "husband" on Jackson's lips making her ill. God, but she couldn't wait for the day when Derrick would no longer hold that title. "He would say them, but I never got off on it the way I did with you last night."

"Why?" He moved one hand to her face, tracing a soft finger along her jaw. "Why is it different with me?"

"I don't know . . . I guess . . ." For the third time in less than a day, tears threatened at the backs of her eyes.

There was just something about being with Jack that turned her inside out, that pushed her to wander the edges of her own emotional landscape. It was what she'd always heard a good dom would do, but she'd never been there, never been forced to look into another person's eyes and know they were seeing straight through to the core of her.

But here she was and there was the answer to his question, floating to the front of her awareness. "I like it because . . . I know you don't really mean it. That, to you, it's almost a compliment."

"It is a compliment." He nodded. "What else?"

"I know you wouldn't say it to just anyone, so it makes me feel special."

"And why wouldn't I say it to just anyone?" he asked, his lips moving closer to hers, so close she was certain he would kiss her, but he stopped when there were still a few inches between them. "Why would I only say it to you?"

"Because..." Nicky sucked in a deep breath, fighting back tears, refusing to let the liquid pooling in her eyes spill down her cheeks no matter how scary and emotional this moment had become. "Because you love me?"

"I do. So much."

Nicky started crying then, she couldn't seem to help herself. She was full-on sobbing as Jackson pressed a soft kiss to her lips and pulled her into his arms, tears rolling down the cheeks she pressed into his chest as he carried her across the room.

ackson laid Nicky down on the soft carpet by the fire and
hovered above her, dropping soft kisses across her face as
she cried, for the first time in his life not freaked out by a woman
in tears. She wasn't crying because she was sad. He knew she was
crying because sometimes it hurt to learn that someone loved you.
When you'd convinced yourself there was no love left in the world,
at least not for you, the unexpectedness of the emotion could be
overwhelming. That kind of love shattered things you'd thought
were necessary to life, replacing them with something so much
better, so much sweeter than the hardness that was there before.

He knew that's how she was feeling because he felt the exact
same thing.

"I love you. I never stopped loving you." He whispered the
words against her lips, feeling close to tears himself as she brought
trembling fingers to his face, her soft touch communicating more
emotion than he'd thought possible.

"I love you, too, Jackson. And I'm so sorry I ever left. I'm
sorry—"

"It doesn't matter." He silenced her with a kiss, a real kiss, slipping his tongue into her mouth, tasting coffee and maple syrup and Nicky before he pulled back to look her in the eyes. "I don't care about the past. I only care about the future."

"God, can we have a future?" she asked, fear creeping back into her voice. "There's so much we don't about know each other, so much—"

"We can have whatever we decide to have." He captured her face in his hands, willing her to see that they had to seize this second chance no matter how crazy it might seem. "More important, we can have whatever I say we can have."

"Because you're the big bad dom?" she asked with a sad, crooked smile.

"Because I'm *your* big bad dom," he said, knowing his eyes were getting shiny and not caring a damn bit. He wasn't too much of a coward to cry, especially when faced with losing the only woman he'd ever loved for a second time. "And you're my girl. I love you so much, Nicky, and I swear to you I will never treat you badly or abuse your trust."

"I know you wouldn't, Jackson. But it's been eight years." She sucked in a breath and shifted her gaze to stare at a place above his head. "And there are things you don't know about me, things that might change your mind."

"We can talk about those things whenever you're ready," Jack said, sensing now wasn't the time to push Nicky to reveal her secrets. "But I can tell you now I don't care about what's happened in the past eight years. No matter what you've done, I would still consider myself the luckiest man in the world if you were mine."

"You would?" she asked, looking on the verge of another round of tears.

"I would, but you've got to stop crying or I'm going to start and that wouldn't be very big and bad of me." He laughed, a tight, strained sound that grew easier when Nicky laughed along with him.

"You aren't going to cry. I don't believe it," she said, a hesitant smile on her face.

He could sense how much she wanted to believe this was a new beginning for them in that smile. But he could also feel the doubt that still lingered in her mind. This wasn't going to be resolved anytime soon and pushing Nick further would do no good. It was time to get them back on more comfortable ground. Even as kids they hadn't been big into talking feelings, no matter how strong they'd been. They had always preferred to let actions speak louder than words.

With one deft movement, he gripped the waistband of her panties and pulled them off.

"What if I said I was going to fuck my pussy? Would you believe that?" As he spoke he trailed one hand up the inside of her thigh, teasing at the crease where leg became something more intimate. He could feel the heat coming from her cunt even before he touched her. It was enough to make him even harder, to make his cock threaten to burst through the fabric of his pants in order to get inside his girl.

"Yes, I would," she said, sucking in a quick breath as he brushed one finger up the length of her, catching moisture from her pussy and moving it to her clit.

"Now, the only question is: How am I going to fuck you?" As he spoke he began to circle her nub, making Nicky squirm beneath him and a moan burst from between her parted lips. "Am I going to take you like this, on top in the ever-popular missionary position? Or am I going to flip you over and lift your hips and take you from behind?"

"Yes and yes," she said, twining her arms around his neck as she spread her thighs even farther, a clear invitation to do with her as he would.

"Or should I pull you on top of me? Let you ride my cock while I suck my tits?" He accentuated the last word by flicking the clothespins still attached to her nipples, making Nicky groan. "Are you ready for these to come off?"

"I don't care. I just want you to fuck me," she said, the strength of her desire clear in her eyes. "Now."

"Are you giving orders?"

"No, but I'm ready to take them." She released her hold on his neck, stretching her arms out to her sides, awaiting his command. "Tell me what you want, Jackson. Tell me how your slut can please you."

His jaw tightened and his aching sac threatened to burst as he looked down at Nicky, for a moment wanting to dispense with the dom-sub play and let this time be different than the other times they'd come together. Amazingly, at the moment, he didn't want to fuck. He wanted to make love. No matter how much he loved the primal pleasure he gave and received in the dom role, right now, all he wanted was to show Nicky with every stroke of his cock how much he loved her. He wanted to kiss her softly as he slid between her thighs, whisper all the things he'd held inside against her mouth as he thrust, slowly, sensuously, in and out of her tight heat.

"If you don't tell me how to please you, I might have to start pleasing myself," Nicky said, a naughty grin on her face as she moved one hand to her stomach and then slid her fingers even lower.

"If you touch my pussy, you'll be punished. And it won't be that spanking I know you're after." Jackson grabbed her wrist and pulled it away from her body. "Turn over. Forearms on the ground, hips in the air. Show me my pussy."

"Yes, sir." Nicky smiled as she said the words, but he read the excitement—and relief—in her eyes.

She wasn't ready to make love, not yet. They were both dealing with some pretty unexpected and heavy emotions. He wanted to deal with them by delving right into the middle of things. She would rather distract herself from the frightening "L" word with a little mindless fucking. Nicky needed to be used, fucked, treated like the slut she'd called herself in order to feel safe from the feelings that were scaring her half to death.

Jackson knew that and was prepared to give her exactly what she needed. There would be time for making love later, he had no doubt in his mind. He and Nicky were too perfect for each other to let a second chance slip through their fingers. They were meant to be together, a matching set, just like their tattoos.

"I think we'll have to leave this exactly as is," he said, leaning over and pressing a kiss to the angel tat on her shoulder. "For some reason, it's not bothering me to have the same ink anymore."

"It's not?" she asked, her voice breathy with excitement as he ran his hands down her thighs to her knees and tugged them a little farther apart.

"No, I like to see my little slut with my mark on her. Now tilt your hips." Jackson sat back on his heels, grunting in satisfaction as Nicky arched her back and shifted her pelvis, giving him a clear view of her aroused sex.

Her pussy was dark rose, and her lips plumped to a point that they looked bruised. At the center of her cunt, her entrance leaked clear fluid down her thighs. She was as aroused as he'd ever seen her. Either the nipple clamps or the love talk had more than done the job of at least a half hour of foreplay.

Call him a romantic, but he hoped it was the mushy stuff that had made his pussy so wet. Still, he made a mental note to invest in a set of high-end clamps as soon as possible. If clothespins made his girl this crazy, he couldn't imagine what a nice set of metal screw clamps would do. He could just imagine them in his new condo in Miami, cooking dinner together, Nicky with her clamps on as they set the table and ate. They'd linger over a couple glasses of wine and then he'd have her dripping pussy for dessert, right there by the windows that looked out over the ocean.

Just imagining the scene made him smile.

"Jackson . . . please." She moaned and arched her back even further, making it clear how desperately she wanted him to touch her, fuck her, fill that empty aching place between her legs. At any other time he would have made her wait, teased her into a state of even greater arousal. But not now, not when her need was so obvious and his cock felt like it was going to explode if he didn't get inside her ten minutes ago.

In seconds, Jackson was out of his pants and kneeling behind her, fingers digging into Nicky's hips as the head of his cock butted against her entrance. He didn't use his hands to position himself or spread the lips of her pussy to ease his way, but simply thrust forward as he tugged her hips back, shoving his engorged length inside her cunt. Nicky's sigh of pleasure made it clear she loved the hint of resistance as much as he did.

Slowly, drawing out the bliss of that first thrust into where she was so tight, so wet, Jackson pushed forward until he was buried to the hilt, his balls pressed tightly against her clit. "God, my pussy is so wet."

Nicky moaned and wiggled her hips, taking him in even deeper. "You make me wet, I can't help it."

"Little slut."

"Yes," she said, a shudder of desire working through her body as her pussy tightened around where he lay buried inside her. "I'm a dirty little slut who likes to get fucked. So go ahead and fuck me al—"

"Watch your mouth, slut," Jackson said, delivering a sharp smack on the cheek of her ass, his cock swelling inside Nicky as she cried out in excitement. "I'll fuck you when I'm ready to fuck you. Do you hear me?"

"Yes," she said, another cry escaping her lips as he swatted her other cheek.

"Yes, sir," he corrected, moving his hands back to her hips and digging his fingers into the full flesh with enough force to make her moan in pleasure at the slight hint of pain.

"Yes, sir." The tension in the muscles trembling beneath his hands made it clear Nicky wouldn't last much longer. A few more cracks of his hand and she was going to come before he had the chance to thrust inside her a second time.

Normally he'd be glad to feel her come at least once before he did himself, but not now. Not even thinking of dead puppies was going to help him maintain control if Nicky's pussy started pulsing around his aching cock. He was too close to his own release.

"I'm going to fuck you, but you'd better not come until you get permission," Jackson said, beginning to pump in and out, slowly at first, but with enough force that Nicky's ass rippled every time he thrust home. "If you come before, I'm going to use those clothespins on your pussy."

"Yes, god, yes." She gasped and her breath came faster as his rhythm increased.

The clear desire in her voice was nearly enough to make Jackson laugh, no matter how close he was to the edge. He should have known Nick wouldn't consider clamps on her pussy lips a punishment. She was into a little bit of pain. He could understand the kink completely. He enjoyed a little pain himself, and couldn't wait to feel her teeth on him again, raking across his lip, digging into his bicep as she writhed beneath him.

"Don't come. Don't come, Nicky," Jackson said, punctuating his words by beginning to spank her in earnest.

"Please, I can't wait. Please," she begged, her breath coming so fast he feared she might hyperventilate. "Please, I can't."

"You can. You will," he said, abandoning the last of his control, holding back nothing as he drove into her slick sheath. "Wait for me. Wait."

Faster and faster he moved, ramming inside Nicky even as he reddened her ass until his hand itched and stung. She cried out and shoved back into his strokes, her fingernails digging into the carpet, desperate little grunts sounding at the back of her throat as she got closer and closer, until finally he knew she couldn't hold back a second longer.

"Come, come on my cock." He groaned as Nicky screamed his name and her pussy squeezed his dick. Seconds later, he lost himself inside her, thick jets pulsing from his aching sac with a bliss that was almost painful. This time, he didn't pull out, but spent himself deep inside her welcoming heat, the sensation of marking her insides with his cum making the orgasm hotter than any he could remember.

Jackson's entire body shook with the force of his release, turning his bones to jelly by the time the waves of pleasure finally began to abate. "God, Nick," he panted as he fell forward, palms landing on either side of Nicky's. He buried his face in the sweat-dampened hair at her neck and inhaled the intoxicating scent of aroused woman. "I love fucking you."

"I think it's clear I love getting fucked," she said, her voice breathy with laughter. "That was . . . perfect."

"I'm just sorry I couldn't make you come at least twice." Jackson wrapped one arm around her waist and pulled her closer, relishing the feel of his cock softening inside her. "I knew I wouldn't last through more than one, you felt too amazing."

"But what a one it was." She sighed as she twined the fingers of her left hand with his. "I'm not greedy—one can be plenty. Though, next time, let's skip the next-to-the-fire thing. Very romantic, but I'm a little dizzy from the heat."

"And here I thought it was my superior fucking skills."

She laughed. "That probably has something to do with it, too." She shifted beneath him, dropping her forehead to the carpet. "I actually don't mind the dizziness, but the dripping sweat I could do without."

"I don't know. I like a little sweat." He ran his tongue along her shoulder, catching the lightly salty taste of her with his tongue.

"Me too, until it dries and starts to get all sticky and gross."

"Hint taken." Jackson pulled out of Nicky and sat back on his heels, watching her as she rolled over to face him. "What would you say to a shower?"

"I'd love one." She grinned as she met his eyes. "I'm assuming this shower will be coed?"

"Of course. I wouldn't want you to have to clean your own back. Or pussy." He stood and then reached down to help Nicky to her feet, marveling that even something as simple as taking her hand sent a shock of electricity through his body. "Besides, someone has to show you how to work the shower nozzle."

"Oh, I know how," she said. "In fact, I think I could show you a few things, mister." She reached her hand between his legs, cupping his sac and rolling his balls in her fingers. "I could do a few very nice things to these in massage mode."

"I bet you could." He groaned and bent down to capture her lips.

She met his tongue with her own, sighing as they explored each other with a sweetness that surprised him. No matter how raunchy the tone of their fucking, it seemed the tender mood they'd established before hadn't been destroyed. In fact, if anything he felt he loved her more than he had a few minutes ago.

"I love you," he mumbled against her lips. "I hope you know I'm not going to stop saying that anytime soon. If it freaks you out, you'll just have to get over it."

"I think I can do that." She wrapped her arms around his torso and hugged him, pressing her breasts and the clothespins still attached to them against his chest.

"Are you ready for those to come off?" he asked, running one hand up to cup the underside of her breast. "They must be stinging a bit by now."

"I like stinging, but, yeah. They need to come off if you're going to soap my nipples." She pulled away from him and removed the clothespins, a mischievous look on her face. "And once you've done my nipples, you might as well get my tits all slick and soapy and fuck them in the shower. I heard something about a man wanting to fuck some tits awhile back. That *was* you, right?"

Nicky squealed and made a run for the stairs as Jackson lunged toward her, squeals that turned to laughter as he chased her straight into the shower. They jumped inside and turned on the water without waiting for it to get hot, clinging to each other for the first few chilly minutes. Then, when the cool stream had warmed, Nicky reached for the soap and turned back to him with a smile. A smile that promised everything naughty and nice, everything Jackson hadn't dared to hope for.

His deepest, most secret wish was coming true. Nicky was going to be his, and this time he was never going to let her go. No matter what he had to do to keep her.

Chapter Eleven

icky indulged in a full body stretch, luxuriating in the softness of Jackson's featherbed. Her body ached in all sorts of forgotten places, but it was the soreness along her jaw muscles that shocked her the most. When was the last time she'd smiled so much it made her face hurt? Had that *ever* happened?

But then why shouldn't she be smiling?

A few feet away, a gorgeous man who had made her come twice in the shower and two more times once they'd stumbled into his bedroom was digging through his suitcase and making noises about cooking tortellini for dinner. Every once in a while, he turned around to smile at her as he plucked jeans and a tight brown sweater from the neatly folded clothes in his bag and pulled them on, the look in his eyes leaving no doubt that he loved her.

He loved her. Jackson still *loved* her, and wanted them to have a future together.

The thought was exhilarating . . . and completely terrifying. Despite the fact that she felt the same way about him and he seemed to be everything she'd ever wanted in a partner, there was still that shred of doubt.

What would he do when he found out the mess she'd gotten herself into with her ex? No matter how much he loved her, she was betting it would be hard for Jackson to respect her knowing she'd willingly turned her entire life over to a man she'd barely known for six months before they were married. He would think she was a complete fool. Hell, *she* thought she was a fool, so she couldn't really blame him.

And even if he could look past her poor decisions, what would Jackson do when he found out she wasn't flying solo anymore? That she came with extra baggage in the form of a nearly one-year-old little girl?

Would he still want her when he found out the truth? And even if he did, would he be able to really *love* another man's child? Nicky couldn't imagine living with and loving a man who couldn't love her little girl as much as she did. And if that meant she was destined to be alone for the rest of her life, so be it. When she finally got her daughter back, she was going to make whatever sacrifices were necessary to ensure Abby had the happy, healthy, idealistic childhood she and Jackson hadn't.

Even if that meant giving up her second chance with the man of her dreams.

"I'm going down to start supper," Jackson said, turning back to her with a pile of clothes in his large hands. Nicky hurried to force a smile back to her face, not wanting him to see the direction her thoughts had been taking. "I brought you jeans, a sweater, and a long-sleeve T-shirt for underneath. In case the sweater's itchy. Size two on the jeans and small on everything else. Is that about right?"

"That's perfect." She took the clothes from his hands, marveling at the softness of the pale blue sweater. It was obviously very expensive, which made her a little sad. She'd been with Derrick for years and he'd never spent money on clothes for her. Pricey lingerie, yes, but those had been more for his pleasure than her own.

"Just about perfect." Jackson reached out and tucked a piece of hair behind her ear with a smile. "A little skinny, but I think I can remedy that. I'm a pretty decent cook if I do say so myself."

"You're an amazing cook, but you can't fatten me up until I get some modeling work first. I've got bills to pay, my friend, and people prefer their models bony."

"What people? I think most men would like to see a little more meat on a woman's bones. Especially a lingerie model's." He smiled and moved toward the stairs. "Besides, I've got enough money to take care of your bills. Don't worry about it."

"Jackson," Nicky said, waiting until he stopped and turned back to her before continuing. "I don't want you to pay my bills. I care about you and I love submitting to you, but I've learned there are aspects of my life that I need to be in control of myself."

He nodded. "Understood. But just know I'd love to help you if you decide to take me up on the offer," he said, the matter clearly dismissed. "Now hurry up and get dressed. I'm going to put you to work chopping vegetables—can't have you thinking you'll be waited on every meal."

"Yes, sir." Nicky smiled and made a show of leaping out of the bed and scrambling into her jeans, making Jackson laugh before he headed down the stairs.

As soon as he was gone, however, she felt her spirits deflate and sank back down onto the bed.

The fact that he'd so easily understood what had been a huge point of contention early in her marriage to Derrick just made her more anxious. Jackson really was the man she'd been dreaming about, the type of dom who understood that being in control of a submissive didn't have to mean taking charge of absolutely every aspect of her life. She just knew he'd never try to make her sign the kind of contract Derrick had, the one that gave the dominant partner complete control over his submissive's finances as well as everything else. Men like Jackson didn't need that kind of stranglehold on another person to feel in control.

"Right, and how stupid is he going to think you are for agreeing to sign something like that in the first place?" Nicky dropped her face into her hands with a sigh. When had this weekend become so complicated? She had a gift for getting herself in impossible situations.

This isn't impossible, just impractical and crazy and probably doomed from the start.

Damned inner voice. No sense in sitting around listening to it prophesy certain disaster.

Nicky stood and shrugged on the long-sleeved tee and sweater—which was one hundred percent angora from Neiman Marcus, so her expensive vibes had been right on the money—and headed to the bathroom to try to do something with her hair.

She worked a little of Jackson's gel through the still-damp curls and then dug through her purse for some lipstick and mascara, determined to look as good as possible considering she had few of her usual weapons of beautification. She wanted to look pretty for Jackson, to just relax and enjoy the rest of their time at the cabin together, but she knew she had to take more aggressive action.

There was no point in stressing out about what he would think of her stupider decisions, or foretelling the end of their relationship before they'd even really begun. She was just going to have to talk to him, tell him everything, and let him make his own decisions about what he could or couldn't deal with in a woman he was dating.

Dating. It was a strange word to think of in conjunction with her and Jackson.

They weren't the dating kind. Their relationship was already far too intense for such a casual term. After only a day, she felt she couldn't breathe as well when he wasn't in the room. Jackson could quickly become a person she depended on, someone she needed as much as she needed anything else in the world.

Dangerous, scary thoughts there, Nicky.

"Well, life can be scary. And not everything worth having is easy," she said to her reflection as she coated her lashes with dark brown mascara.

That's what you said about Derrick. Look how that turned out.

"Oh, shut up. Just shut up." Nicky threw her gloss back into her purse.

Great, now she was yelling at the voices in her head. She had to nip this insanity in the bud.

Before she could talk herself out of it, Nicky turned toward the stairs. She would go down to the kitchen and tell Jackson everything. Right now. Before they ate tortellini, before she fell any more head over heels for him than she was already. Even if telling the truth meant she would lose him, at least she'd know how this was going to end. She couldn't handle any more suspense.

Suspense was one of her least favorite things . . . unless it was of the sexual variety.

She was nearly to the bottom of the stairs when she heard Jackson talking and froze in place. For a second she thought someone else must have arrived at the cabin, but after a few seconds it became clear he was on the phone. She hadn't seen a landline in the any of the rooms, so it must be his cell. Which made her wonder if her own cell was getting reception.

Some smarty-pants she was. And here she'd thought that stellar grade on her GED and the A's in the classes she'd taken at the community college had meant something. Checking her cell reception should have been the first thing she did as soon as she was alone if she'd really been focused on getting out of here and away from her captor.

Of course, that was the problem right there. She hadn't wanted to get away, not really. Not even when she'd run from Jackson when they'd parked on the side of the road. Even as she'd run like hell for the headlights coming around the corner, she'd wanted him to catch her.

"Yeah, I need a complete background check. I want to see what she's been up to," Jackson said to the person at the other end of the line.

Background check? On her? Dear god, what did he think she'd been doing for the past eight years that required a *background* check? *He* was the one who had turned into a kidnapper.

"See if there's any criminal record, and if so, what she was charged with."

Oh. My. God. He thought she was a criminal, and was making sure she wasn't dangerous before he took things any further in their relationship. The lack of trust implied by that action was . . . staggering. She'd trusted him not to hurt her and submitted to him without question, even after he'd told her he intended to permanently mark her body without her permission. And still *he* was the one who felt the need to do a background check.

It didn't just hurt her feelings—it made her angry. Really angry. With Jackson, but more important, with herself.

She should have known better. After years in a horrible dom-sub relationship, she'd been ready to jump right back into another one in less than a day. It didn't matter that Jackson wasn't a stranger, he was still a person she'd had no contact with for the past eight years. She should have insisted on moving forward slowly if they were going to move forward at all. Going to bed with your kidnapper mere hours after getting into his car and professing your love for him twenty-four hours later was insane. She obviously needed some kind of intensive anti-sub therapy.

Which she was going to make sure to get, as soon as she got the hell away from here.

Jackson went ahead and chopped the tomatoes, garlic, and fresh basil himself. Nicky was taking forever upstairs, but he didn't want to rush her. She'd said something about wanting to fix her hair and makeup before dinner and he knew how long those girlish things could take. And even though he thought she was just as beautiful without makeup on and her hair in crazy curls, knowing she wanted to dress up just for him made him smile.

A lot. Smiling and humming a little tune, he put the tortellini on to boil and fetched the pine nuts, fresh mozzarella, and baby green beans from the fridge.

Everything was working out perfectly. This weekend was turning out to be one of the best of his entire life. He felt so comfortable with Nick. Spending time with her was like going home, to a real home. To that place of warmth and love and happiness neither one of them had ever known.

And the sex was . . . indescribable. He hadn't known he could come so hard, so often. She made him wild with a single look, the slightest touch. He could fuck her every day for the rest of his life and never get tired of feeling her body pressed against him. She was everything he'd ever dreamed of and everything he'd ever need.

He knew he was crazy, but he was already thinking rings, wondering how long he'd have to wait before it would be at least somewhat rational to pop the question.

Jackson's phone buzzed in his pocket, interrupting his stream of insanity. It was Christian calling him back. It hadn't been more than fifteen minutes since they hung up the first time, but then, his partner did have some excellent sources. Christian's ability to get the dirt on just about anyone had often made Jackson a little suspicious.

Despite the fact that he used to be a police officer before he quit to do the tattoo artist thing full-time, sometimes it seemed a little too easy for Chris to find out the intensely personal details of other people's lives. Even police officers had to work to get access to things like juvenile arrests and medical records. Especially medical records.

But when Christian had discovered a girl Jackson was casually dating was HIV-positive and hiding it from her lovers in order to convince them to indulge her passion for blood play without reluctance, Jackson hadn't asked questions. He hadn't cared how Christian had gotten the information, he'd just been glad to learn the truth before he'd put himself at risk.

The same was true now. Before he got in any deeper with Nicky, he had to know what she was hiding and whether he could help her out of whatever trouble she was in. If not, he didn't know if he could handle getting any closer to the woman upstairs. If she'd gotten herself into a bad situation beyond his control to remedy, it would drive him insane to see her suffer and not be able to keep her safe.

"What did you find out?" Jackson asked, keeping his voice low in case Nicky made a sudden appearance. Surely she was nearly ready by now and could be headed down the stairs any second.

"Nothing much. It's like the woman just dropped out of her life two years ago," Christian said. "I found a couple of pictures from her wedding to this Derrick Sack of Potatoes guy, but—"

"What?"

"Sakapatatis. No wonder Nicky didn't change her name. That has to be one of the least sexy last names I've ever heard. It would have been lingerie model suicide."

Jackson sighed and rolled his eyes. "So that's it? Her ex has a lame last name? That's all you found out?"

"No, that's not all I found out. This is me you're talking to." Christian sniffed, clearly offended. "She has a clean criminal record. Never even had an unpaid parking ticket, which probably wasn't too hard considering she didn't have a driver's license until about two months ago."

"No driver's license?"

"Not in California, and the Nevada license expired when she turned twenty."

"That's strange." Nicky had always loved to drive his car and had been at the DMV the morning of her sixteenth birthday ready to test for her license.

"And it gets stranger, my friend. According to her and the Sack of Potatoes guy's tax records, she reported no income from the time she quit modeling until she started working at the bar. Absolutely nothing."

"Maybe he didn't want her to work. He sounds like the type from what I've heard."

"Maybe. But he didn't want her to spend, either. She didn't have her name on any of his four bank accounts or have an account of her own. Hell, she didn't even have a credit card. There's no credit history on the chick for the past two years."

Jackson grunted, putting the pieces together before Christian spoke again.

"Which probably means she's flat-ass broke unless she's been stashing cash under her mattress or something."

"What about the money she earned modeling?" Jackson asked. "What happened to that? She must have had an account before she was married."

"She did, but she closed it out before she hooked up with her husband. She's broke, man."

"So what?" Jackson snapped.

"So nothing. Don't shoot the messenger. It's no big deal, as long as you don't mind being her sugar daddy. But . . . there is something else."

"And what is that?" Jackson asked, trying to keep the frustration out of his voice as he turned off the burner on the stove and poured the tortellini into the colander to drain. "I don't have a lot of time right now, Christian."

"Fine, I'll cut right to it. She's got a kid."

"What?" Jackson dropped the pot into the sink with a clatter, feeling his stomach bottom out. If Nicky had a kid, who was taking care of him or her while she was up here?

"A baby girl about eleven months old, Abigail Diana Sakapatatis. From what I can find, it seems like the kid is still living with the husband."

"But that guy's bad news. He was abusive to Nicky—I'm almost certain of it."

"Yeah, well, maybe she had to get out of the situation, but couldn't take the kid with her. If she has no money, she wouldn't be very well equipped to—"

"No way. She would never leave her child with someone who would hurt her. She wouldn't do that, Christian."

"Listen, don't freak out on me. I'm just telling you what I learned." Christian sighed, and Jackson could tell he wasn't going to like the next words out of his partner's mouth. "And I'll tell you something else: I think you're crazy. You don't know this woman anymore. She is not the same sweet little girl you fell in love with."

"You don't know anything about her."

"No, but I do know a thing or two about you. And I know that, beneath that big bad act, you're a softie, man. You're a prime target for a woman like her."

"Choose your next words very carefully," Jackson said, hoping Christian heard the warning in his tone.

"I'm not saying anything bad about your precious Nicky. I'm just saying she's a woman who is obviously in some sort of trouble. Financial trouble for certain and probably more if this soon-to-be ex is as bad as you think."

"Again I have to say, so what?"

"So help her if you want to help her, but don't let yourself think you two are headed for happily ever after or something. She's obviously not in a place where she can be loving anyone."

"I'm going to hang up now." Jackson could barely force the words out, his jaw was clenched so tightly. Christian didn't know what the hell he was talking about. He'd never dated the same woman for more than a month at a time. What the fuck did he know about love?

"Fine, but when she uses you and then leaves your ass a second time, don't say I didn't warn—"

Jackson snapped the phone closed and threw it on the counter. He shouldn't have brought the damned thing. He hadn't wanted any distractions when he came to the mountains. That's why he hadn't had a landline installed in the first place.

The last thing he'd needed was a dose of reality via Christian, the biggest cynic in his personal acquaintance. Jackson was the one whose mother had dumped him on his dad's porch before he could even walk and never come back. Then his dad, the only adult who had ever made Jackson feel safe and cared for, had kicked it when he was ten and he'd been shuffled from shitty foster home to shittier foster home until he was eighteen. Still, Christian was the one who acted like life had betrayed him. Jackson had never met the other man's family, but they must be some pieces of work to make Christian distrust people even more than he did.

"Nicky? Are you about ready?" Jackson shouted to be heard upstairs as he fished the wok out from the cupboard and dumped the tortellini and vegetables inside. "We're about two minutes from estimated pasta arrival."

Silence. Not so much as the sound of footsteps crossing the floor or water running in the bathroom. "Nick?" he called again.

Still nothing, the kind of nothing that made the hairs stand up on his arms and his throat grow tight. Jackson set the wok on the stove, but didn't turn on the burner. Instead, he headed for the stairs, wiping his damp hands on his jeans as he went.

There had to be a logical explanation for this. Maybe she had found the iPod in his suitcase and was checking out his favorite playlists. Nicky had always loved to play her music loud and he doubted becoming a mom had changed that.

A mom. Nicky was a mom.

A mom who had left her little girl with a potentially dangerous man. The knowledge all but killed the spark of pleasure the idea of meeting Nicky's daughter had inspired.

What could have driven her to make that kind of decision? Was she so traumatized by her marriage she wanted out any way she could, even if that meant leaving her daughter behind? Maybe she'd wanted to take her baby with her, but hadn't had the money, as Christian had suggested.

Or maybe she just hadn't taken to being a parent the way he'd always thought she would.

They'd never really talked about kids in-depth, but even as a teenager Nicky had seemed like the kind of woman who would grow up to be a great mother. The way she'd taken care of the younger foster kids in Phil's house had always impressed him. She hadn't just made sure they had something to eat or helped them with homework, she'd done her best to make them smile, to lessen the negative impact of living with Phil in her own small way.

Could that have really changed so much in eight years?

Jackson knew he was going to find out. She'd probably be pissed that he snooped around behind her back, but—

"Nicky?" He said her name one last time, even though the open window next to Nicky's bed assured him she wouldn't be answering his call. She was gone.

Chapter Twelve

icky burst out of the woods just as the sun was setting, panting from her run down the side of the mountain. She sported several scratches on her face and her jeans were soaked through to the knee from where she'd waded through the snowdrifts, but at least she'd made it to the edge of the little town whose lights she'd glimpsed the night before.

She hadn't dared take the road. It would have taken too much time and Jackson would have found her for sure. Even now, he might still find a way to stop her. He had to have realized she was gone and put two and two together to guess where she'd run. The town at the bottom of the ravine was the only sign of civilization nearby, and the only place where she might find someone to help her.

"Or a bus station if I'm lucky." Nicky took a deep breath and exhaled a puff of white. The temperature was falling fast.

Even warm from her run and wearing a heavy sweater, she was starting to feel the cold. Luckily the boots Jackson had brought for her seemed to be waterproof, but her jeans were not. The damp fabric felt like it was freezing to the skin beneath. She had to find somewhere to get inside and get warmed up before she risked frostbite—hopefully that bus station she was dreaming about. A bus ticket and a snug little waiting room that served hot chocolate would be heaven to her right now.

Or maybe something a little stronger than hot chocolate. An Irish coffee sounded pretty good. Anything to help numb the pain and anxiety flooding her system. She'd only spent a *day* with Jackson, but leaving him was as horrible as it had been the first time. Far worse than leaving the man she'd been married to for three years.

But she couldn't think about that now. She had to focus on getting the hell out of Dodge.

Nicky set a swift pace down the street toward a line of wooden buildings resembling the main drag of an Old West town. She was still too far away to know for certain, but the businesses appeared to be mostly souvenir shops and the occasional outdoors supply store. There were only a few cars parked alongside the street, but hopefully that meant there were at least a few townspeople who hadn't headed home for dinner yet. Surely one of them would be willing to give her a ride to the bus station. Or at least let her use their phone to call someone to help her if there wasn't a station in town.

Her cell had died sometime between leaving L.A. and arriving in the mountains. She must have forgotten to charge it before she went to work Friday night. Stupid and careless, but then she hadn't anticipated being gone from home more than a few hours. She certainly hadn't imagined being kidnapped and ending up in a sleepy mountain town desperate to make contact with one of her few friends in Los Angeles.

They hadn't known each other long, but she was guessing Cassandra wouldn't mind driving a few hours to pick her up as long as Nicky paid for her gas and spilled all the sordid details of how she'd ended up stranded in the middle of nowhere. Cassie lived for gossip, whether it be the Hollywood variety sold at grocery store checkouts or the intimate details of her friends' and coworkers' lives. She'd break every speed limit between L.A. and wherever the hell Nicky was calling from as soon as she heard the words "kidnapped" and "ex-lover" in the same sentence.

The idea of the ride home with Cassie, however, made Nicky pray there was a bus station close by. She didn't want to talk about what had happened with her and Jackson. Not now, maybe not ever.

She broke into a jog once more, swiftly closing the distance between herself and the only business still open this late in the winter months. Skiing was a big tourist draw in these parts, but a little town at the bottom of a ravine too steep for the skiing and snowboarding enthusiasts to maneuver probably didn't see much action once the sun went down. The tourists all flocked back to Arrowhead or Big Bear to eat and drink away the chill from a day spent on the slopes.

But even a tiny town like this one had the requisite mom-and-pop diner, serving eggs and pancakes in the morning and other down-home favorites the rest of the time. The blackboard nailed to the outside of the diner proclaimed today's special to be chicken fried steak with potatoes and gravy and green beans.

Nicky's stomach rumbled, despite the fact that chicken fried steak would no doubt be a pathetic meal compared to the pasta Jackson had been preparing for them up in his cabin. He'd told her he'd brought a bottle of Merlot to go along the food and cheesecake for dessert, and sounded so excited to share both with her. To share the evening with her, period.

But how could he have really felt that way if he'd been so desperate to invade her privacy the second her back was turned? And not just invade her privacy himself, but ask some friend of his to do it, to delve into her past and find out if she was a *criminal*, for god's sake.

It made her wonder what he'd really thought of her all those years ago. If he'd known her as well as she'd thought, surely he would have realized she would never do anything illegal. Scandalous and wild, yes. Reckless and stupid, probably. But not illegal. That wasn't her. Never had been, never would be.

The sound of a car pulling down the road behind her made Nicky press closer to the wall of the diner, hoping the awning shading the entrance would help conceal her. With her blond hair and light blue sweater, it wouldn't be that difficult to spot her from the road. And if Jackson saw her, she was as good as caught. There was no one on the street to hear her scream for help, even if she managed to call out before he hustled her into the Expedition.

A quick peek over her shoulder revealed a beat-up Jeep trundling down the road, not Jackson's monster truck. She was safe for now, but the clock was ticking. Jackson was coming for her, she could feel it in her gut. Hell, if she didn't know better, she'd think he was already inches away, ready to throw her over his shoulder and tote her back to his lair.

He wouldn't let her get away with leaving, she knew that much for certain. He'd feel betrayed that she'd run, as betrayed as she'd felt when she'd discovered how very little he trusted the woman he professed to love.

A bell rang above the door as Nicky pushed inside the diner.

The smells of frying meat and homemade bread engulfed her, making her stomach rumble again. It had been quite a while since brunch and she and Jackson had certainly done their part to build up a hearty appetite.

Nicky's muscles ached from their marathon lovemaking as much as her dash down the mountainside. But those aches would fade in a few days' time. No telling how long the aching in her chest would last. Her stupid heart had already grown ridiculously attached to Jackson again. So attached it raced with excitement, not fear, when a large hand suddenly closed around her wrist.

"I figured you'd come here. Only place in town open after five during the winter." Jackson's eyes were dark and expressionless, but Nicky could feel the anger in the iron grip of his fingers.

"Let go of me. I'm going home," Nicky said, keeping her voice low so as not to attract any more attention from the few diners scattered throughout the small restaurant. People were already staring, no need to make a scene. Yet.

If Jackson didn't take no for an answer, however . . .

"You're going back to the cabin with me. I'm going to do what we came here to do. Right now. Afterward, I'll drive you home myself. Tonight if you want."

"What I want is for you to let me go." Nicky tried to jerk away, but he held her tight. "I'm not going back to the cabin, and I'm not letting you touch me again. With a tattoo needle or anything else."

"You'll do what I ask you to do for the next few hours."

"I'm not playing games anymore, Jackson," Nicky said, hoping he read the truth in her eyes. "I will not obey you, I will not submit to you, and I'm not going anywhere with you willingly. You'll have to use force."

"I don't have a problem with that." His eyes glittered with anger and something else, something that looked a lot like ... hurt.

"Well, I do. Try to take me out of here and I will scream for help," she whispered. "I'll tell these people to call the police and you'll end up spending the night in jail."

Jackson made a sound halfway between a grunt and a growl. "That was your plan all along, wasn't it? Act like you cared about me, get me to lower my guard, and then make a run for it?"

"Yep. Sure was," Nicky said, hoping the words hurt him as much as he'd hurt her. That *had* been her plan at first. No need to let him in on how her plan had changed, how she'd started to dream about the future they were going to have together.

"Like I said before, you're a great actress. You had me completely fooled."

Nicky flinched despite herself. Angry Jackson she could deal with, but hurt Jack ... She felt like she was being gutted by the pain clear in his words. It was almost enough to make her tell him the truth—that she'd been as fooled as he was until she'd heard him on the phone checking into her criminal background.

Criminal background. The thought made her grit her teeth and the anger helped banish the last of her guilt. This man didn't know her and didn't trust her. Talking would be futile.

"That must have been hard for you, pretending to be attracted to me, to love me," Jackson said, his grip on her wrist growing so tight Nicky flinched again, this time in pain.

"You're hurting me."

"Good." His eyes grew even colder but his fingers gentled on her arm. Nicky took the opportunity to jerk her hand free and back a few steps away.

"I think you should go." She crossed her arms and stuck her chin in the air, willing herself not to show how upset she was. "People are starting to stare."

"Let them stare. I'm not going anywhere without you, even if I have to throw you over my shoulder and carry you back to the car."

"So I guess you want to go to jail," Nicky said, a part of her wanting to slap the stubborn expression off his face. What was he thinking? This was insane. He couldn't abduct her *again* in front of half a dozen people and expect to get away with it. He really would be arrested if he tried that. "Is that why you kidnapped me in the first place? You have dreams of a life behind bars and a little boyfriend you can make your butt monkey?"

"I'll give you one last chance, Nick. Walk with me to the car, or I'm going to carry you out."

"You're crazy if you think—" Nicky's words ended in a squeal as Jackson did exactly as he'd threatened, scooping her over his shoulder in one smooth movement and turning toward the door.

"No! Put me down!" She yelled and pounded on his back with her fists.

How dare he? She was not a fucking child! She was an adult who—no matter what her sexual preferences were—deserved to be treated with respect and to have people listen when she said "no." Her husband might never have gotten that message, but Jackson sure as hell would. She'd send the bastard to jail and see how *he* enjoyed having his free will stolen away.

"Help! Someone, call the—"

Jackson's hand covered her mouth, cutting off her words as he swung through the door. Nicky could only pray someone in the diner knew where Jackson lived and would call for help. In the meantime, she would just have to do her best to fight for her freedom. No matter what, she wasn't going to passively submit to Jackson—or anyone else—ever again.

She was nearly naked again, wearing nothing but tiny black panties. Her jeans had been soaked through or he wouldn't have taken them off. He needed her shirt off to get to the tattoo, but not her pants. It certainly would be a hell of a lot easier to concentrate if she were wearing more clothes. The time for making love or fucking or whatever they'd been doing was over. From this point on, he was all business.

Too bad this business had an awful lot in common with one of his favorite pleasures.

Bondage had been a huge turn-on even before he discovered the BDSM lifestyle. Either binding another or being bound himself, it didn't much matter. Both made him hard enough to shatter rock. So it was no surprise his cock swelled uncomfortably within the confines of his jeans as he cuffed Nicky's wrists to the mission-style headboard of the bed.

He couldn't help being aroused, but he could have helped the way his fingertips traced the column of her spine, past the small of her back and down her legs. He should have refrained from gripping her just above the knees and pulling her thighs slowly apart, digging his fingers into the soft flesh.

Wider. Wider. Moving his fingers to wrap around her ankles.

A soft moan of excitement escaped Nicky's lips, making Jackson's breath rush out in a sigh of relief. He'd felt like a monster since the second he'd thrown her over his shoulder at the diner, a feeling that had only gotten worse as she continued to fight him all the way up to the cabin. With every passing second he'd become increasingly convinced that he'd gone too far, and truly crossed the line into abusive territory.

But that sigh of arousal helped calm his fears. No matter what she'd said in the diner or on the road up to the cabin, she hadn't been faking her physical responses to his touch.

Her emotional response, however, was another thing altogether.

"See there, Nicky. Aren't you glad I caught you in time?" His voice was as rough as the rope he used to secure first one ankle and then the other to the baseboard near her feet. He'd only brought the one pair of cuffs, so rope would have to do. At this point the idea of rope burns on Nicky's delicate skin didn't cause him much inner torment.

It was amazing how badly it had hurt to realize she'd been lying to him from the moment they'd arrived at the cabin. But then he'd been a fool to believe the woman he'd *kidnapped* could really come to love him again in less than a day. No matter what he felt for her, no matter that it had seemed she felt the same way, it had been pure stupidity to drop his guard. He should have stuck to his original plan from the beginning and spared himself the heartache.

And abducting Nicky again from a public place, asshole. You've really lost it, and chances are better than good you'll be facing criminal charges.

His inner voice was channeling Christian this evening.

It was irritating as hell, and unfortunately, probably right on the money. Even if the people in the diner didn't call the police to report what they'd seen, Nicky now had several witnesses to corroborate her claims of being kidnapped.

A day ago, he would have said that it didn't matter, that he wouldn't have denied the charges anyway. But now a part of him would be sorely tempted to insist their weekend trip had been a consensual affair. He was *that* angry about being taken for a ride. Or that devastated, take your pick.

He preferred angry. It hurt a hell of a lot less.

"Tell me, Nicky," he whispered, his voice thick with anger. "Now."

He finished up at her ankles and moved over her prone form, bracing his hands on either side of her shoulders, hovering close enough that he could feel the heat of her body but not the silky softness of her skin. He moved his mouth just the barest bit closer, letting his lips brush softly against the back of her neck as he spoke again. "Tell me what you want."

Nicky shivered, but he could tell it wasn't from the cold. She was aroused, he would bet his hands on it. If he let his fingers slide into those tiny black panties, he'd find her wet and ready, no matter how much of a fight she'd put up as he carried her up the stairs and wrestled her onto her stomach on the bed.

"Fuck you," she whispered, anger clear in her tone as well.

So she was pissed as well as turned on. Good. That made two of them.

"I don't think so. No more distractions. We're going to finish this," he said, reaching over to where the tattoo machine sat beside the bed.

Jackson flipped the switch on the motor then pulled on his latex gloves. He'd already prepped the gun with black ink, so they were ready to go. All he had to do was put the needle to her skin. He'd planned how he would modify the tat if Nicky refused to give him her input, so there was no reason to stall any further.

In half an hour, he could be finished and they could both be getting ready to head back to L.A. He should get on with it already.

But for some reason, he couldn't force his hand to move any closer.

"Tell me what you want, Nicky. This is your last chance," he said, hoping she heard the resolve in his voice. If she didn't talk now, she would lose the opportunity.

But she didn't say a word, only pressed her face into the quilt beneath her, every muscle tensed, braced for the feel of the needle piercing her skin. The position only emphasized how small she was. Her wrists were tinier than ever, and her shoulder blades and the knobs of her spine were clearly visible through her skin, once more inspiring the desire in Jackson to get to work fattening her up.

He should just forget this tattoo madness and go down and reheat the pasta, bring it up here so they could eat it together in bed. They could feed each other tortellini and sips of red wine, then have each other for dessert. After all, who needed cheesecake when you could have your tongue buried in something as sweet as Nicky's pussy?

The imagined scene made his cock ache even as his throat grew uncomfortably tight. Nothing like that was ever going to happen again. It had all been a lie, every touch, every word.

What a fucking fool he was.

Jackson's anger sharpened to a knifepoint. She'd let him think they had a future, made him happier than he'd been in years, only to tear him down hours later. She'd *cried* in his arms, for god's sake, wept because she was so overwhelmed by what she was feeling.

Except now he knew she hadn't been feeling anything at all. It had been an act.

Seconds later, without him having made the conscious decision to move, the tattoo gun was on her flesh, tracing the edge of the wing he intended to expand. He'd add enough feathers to cover the angel's body, then go to work on the face, covering the ethereal features with wild strands of black hair. By the time he was finished, no one would recognize his tat and Nicky's as similar, let alone matching in every detail. And when the resemblance was gone, he'd finally be free of this obsession with a woman who couldn't care less.

"Stop."

"Sorry. I can't," he said, clenching his jaw and refusing to acknowledge the guilt that whispered through his rage. Screw guilt. It wasn't going to get this job done.

"Don't. Stop it. Stop!" The words started as a whisper, but ended in a scream. Nicky's shout echoed off the walls of the bedroom, followed closely by the horrific sound of a woman crying.

No, she wasn't just crying. She was wailing like her heart was breaking, weeping so hard her shoulders shook as the sobs wracked her body. She seemed to be trying to speak through her tears, but the words were unintelligible.

One thing was for certain, however—there was no way he could continue the tattoo with her shaking like a leaf and clearly so upset. He might be angry with her, but he wasn't that monster he feared he was becoming.

You're not? So, you'll strap a woman down, but not sit on her to force her to hold still. What a fucking gentleman.

Shame swept through Jackson's body like a blast of cold air, shocking him to the core. What was he doing? How could he really go through with this? It was madness. What's more, it was cruel. No matter what Nicky had done, no matter how she'd made him feel, he was supposed to be a better person than this. At least, that's what he'd always told himself.

Now . . . he wasn't so sure.

The way he'd acted bore a strong resemblance to every piece-of-shit foster father he'd ever known. Looked like he'd grown up to be more like the men who had beat him, the men who he'd watched starve their own biological kids to pay for beer, the men who had hit their wives and terrorized their families. He'd once watched his first foster dad chain a seven-year-old girl in a dog-house for a night because she'd taken the change from the couch cushions to buy candy.

That night, as ten-year-old Jackson had listened to his foster sister cry and beg for someone to come get her, he had vowed he'd never hurt anyone the way he'd watched so many people be hurt. He'd sworn he would be the type of man who helped people, who made their lives better.

But now he was standing above a woman he'd forcibly bound to a bed, listening to her cry hysterically.

In that moment, something inside him snapped. He had to stop this. Now. Before he hurt Nicky any more than he already had, and before he committed an act of violence that would haunt him forever.

Chapter Thirteen

"I'm sorry, Nick. Please, don't cry." Jackson flipped off the tattoo machine and stripped his gloves off with two angry motions. "I don't know what's wrong with me. I never should have tried to do this."

Nicky felt him working to untie the ropes at her feet a few seconds later, but even knowing she was soon going to be free didn't help stop the tears. If anything, it made them worse. She was crying so hard her entire body ached and her chest felt like it might explode. The sobbing sounds echoing through the room didn't even sound like her. She sounded like a wounded animal, a creature that had been caged for too long.

All the pain of the past three years, all the fear and anger and despair, hit like a physical blow. Jackson's tattoo needle had made a hole in her heart and everything she'd held inside was spilling out all at once.

"Please, babe. Please, I'm sorry," Jackson whispered into her hair as he plucked the key to the cuffs from beside the bed and unlocked her wrists. "I'm sorry."

Nicky wanted to tell him it wasn't his fault, at least not all of it. His betrayal was only the cherry on top of a huge messy shit sundae of hurt. She wanted to tell him that it was okay, that he'd stopped in time and she wasn't as wildly angry as she'd been before. She wanted to say it wasn't the tattoo modification but the lack of respect for her free will that had finally pushed her into major meltdown mode.

But she couldn't stop crying long enough to say any of those things.

So she did the only other thing that felt right. As soon as her arms were free, she rolled over onto her back and reached for him, holding both arms out like Abby did when she wanted her mommy to pick her up. She was still crying and could feel her nose beginning to leak, but for once she didn't worry about what kind of face she was putting on for the man in her bed. She just needed Jackson to hold her, to wrap her in those strong arms and tell her everything was going to be okay even if that was a lie.

"Nicky." All he said was her name, but she saw the shine in his eyes before he pulled her close, crushing her against his chest.

He loved her. He really did.

The thought made her sob even harder, more tears pouring out to soak his sweater. He was weirdly obsessed with their tattoos, thought she was a criminal, had kidnapped her—twice—and was probably a prime candidate for some sort of serious therapy, but he loved her. Jackson loved her in a way she could feel every time they touched, in a way that made her heart ache thinking about all the loveless years she'd wasted with a man who thought of her as nothing more than another decoration for his Bel Air mansion.

Nicky snuggled closer to his chest, reveling in the foreign

sensation of being home. The urge to cry slowly vanished in the wake of that warm, safe feeling, the feeling she always had when she was this close to Jackson. He was the only man who had ever been able to turn her on and calm her down at the same time.

"I'm so sorry." He dropped kisses onto the top of her head, the tension in his voice making it clear how grueling he'd found her epic crying jag. Poor Jack, he'd never been able to handle seeing a woman cry. "I've obviously lost my mind. I never wanted to hurt you, I never—"

"It's okay," she whispered, not wanting to lift her face from his chest.

"No, it's not okay. But I'm going to make it okay. We'll leave whenever you want and I'll take you wherever you want me to take you. I'm just sorry I—"

"I'm sorry, too," Nicky said. "This wasn't all your fault, you know. That was coming for a long time. I mean, I've done my share of crying the past three years, but nothing like that."

Jackson's muscles relaxed a bit and one hand began to smooth idly up and down her bare back. "Your marriage was that bad, huh?" He reached over to the side of the bed and plucked a Kleenex from the box. Nicky took the tissue and did her best to mop up her face without moving too far away from Jackson. She needed to be close to him right now. It made her feel stronger for some reason.

"Yes, it was that bad." She sighed, amazed that thinking of Derrick no longer summoned the familiar rush of hurt and rage. It was as if she'd finally cried him out of her system. Now she just had to get him out of her life and she would truly be ready to move on.

"You want to tell me about it?"

"Not really, but I probably should," she said. "I haven't told anyone. I've been too ashamed."

"I'm sure you have nothing to be ashamed of."

"Oh, I do." Nicky laughed, a short, sad sound. "I was really twisted, and really, really stupid."

"Hey, you're talking to the guy who kidnapped his high school girlfriend." He hugged her and softly kissed her forehead. "You can't get much more twisted or stupid than that."

This time her laugh was genuine. Jesus. Only Jackson could make her laugh just a few minutes after crying her eyes out.

"So spill it, all the gory details."

Nicky took a deep breath, not certain how to begin. So she started with the basics, how she'd met Derrick at one of the classier BDSM clubs in town. How he'd captured her interest from the start, seeming so much more truly dominant than any of the other men she'd met. She told Jackson how Derrick had swept her away for long weekends at posh resorts up and down the California coast, and then surprised her with a giant rock four months into their relationship.

"We were married two months later up near Santa Barbara at a winery," Nicky said, feeling oddly detached from the story of her life. All of that just seemed so long ago, like it had happened to a different person.

"Sounds pretty fairy tale so far," Jackson said. "I mean, if you're a submissive woman who's into really rich guys."

Nicky smiled. "Yeah, it was pretty good. We had a great time together, and he was always very nice to me. Derrick kept the dom thing going just about all the time, but he never pushed my limits. So I guess that's why I had no issue with signing the paperwork he had his lawyers draw up before our wedding. And I was twenty-one and stupid—that was probably a big part of it, too."

"A prenup agreement?"

"Well, there was that, but there was also a master-slave agreement. You ever heard of those?"

"I have," Jackson said, the dark note in his voice making it clear he didn't like the sound of them. "I don't know too many long-term dom-sub couples, so I don't have any personal experience, but I've heard of them."

God, how she wished *she* didn't have any personal experience with them. If she could go back in time and refuse to sign the thing, she'd do it in a heartbeat, even if it meant she had to relive those years with Derrick. No matter how awful they'd been, Abby had come out of that time, so Nicky could never count them as a total waste.

"From what I understand, there isn't really a standard boiler-plate contract for the master-slave agreement. It's either as open or restrictive as the dom and sub decide for it to be." Nicky sighed, not in a hurry to get to the next part of the story.

"Let me guess. This guy wanted it nice and restrictive."

"I signed over control of just about everything. My money, my right to drive a car, to leave the house without Derrick chaperoning—all kinds of things that should have rung alarm bells, but didn't."

"But those contracts aren't really legal, Nick. It's not like a dom-sub agreement would stand up in a court of law."

"Oh, I know. But that didn't really matter once we were married. I had no money, no car to drive. Basically no way out. Not that I wanted out, not then anyway. I started to get a little tired of the full-time control thing, but we were making it work," Nicky said, her chest getting tight. It was time to drop the big bomb. She wondered what Jackson would think about her having a child. "Things didn't get really bad until I accidentally got pregnant."

She risked a peek up into his dark eyes, shocked to see he didn't look at all surprised.

"You knew?" she asked, her brow wrinkling in confusion.

"I had a friend check up on you while you were getting ready. He told me you had a one-year-old little girl. Abigail is her name?"

"Abby, she's going to be one in a few weeks," Nicky said, anger spiking in her blood. "And I heard you talking to your *friend*, trying to see if I had a criminal record. What the hell were you thinking? I've never done anything illegal except get a tattoo without parental consent when I was sixteen. I never even drank until I was twenty-one."

"Is that why you ran? Because you heard me on the phone?" He looked so hopeful Nicky couldn't seem to stay mad.

"It made me feel like you didn't trust me, and I felt I'd been pretty cool about trusting you even though you were the one who—"

"Abducted you and hauled you off to my mountain lair." Jackson kissed her on the lips for the first time since they'd fought.

Electricity swept over Nicky's skin, tightening her nipples, making her very aware that she was nearly naked in Jackson's arms. By the time he pulled away, she could feel the hard ridge of his cock swelling against her stomach, and was tempted to forget the rest of her story and go straight for the zipper of his fly.

"I'm sorry I upset you, but I was only trying to help. You said you had secrets and I wanted to make sure that, whatever those secrets were, I could still make things okay for us."

"You should have trusted me to tell my secrets when I was ready," she said, "not gone behind my back."

"I know that now. I'm sorry. And I should never have forced you to come back here with me. It was wrong . . . very wrong."

"Well . . . don't let it happen again," Nicky said, trying very hard to resist the urge to wrap her leg around his hips and grind her center against his swollen length. After years of celibacy, her libido still hadn't gotten enough of this man.

Celibacy. Unfortunately that brought her back to her story. Might as well finish it and get the damn thing over with.

"So I got pregnant with Abby and was so excited. She wasn't planned, but I'd always wanted kids so I figured it was a happy surprise."

"But Derrick didn't?"

"He tried to convince me to have an abortion." She gritted her teeth, some of the familiar anger she always felt when thinking about her ex returning. "When I wouldn't, he just . . . shut off. He would barely speak to me and certainly wouldn't touch me or sleep in the same bedroom. He said he found a pregnant woman's body disgusting."

"Son of a bitch," Jackson growled.

Nicky laughed. "I think that was part of the problem. His mother is a real freak show and he was an only child. I think he equates women who are mothers with evil or something. At least that's the hypothesis I came to in my freshman psych class."

"You went to college?" He smiled, obviously proud of her. What a difference from Derrick, who had mocked her attempts to start school when she was already older than most of the graduating seniors. He'd insisted he made plenty of money and she was better off at home, serving her husband like a good submissive wife.

"I only did two semesters. One when I was pregnant with Abby and one after. They had a really good child-care room at the community college and it was close enough for me to walk there from our house."

"Still, that's great and you could go back. You always were so smart."

"Thanks," she said, her eyes tearing up at the simple compliment. Jackson was the only man she'd ever known who seemed to value her brain as much as her body. Hell, the only one who even realized she *had* a brain.

"Oh, god, don't cry." He laughed, but she could tell he meant every word, so she did her best to pull it together. "So what happened after Abby was born?"

"Derrick didn't like my after-pregnancy body any more than he liked my pregnant one, but that was fine by me. At that point I was looking for a way out." Nicky traced the pattern on Jackson's sweater, concentrating on the swirls instead of her own words. "But Abby was so tiny and helpless and I was scared. I didn't know how I'd survive with a newborn, no job, and not a dime to my name. And to be fair, Derrick did seem to love her in his way, once she outgrew the colic and started smiling and playing a little more."

"But that doesn't sound like a very good life. For either of you."

"It wasn't. Derrick had grown even more distant with me after Abby was born. At first he just ignored me, but then he started to . . . say things."

"What kind of things?"

"Anything that would hurt. I think he blamed me for ruining what we had by getting pregnant and wanted to punish me for it. He'd talk about how my looks had gone downhill, how I was a lazy housewife—even though he had a maid come in twice a week so there wasn't much cleaning for me to do. He'd say I was a high school dropout not fit to teach Abby anything and—"

"He's a piece of shit. Where does he live? I've suddenly got a strong desire to punch his face in."

"No!" Nicky immediately realized her response was too strong, but it was too late.

"You're still afraid of him," Jackson observed, rage in his eyes. "You don't have to be. Not anymore."

God, could she tell him? Would Jackson help her, or would he think she was a piece of shit herself for letting Derrick get his hands on her child?

"I promise you, Nick. I'll make sure he never hurts you again."

"It's not me I'm worried about," she said, rushing on before she could second-guess herself. "When I finally left him, I took Abby. I changed our names and tried my best to hide, but I didn't run far enough, I guess. He found us and he . . . took her."

"Took her? How could he just take her? You're both her parents, no court in California is going to—"

"We haven't gone to court and we probably won't. Derrick had his lawyer draw up a divorce decree that he expects me to sign as is. It gives him full custody of Abby."

"That's bullshit. You and your lawyer will fight him. I'm sure a bastard like that will—"

"I don't have a lawyer."

"Why not?" Jackson captured her face in his hands, urging

her to look up and meet his eyes. The doubt she read there made her sick to her stomach. He wasn't sure she wanted her own child. Just another case of Jackson not knowing her nearly as well as she'd hoped, no matter how much he loved her.

"Derrick is a dangerous man," Nicky said, trying not to let his doubt cut her too deeply. He didn't understand the situation. And he *wouldn't* understand until she got up the nerve to tell him. But for some reason, it was nearly impossible to bring herself to say the words. As if saying them out loud for the first time might make the danger to Abby more real.

"I can understand that, but you can't let this creep bully you out of your child's life. I can understand that you're scared, but you have to fight for her."

"Believe me, there's nothing I'd like more, Jackson. I love Abby more than anything in the world and I want her with me. I promise you that." The back of her throat grew tight, as if it would physically prevent her from telling Jackson anything more. "I know living with Derrick isn't a good situation for anyone, especially a baby."

"Then let's go get her. I'll drive you there tonight. We'll walk in and take Abby and I'll beat the living hell out of the man if he tries to get in our way."

"Great, Jackson. And then he'll call the police and you'll be arrested and I'll look like an unfit mother for bringing my boyfriend to beat up my husband. This is not something that can be solved with fists. We're not in high school anymore."

Jackson sighed. "You're right. I just can't stand to think of that man having your little girl. I've got a bad feeling about it. I know you used to think I was crazy with the bad vibe shit, but I swear I—"

"No, I didn't. Your vibes were usually dead-on. And they're definitely right on the money in this situation." Nicky swallowed past the lump in her throat and licked her dry lips. "Derrick said he would kill Abby before he'd let me be a part of her life."

"What?" Jackson's voice was thick with equal parts rage and disbelief.

"If I fight for custody in court or try to take her again, he promised me he'd kill her. That he'd do it in a way no one would ever suspect was murder and not an accident."

"He wouldn't. He's just bluffing to—"

"No, he's not, Jackson." Her voice shook and her skin suddenly felt the chill lingering in the cabin. "If there's one thing I learned about Derrick Sakapatatis in the years we were married, it's that he always keeps his promises. Especially the scary ones."

Chapter Fourteen

Jackson was quiet for a few minutes, his mind racing as he pulled a trembling Nicky so close it felt like the fronts of their bodies would fuse together. Not only was he a head case, he was a fool. He should have known Nicky would never lie and say she loved him just to gain her freedom. She wouldn't have reached for him after he set her free, or be spilling her guts right now if she didn't love him. She wasn't the type to talk emotional stuff with anyone but her nearest and dearest. Her feelings were as real as the passion between them.

And as real as the hellish position she was in with her husband.

No wonder she'd let the bastard take their daughter. Even if the man was lying, what mother would be willing to risk the chance—even the slight chance—that he wasn't? He was threatening her child's life, for god's sake.

Derrick was a fucking monster, whether he was bluffing with the death threat or not.

"I don't know a whole lot about how the legal system works,"

Jackson said in a low, soothing voice. "But couldn't you testify to what he said? Wouldn't that be enough to throw suspicion on whether he'd be a good—"

"I wouldn't get to testify. He said he'd kill Abby first, so the only way I'm getting on a stand is if she's already dead." Nicky's breath rushed out on a shaky breath. "Besides, who would take my word over Derrick's? I'm a high school dropout who's worked as a waitress, a lingerie model, and now a bartender at a semi-sleazy bar. He's a rich real estate investor who graduated top of his class at Stanford."

Jackson wanted to tell her things like that wouldn't matter, but he wasn't a fool. How many times had he been looked down on for owning a tattoo parlor or sporting two full sleeves of ink down his arms? Things had started to change after the reality show, but he still got the hairy eyeball from store clerks from time to time.

"Your silence is very reassuring," she said, shifting in his arms, the way her breasts pressed against his chest reawakening things that had been deflated by the news of her ex's death threats. Even now, more anxious than he could remember being in years, he still wanted to be inside Nicky.

When they were making love, when he was buried to the hilt in her gripping heat, he didn't have to think about anything. Not the danger her little girl was in, not the uncertain future, and certainly not the fact that he wasn't at all the man he'd thought he was only a few short weeks ago.

He'd not only followed through on his plan to kidnap Nicky, he'd chased her down like an animal when she'd run and used brute force to haul her back to his cabin. He obviously wasn't right in the head, and was displaying far more similar traits to her bully of an ex-husband than he wanted to admit.

Even if he figured out a way to help her and cleared the path for them to start dating seriously, how could he be sure he was any better for her than the man he'd helped her get free of? He knew he'd never dream of threatening a child, but then ... not so long ago he'd been certain he'd never kidnap a woman and tattoo her against her will, either.

Did he even know what he was capable of anymore?

"Jackson? Is something wrong?" Nicky's eyes were wide and worried, but she still clung to him the same way she had since he'd untied her.

When she'd reached for him in spite of what he'd done, Jackson had thought his heart would explode. She really did care—it hadn't all been a lie.

But maybe she would have been better off if it had been.

He loved her more than anything in the world, but who knew if that love would be enough? This Derrick creep had obviously loved her in his way, and look how that had turned out. Could Jackson be certain he'd do any better by Nick? Sure, he'd never ignore her or tear her down with words, but who knew what else he'd do once he'd settled into being the dominant man around the house.

No matter how strong Nicky was, she was a submissive through and through. She would place her trust in him and have faith he would make the best decisions for them both. But what if he couldn't handle the responsibility for two lives—three including her daughter's? What if he wasn't the man he thought he was, and ended up bringing even more hurt into the life of the woman in his arms?

"I really wish you'd talk to me. You're starting to freak me out a little."

Jackson winced inwardly. Freak her out. He *should* freak her out. He'd been acting like a maniac since the night he headed out of Vegas, bound for California. "Sorry, I was just thinking."

"About what?"

"About how we can make sure Derrick is the one considered an unfit parent," he said, the lie sliding easily from his lips. He couldn't tell Nicky about his doubts about himself. Not now, not when she obviously had no one but him to turn to. "My partner and I opted out of another season of *Sin City Ink*, but I'm still in touch with a lot of the cameramen who used to work on the show. Most of them live in L.A., so it shouldn't be hard to find someone willing to loan us the proper equipment."

"What kind of equipment?" she asked, a hint of hope in her voice.

"A hidden camera or two, a couple of microphones so tiny you can barely see them. Just a few things we'll need for a little sting operation." Jackson smiled when her eyes lit up. "If we can get Derrick on film threatening Abby, I think just about any judge out there will give you full custody until you go to trial and a nice restraining order, at the very least. If we're lucky, the bastard might even get jail time."

"You really think so?" Nicky asked, the excitement clear in her voice. "But we'd have to make sure Abby was safe before we showed anyone the film."

"I think we can make that happen pretty easily. I'll talk to my partner, Christian. He used to be a cop and will probably have some good advice on how to handle your ex."

"He has experience with domestic disputes as well as digging up private information on people in a matter of minutes?" Nicky narrowed her eyes, making it clear she didn't think much of

Christian already. "I'm not sure I want this guy's help if it's all the same to you."

"Christian's a good guy. I'm the jerk who was nosing around behind your back. Give him a chance," he said, feeling every inch a jerk. What had happened to the levelheaded man he'd always prided himself on being? It was like every ounce of restraint or common sense went out the window as soon as Nicky was in the picture. "If you don't like him once you meet him, we'll go it alone. We probably won't need that much help anyway. Derrick has to go to work and leave Abby alone sometime, like at a day care or—"

"He has a nanny. Two of them, actually, a day nanny and a night nanny. But I still have the key to the house, so we should be able to figure something out." She chewed her lip, obviously working through the scenario in her mind. "I'm sure he hasn't changed the locks or the code on the security system. He doesn't expect me to go against him in this."

"So we'll just wait until Derrick's out of the house and go in and take Abby. Since we'll have proof of Derrick's threats by then, I doubt you'll catch any legal flack for doing whatever it takes to protect your little girl."

"Oh, and I know exactly when to do it!" She vaulted into a seated position, treating Jackson to a very distracting view of her breasts.

"When?" Nicky noticed the direction of his stare, but didn't move to cover herself. Instead she just smiled, a secret little smile that made his cock even harder.

"There's this new BDSM club Derrick was visiting pretty regularly before I left. It's out in the Valley, but a lot of the girls who go there don't mind partner swapping or performing with another man for their dom." Nicky's expression left little doubt how distasteful she found the practice. Good. Jackson wasn't into sharing and had never understood doms who got off on watching their submissive partner perform sexually with other men. "We can stake out the club. Then, when he shows up, we head back to the house and get Abby. By then she and the night nanny will probably be asleep, so we can just sneak in and out without anyone even knowing we were there."

"Sounds like an excellent plan," Jackson said, reaching for Nicky in spite of himself.

With all the doubts still swirling in his mind, the last thing he should be doing was making a move to continue their sexual relationship. They should be friends and nothing more until her little girl was safe and they'd had time to talk about what they each wanted for the future.

But then Nicky took his hands and pushed them above his head, straddling him with that naughty smile. One look at the heated look in her eyes and he knew he was a goner.

"It does. Thank you. You don't know how much this means to me." She leaned over him, teasing him with her breasts, brushing the soft skin against his face as she lifted first one wrist and then the other to the headboard.

Jackson didn't fight. He let her cuff him, figuring she deserved the chance to turn the tables after all he'd done. After he'd manhandled her and tied her down without permission.

The thought was nearly enough to make his cock soften, but then Nicky was kissing him, pushing her tongue into his mouth, making him groan. She tasted so fucking sweet, like everything he'd hungered for in his entire life. He met her strokes with his own, exploring every inch of her mouth. Both of them were breathing fast by the time Nicky pulled away with a quick nip at his lower lip.

Seconds later she was busy at his belt buckle, tearing off his belt, fumbling with his fly, her hands shaking like she hadn't been laid in years.

"No foreplay?" he asked, groaning again as his swollen length sprang free.

Nicky shoved his jeans and boxer briefs to his knees and then made quick work of her little black panties. "No foreplay. I want you inside me. Now."

She rose up over him in one smooth motion, spreading the lips of her sex and positioning his cock at her entrance. Seconds later he was inside her silken sheath, encased all the way to his aching balls.

"God, Nick." He moaned as she leaned forward, her hair spilling in silky waves around his face as she captured his lips once more.

They kissed for what seemed like forever, a slow, sensual meetings of lips, teeth, and tongue that communicated so much more than words. Less than a half hour ago, he'd thought he'd never know this kind of connection with Nick ever again. That sense of loss was still so close to the surface, intensifying the pleasure of every kiss, setting every place they touched on fire.

And slowly driving him even further out of his mind.

Of course, it didn't help that Nicky limited her movement to tiny circles of her hips, grinding against him so only the base of his cock felt the friction of sliding in and out of her tight heat. The slight movement made him impossibly thicker, harder, until things low in his body cramped with an almost painful pleasure.

It was a sweet breed of torture, lying there beneath her. He was dying to buck his hips, to drive inside her, hard and fast. But he only hummed into her mouth, forcing himself to follow her lead, to let her set the pace.

"Jackson." She breathed his name, the arousal clear in her voice making his jaw clench.

Damn, it was hell to hold back, to force his movements to mimic Nicky's own. But he could feel how her pussy clenched each time he nudged against her clit. She was close to the edge, her muscles strung tight and her breath coming in desperate little pants. The arms braced on either side of his face trembled and her hands fisted in the pillow beneath him. She only needed the slightest push and she'd shatter, her cunt clenching around his cock.

Thankfully he had just the perfect push in mind. "I want to suck my tits. Move for me."

Nicky obeyed with a moan, shifting on top of him so that her breasts and her tightly puckered nipples were within easy reach. Jackson's breath caught at the erotic beauty of her flushed skin. She was so perfect, the only woman who had ever literally taken his breath away.

He captured one rosy tip in his mouth, sucking and nibbling, tracing the pebbled flesh with his tongue until Nicky writhed on top of him. She picked up the pace of her movements, more wet heat gushing from her sex as he transferred his attention to the other breast, dragging his teeth over her nipple before licking away the sting.

"Are you going to come for me?" he asked, in between flicks of his tongue. "Are you going to come on your cock?"

"Oh, god. Oh, god, yes." She moaned, the circling of her hips growing more and more frantic until finally she threw her head back with a wild cry. Her back arched, pressing her breasts closer to his face as she came.

Jackson sucked even harder, pulling at her sensitized flesh until she screamed his name and began to move again. In seconds she was coming a second time, fingernails digging into his shoulders with enough force for it to sting, even through the thick fabric of his sweater. The feel of her slick, hot pussy clutching at him a second time was almost more than he could take.

"Fuck, Nick," he mumbled against her soft, damp skin. "Ride me. Ride my—"

She sucked in a deep breath, braced her hands on his chest and lifted her hips, slamming them back down before he could finish his sentence. Without the slightest urging, she set a brutal rhythm, sheathing him inside her again and again, as if she'd read his mind and knew exactly what his body craved.

The sound of flesh slapping against flesh filled the room as her ass made impact with his thighs, underscored by the grunts and groans as each of them neared the edge. Jackson arched to meet her as she dropped her hips, intensifying their connection, reaching all the way to the end of her and still not feeling as if he'd ever get close enough.

The smell of her arousal spun through his head, making his hands itch to reach between them, to gather some of the wet heat dampening her thighs and bring his fingers to his mouth. He wanted to taste her at the same time he lost himself inside her, wanted to drown himself in every aspect of Nicky.

"Jack. God, Jack," she gasped, her rhythm starting to falter.

"Harder, faster. Don't stop." He watched her breasts bounce as she began to ride him once more. His swollen balls ached, throbbing with the need to come, but he forced himself to hold back his release, to savor every last moment of being inside his girl.

"I'm going to come, Jack. I can't, I—"

"Come," he groaned, the sound transforming to a cry of surrender as orgasm hit them both at the same moment. His cock jerked inside of her even as her pussy clenched around him, milking every last drop of seed from his body. Things low in his body twisted in ways that didn't feel natural, but they sure as hell felt good. He couldn't remember ever coming so hard his vision blurred and his skin felt too small to contain the pure pleasure exploding inside his every cell.

His ears were ringing by the time body and soul finally reconnected, the blood pounding through his veins making him decidedly hard of hearing.

That was the only explanation as to why he hadn't noticed the men in the door sooner.

"What the fuck are you doing in my house?" he asked, his voice at its deep and most threatening best despite the fact that he was cuffed to a bed and not in a position to be doing anyone much damage. He must have forgotten to lock the door. A pretty stupid call out in the middle of nowhere, where they had more than their share of backwoods crazies.

"Shit!" Nicky shrieked and leapt off of him, burrowing under the covers before poking her head back out. "You scared the hell out of me," she said, breath coming fast as she flipped one edge of the blanket over Jackson's now exposed cock. Still, she didn't sound afraid.

Probably because the men were cops. After a second look at the door, Jackson too noticed the khaki uniforms and the holsters, complete with walkie-talkies and standard-issue fire-arms. Shit indeed. Nicky had hit the nail right on the head.

"We were just leaving, ma'am," the younger man said, tipping his hat and directing his eyes to a spot somewhere on the ceiling. "We'd gotten a report there might be a woman in trouble up here, but obviously we were mistaken."

"Unless you're the one in trouble, sir," the older man said, a grin on his face, though he too had the decency to avert his eyes from the bed.

"Nope, no trouble." Jackson willed his voice to be calm and collected, to not betray the anxiety he felt. If Nicky was going to turn him over, she would have done it already. Right? "At least not any trouble I don't want to be in."

"And you, ma'am? If you want out of here, we can wait while you get dressed and escort you back down to town." The younger man stepped a little farther into the room and let his hand stray casually to his gun, making it clear he was ready to do whatever it took to protect and serve.

"No, I'm fine. We were just having a little argument earlier. Disagreeing about wedding plans." She laughed, such a genuine sound Jackson would never have guessed she was lying if he didn't know better. "You know how stressful that kind of thing can be."

"All right, but keep the arguments in the privacy of your own home next time. You had a few people worried." The older cop sighed, but didn't seem overly annoyed. He and his partner probably hadn't had much else to do tonight in a community like this one.

"Will do. Thanks, Officers." Nicky smiled and actually waved as the two men turned and tromped down the stairs.

Jackson lay beside her, holding his breath until he heard the door slam below them. That had been entirely too close. What if he hadn't stopped modifying Nicky's tat in time? What if the policemen had entered the room to find a sobbing woman tied to his bed and him jabbing at her with a needle? Getting arrested wouldn't have been anything he didn't deserve at that point, but still. . . .

The enormity of his risk finally hit him in the face. Christian had been right. It had been a form of suicide to go ahead with his plan to kidnap Nicky. Even the fact that she seemed happy to be with him most of the time they'd been together didn't make up for it. He was a madman, a criminal, and not nearly good enough for the woman giggling as she rolled over him to fetch the handcuff keys.

"Ohmygod, that was hysterical. I've never been caught in the act before. How embarrassing. I nearly peed myself I was so scared." She unlocked the cuffs and then hurried into the bathroom, still laughing.

Jackson heard the water running and then the toilet flush, but not even those normal sounds could thaw the cold fear in his heart. He was going to have to watch himself very, very closely. Whatever madness had driven him to this point was probably still swirling around in his brain, waiting to come out and play. His job now was to make sure it didn't get the chance, that he never committed another criminal act around Nicky or anyone else.

He'd help her, make sure she and her daughter were safe, and then he'd get the hell out of her life. It was the best thing he could do. There was no doubt he loved her, but she deserved a sane, rational man who would never think of doing half the things he'd done the past two days. Including taking advantage of a woman in a vulnerable position.

"So, I'm starved. What about you?" Nicky asked as she plucked her clothes from the floor and dressed. "Do you think that pasta you made is still good?"

"We can reheat it, and eat it on the road. Let's get everything packed up." Jackson rolled from the bed and tugged his pants up around his waist.

"Okay," Nicky said, her tone wary. "Are you all right?"

"Yeah, I'm fine. I just . . . I think we should get back to L.A. The sooner we get things moving, the sooner we get your daughter back."

She nodded and walked toward her room, but stopped in the door to the bath and turned back to him. "I was never going to tell the police, Jackson. Even if you'd forced me to change the tattoo, I wouldn't have. I care too much about you to ruin your life."

Jackson's heart lurched in his chest as he watched her disappear. Her words only cemented his decision. He had to get out of her life, as soon as possible. He didn't deserve a woman like Nicky. Never had, never would.

Chapter Fifteen

"So we're all straight on where we need to be when?" Jackson asked, pacing around the luxury hotel suite where they'd been staying since their return to L.A. He'd thought it would be best if they stuck close to plan their strategy, which had been more than fine with Nicky.

The suite was twice the size of her studio apartment and she still couldn't get enough of Jackson. Even after the sex marathon they'd had at the cabin, she'd been eager to get back between the sheets with the man. Making love to him was swiftly becoming an addiction.

Too bad he didn't feel the same way.

He hadn't touched her in three days. Instead of joining her in bed, he'd sacked out on the couch, leaving her one of the suite's bedrooms and his partner, Christian, who had flown in from Miami, the other. Something was obviously bothering him, but she hadn't had the chance to talk to him about it. Christian or his other friends always seemed to be around. They hadn't had ten minutes alone together since the ride back to L.A.

But if she was honest with herself, she'd felt him pulling away even then. Ever since their brief and embarrassing encounter with the police, he'd been acting differently. He was still committed to helping her get her daughter back, but he didn't seem interested in continuing what they'd begun up at the cabin.

Nicky knew she shouldn't let that hurt her so much. Three days were nothing in the scheme of things, and saying you loved someone didn't necessarily mean you were ready to settle down and live happily ever after. Hell, she wasn't even sure *she* was ready. She only knew she missed the connection they'd had, missed it so much it made her feel strangely hollow inside.

But she had to pull herself together. Jackson had his own life, his own plans for the future, and they had nothing to do with her. She should just be grateful he was using his connections to help her get Abby back.

And she was. But she was also disappointed. Profoundly.

"Christian, do you remember where you're supposed to wait for the call?"

"Jackson, we've been over it a hundred times," Christian said, reaching for the television remote and sinking farther down into the overstuffed couch. "Let's check out what's on pay-per-view and relax for a couple of hours, man."

His blasé attitude bugged Nicky. A lot. This was her daughter's life on the line, after all. "If you don't want to help out with this, Christian, I totally understand. We can change the plan. Jackson and I can do the bit at the club then—"

"Of course I want to help, and I'm your man for breaking and entering. Believe me," Christian said, turning his attention back to where Nicky and the two cameramen sat at the mahogany dining table.

The monstrosity was bigger than her bed back at her studio apartment, and reminded her way too much of the ostentatious furnishings in her former home. Derrick had picked out all their pieces himself and his tastes ran to the large and overly embellished. Just another thing they hadn't had in common. Nicky had felt more at home in Jackson's cabin after two days than she had in three years of wandering Derrick's garish showplace.

"This isn't breaking and entering," Nicky said. "I have a key and the code to the security system."

"And what if the code has changed? What would you do then?"

"I don't know," she said, trying to keep anger from her tone. The man wasn't trying to be argumentative, he just rubbed her the wrong way. "I'd figure something out."

"Figure something out. Good plan." He snorted, a derisive sound that made her grit her teeth.

Maybe the bastard *was* trying to be argumentative. Fine with her.

"Well, what are you going to do if Abby starts crying and wakes up the nanny?" Nicky asked. "She doesn't know you, and I'm betting she's not going to like you very much."

"I'll have you know I'm good with ladies of all ages," Christian said, that smirk on his face she knew most women would find sexy, but only made her want to strangle him. "You want references? I'm sure Jackson would be willing to testify to my many successes with the fairer sex."

"Christian." He spoke his partner's name, but Jackson's tone was a warning to both of them to cut the crap. He was right. They didn't have time to argue.

Nicky sighed, all the anger flooding from her as the cold reality of what they were planning set in once more. She was placing way too much trust in a man she didn't really know, and it scared her. "Listen, I'm grateful for your offer to help," she said in a softer voice, "but I honestly think it would be better if I went."

Christian met her eyes, the hard look on his face softening for one of the first times since she'd met him Sunday morning. She'd been surprised to find Christian fairly hostile toward the woman his best friend had promised to help, but tried not to take it personally. She wasn't here to make friends. She was here to get Abby back.

"I grew up helping out with six little brothers and sisters," Christian said, rising and coming to lean on the back of the empty chair across from her. "I'm good with kids, and if Abby is like most babies she sleeps like the dead once she's down. Am I right?"

Nicky bit her lip, not wanting to admit he did indeed have a point. Whenever Abby fell asleep in her car seat, Nicky had to move heaven and earth to get her awake enough to sit up in the buggy when they went grocery shopping. It had driven Derrick so crazy she'd started riding in the backseat so she could play with Abby while they drove, keeping her awake until they reached the store.

"See. I know a few things about kids," Christian said with a smile. "And I promise you I'll have your baby here by the time you crazy kids get back from your kinky time."

"Speaking of the kinky time, I'd like you dressed in about an hour." Steve, the sound guy Jackson had convinced to help them, reached for another slice of pizza as he spoke.

He'd been eating nonstop since he arrived at the hotel room three hours ago and showed no signs of slowing down. It was obvious he came by his impressive bulk honestly. With his thick brown beard, friendly face, and giant belly, he resembled a twentysomething Santa Claus.

If Santa was a big porn fan.

Steve had grilled Nicky for over an hour for all the details on the former porn stars she worked with at the Hard Way, keeping at it until she'd fled to the deck pleading a need for fresh air. She wasn't a prude by any means, but porn wasn't really her thing. Why spend hours watching badly staged sexual scenarios that catered to the male of the species when you could actually be having sex?

Or maybe even making love, sharing more than a body connection with another person. The way she and Jackson did when they—

Not going there, remember?

"Do you want both of us dressed or just me?" Nicky asked, blinking away the mental images inspired by thinking of her and Jackson making love.

"Both of you. It could be tricky making sure the mics don't show in tight clothing," Steve said around a mouthful of pepperoni and olives. "It's going to be tight, right? I can't wait to see Jackson in some second-skin leather pants."

"Thanks, Steve," Jackson said. "And here I'd thought none of the girls on the set would date you because of that sicko porn collection you're so proud of. I didn't know you were gay."

"Only for you, Jackson. Only for you." Steve batted his eyes and all the men laughed. Even Ken, the rather quiet Asian man in charge of the cameras, chuckled into his giant mug of coffee. Nicky probably would have laughed, too, if she wasn't so nervous.

"I think I'll go ahead and shower and get dressed now," she said, taking her coffee mug to the sink and dumping the last of the contents down the drain. She was already hyped up enough, the last thing she needed was more caffeine.

"Me, too. I'll use Christian's bathroom." Jackson shot her a reassuring smile as they crossed paths. Nicky smiled back, trying not to think about how much more she'd enjoy the process of getting clean if they were to share a shower. She could use a little stress-relieving quickie right about now.

Who was she kidding? She could always go for a quickie if Jackson were the man in question. She craved his hands on her, his voice whispering in her ear, telling her how to please him, taking away all fear and doubt with the quiet assurance of his dominance. She really was hopeless, head over heels for another dom before she'd even started divorce proceedings with the first man who'd taken control of her life.

Maybe *that* was why Jackson didn't want her anymore. He'd seen how weak she was and wanted no part of it. He'd said a submissive's role required a lot more strength than a dom's. Maybe he'd decided she didn't have what it took to be his girl.

So what? If that's what he's decided, it's his loss.

Nicky froze in the doorway to what had been her bedroom for the past two nights, shocked to her core. How long had it been since she'd felt enough pride in herself to assume anyone would be better off with her than without her?

Years. At least two years.

A part of her knew she had Jackson to thank for that, too. If he hadn't made her feel so intensely desired, who knew how long it could have taken to recover her lost confidence? The guys at the Hard Way had made sure she knew her body was still worthy of interest, but it was Jack who had made the person inside the body begin to feel whole again. She owed him for that. Big-time, no matter what craziness had driven him to kidnap her in the first place.

So if he wanted out of what they'd started without a bunch of drama, she'd do her best to let him go.

Nicky sighed as she turned on the shower, ignoring the aching in her chest and the tightness at the back of her throat. She couldn't let herself dwell on the likelihood of losing Jackson. There was too much riding on her ability to pretend they were a happy little BDSM couple.

With the help of one of Christian's many mysterious connections, they'd scored a copy of the guest list and a pair of tickets for a special scene being held at Under My Thumb, the club in the Valley Derrick had been frequenting before he and Nicky split. Derrick Sakapatatis was on the VIP list for the "Knights in Black Leather, Ladies in White Lace" costume event.

The knowledge made her shudder. Barring some unforeseen change of plans, she'd be seeing her husband in a few hours. But this time she wouldn't be alone. She'd be accompanied by her new dom, a man determined to help her get custody of her daughter. Though they weren't going to let Derrick in on that fact right away.

The plan was for her and Jackson to engage in some very public play, doing their best to capture Derrick's attention and hopefully inspire some good old-fashioned jealousy, a tactic Nicky was cautiously optimistic would work.

Even though he'd found her undesirable for the past couple of years, that didn't mean Derrick was ready to see her serving another man. After all, *she* was the one who'd left *him* and she knew how that stung. Above all else, Derrick craved control of the people in his life. That craving had even led to an offer to take her back the day he'd tracked her down at her new apartment. It was only after she refused that he'd flown into a rage and snatched Abby from her crib.

So hopefully he'd get nice and angry when he saw Nicky letting Jackson do so many of those things she'd never wanted him to do to her in public. Because the angrier he was, the more likely he would be to incriminate himself. On the off chance the threats he'd made had been a heat-of-the-moment thing, they needed him nice and heated tonight.

Then, once his temper was boiling, she'd fan the flames by asking him to step outside for a talk. A talk in which she'd tell him all about her new knight in shining armor and do her damnedest to get any threats he made on tape.

Once that was accomplished, the men monitoring the camera and sound feeds from a nearby van would call Christian and give him the go signal. He'd be on the move from his location near Derrick's house seconds later. Even if Derrick left the club right after his chat with Nicky, Christian would still have plenty of time to get in and get Abby and get out before Derrick arrived home.

They'd decided it was too risky to wait and go after Abby a night or two after Nicky and Jackson's appearance at the club. Derrick would be on his guard and suspecting something from his soon-to-be ex. If he hadn't changed the locks and security code previously, he certainly would then, and that would make gaining access to the home that much trickier and illegal.

This was the best plan they could come up with and it seemed to be a good one.

"Then why are you so nervous?" Nicky asked her reflection in the steamy mirror as she stripped out of her white T-shirt and jeans.

Was it the chance of failure? The fear that she wouldn't really be holding Abby by the end of the night? Was it anxiety over seeing Derrick for the first time in weeks?

Or maybe it was the way her heart rate accelerated when she looked at the white, nearly see-through peek-a-boo chemise and matching frilly shorts she'd be wearing in front of an entire room of people. They hung on the rod near the hotel towels, taunting her.

Even in her club days, she'd never been the type to go to a scene so scantily dressed. Leather shorts and a tank top with thigh-high boots had been more her style. She'd feel naked in the outfit Jackson had picked out for her. And even more exposed because *he* had been the one to choose the ensemble. It was obviously the kind of thing he would have wanted his girl to wear.

Tonight she would be his girl. He would finally touch her, tease her, dominate her, for what might very well be the last time. And he'd do it all in front of a room full of people.

Public displays weren't usually her brand of kink, but Nicky vowed she was going to make the most of the coming hours with Jackson. Nerves be damned. She wasn't going to let her last chance to be mastered by Jack slip through her fingers. She had to put on a good show for Abby's sake, and she needed to feel Jackson's strong hands upon her for her own sake. She needed the chance to say good-bye with more than words, to have one last kiss, one more chance to bask in the bliss of pleasuring the man she loved.

God, she did love him. It hadn't been some madness inspired

by their decidedly odd weekend. The feeling was still there now, simmering inside of her, growing stronger every day.

"Nicky?" Jackson's voice at the door made her jump and her heart race a little faster.

What was he doing here? Had he decided a team shower made more sense as well?

Before she could second-guess herself, Nicky turned to the door without bothering to wrap up in a towel. She was still wearing her bra and panties, and it wasn't like Jackson hadn't seen everything she had to offer.

"Hey. What's up?" She opened the door, breath catching to see Jack standing in front of her wearing nothing but his faded black jeans.

His massive chest was bare, every muscle sharply delineated from his morning workout at the hotel gym. It was hard as hell to resist the urge to lean forward and trace the lines of his six-pack with her tongue. She wanted to taste the light salt of his skin, wanted to kiss her way past his navel while her fingers worked the close of his jeans. It felt like ages since he'd had his hand fisted in her hair and his cock down her throat. She wanted to feel his hot, steely length shoving between her lips again, wanted to—

"Um, Ken said . . ." Jackson's voice trailed off, his breath rushing out between his parted lips.

His dark gaze met hers and Nicky had no doubt he knew exactly what she'd been thinking. He swallowed hard and let his eyes flick down to take in her simple white bra and cotton panties. They weren't nearly as scandalous as what she'd be wearing tonight, but apparently Jackson found them plenty interesting.

Nicky smiled as she watched the crotch of his jeans grow tighter. "Ken said?"

"He said to make sure to wear your hair up," Jackson said, his eyes lingering on her breasts until Nicky's nipples pulled tight inside her bra. God, he could make her ache with just a look, make her pussy slick without laying a hand upon her. "The cameras are hidden in the earrings he brought and he doesn't want your hair getting in the way."

"Okay. Not a problem." She stood in the doorway, unmoving, wondering if she should risk making the first move. "Is there anything else?"

"No. Nothing else." He shook his head and stepped back, his gaze dropping to the floor. Nicky's heart sank in spite of herself. They were going to be together in a couple of hours, she should just suck it up.

But in a couple of hours they were going to be putting on a show for Derrick. She wanted Jackson to touch her before the pretense, to let her know he still felt something for her. Even if it was only lust.

"Jackson, I—"

He was gone before she could finish her sentence, fleeing from the bedroom like his hair was on fire. That was how desperate he was to get away from her. His cock might still respond to the sight of her nearly naked body, but that was the end of it. Jackson didn't want her anymore. It was as if he'd completely forgotten the passion that burned so hot between them just a few short days ago.

"Then I'll just have to make sure he remembers," Nicky whispered as she closed the door and flung her bra and underwear onto the floor.

She stepped into the shower, determined to scrub, soap, shave, and loofah herself into a state of unparalleled desirability. She'd show Jackson what he was missing and give him a night he'd never forget.

Even if she couldn't change his heart, at least she could make certain she would haunt his mind. Jackson would never enter another BDSM club again without thinking of what they'd done together. She was going to make sure of it, or die trying.

Chapter Sixteen

nder My Thumb was a lot classier than Jackson had anticipated. Compared to most of the clubs he'd frequented in Vegas, the joint was downright restrained. Gold-and-brown-swirled fabric adorned the walls of the main room, lending a cozy feel to the lounge area. Dozens of low tables and upholstered black-and-gold chairs surrounded the circular bar at the center of the room, and a waterfall on one wall all but eclipsed the music coming from the other rooms with the soothing sound of water tumbling over rocks.

If it weren't for the glimpses of bondage equipment and spanking tables in the darker rooms to his right and left, and the scantily clad submissive chained to a revolving platform above the bar, he and Nicky could have been in just about any bar in L.A.

Well, any bar that allowed its patrons to bring their dates in on leashes.

Just ahead of them, half a dozen collared women and a couple of collared men knelt on the floor next to their dominant partners' chairs, eyes downcast and secretive smiles on their faces.

The sight immediately put Jackson's mind at ease about the personality of the club itself. Safe, sane, and consensual seemed to be the rule. The laid-back vibe of the place revealed its patrons weren't concerned for their own safety or anyone else's.

In fact, many of the couples were laughing and chatting, the subs fetching plates from the hors d'oeuvres table and the dominants feeding their partners while they knelt at their feet. There was an almost . . . loving feeling in the main room. It was a pleasant surprise, and Jackson knew he would have completely enjoyed spending a night here playing with Nicky if they weren't positive they would encounter her ex.

"Looks like I'm missing an important accessory," Nicky whispered, glancing at the rhinestone-inlaid collar of a very young blond sub as they made their way to the bar.

"Do you think I should have found you a collar?" Jackson leaned down and breathed the words against Nicky's neck, relishing the clean smell of her. She looked so beautiful with her hair up, her neck long and graceful. He could amuse himself for at least half an hour just letting his lips play up and down that smooth column of soft flesh.

"There's a woman selling gear at one of the tables in the corner. It's not too late to buy one. I'd certainly enjoy following you around on my hands and knees, sir." Nicky angled her body closer to his, the tips of her breasts brushing against his chest as he ordered them each a snifter of brandy.

He could catch just the faintest glimpse of her berry-colored nipples through the white fabric of her lacy little top. It had been driving him wild since the second she stepped out of the bathroom and every male jaw in the hotel room had dropped to the floor. Even Christian, who had done his best to make his dislike of Nicky known, had gotten that wolfish look in his eye. Like he wanted to pounce on Nick and devour her whole.

It had been all Jackson could do to keep from driving his fists into the faces of the very men who had been generous enough to help him. Friends or not, he couldn't stand to see anyone else look at Nicky with desire. She was *his*, and no other man should touch her, even with their eyes.

No, she's not yours, bucko. She deserves a better man and you're going to make sure she's free to find him.

Jackson paid the bartender and took a deep pull on his brandy, wincing as the liquid burned a trail down his throat.

He'd seen the way Nicky looked at him since they'd returned to L.A. She wanted to pick up where they'd left off at the cabin. Hell, he did, too, but it wasn't best for either of them. He needed to get his head on straight and she needed the chance to be with a man who wouldn't do crazy things like threaten her daughter's life or kidnap her and try to tattoo her against her will. He and Nicky just couldn't have that second chance he craved with every cell in his body.

But they could have tonight. One last night that would have to last them a lifetime.

"So what do you say? She's got whips, too." Nicky sipped her drink as she traced soft fingers up his stomach to his chest, making him shiver. Even through the thick leather of his sleeveless shirt, he could feel the heat of her touch. "I want you to spank me in front of everyone. Isn't that why the legs on these little shorts are so loose? So you can flip them up on either side and see—"

"Soon." Jackson's hand tightened reflexively on Nicky's hip. He wanted nothing more than to find a bench and make her fantasy a reality, but they needed to take stock of their surroundings before they chose a place to play. His next words were even softer than a whisper. "Do you see him anywhere?"

Nicky's wicked smile faltered for a moment. "Not in here. But he might be in one of the playrooms."

"Then let's take a tour." They tossed back the last of their drinks.

Jackson put one hand at the small of her back and led her into the room on their right. Eyes followed them as they walked, but he wasn't surprised.

Nicky was easily the most gorgeous woman in the room, and he wasn't ignorant of the effect his own imposing bulk had on the average submissive. He and Nicky together were the poster children for the stereotypical fantasy BDSM—the tiny, delicate sub and large, muscled dom.

They were going to have their share of observers once they settled in to play, there was no doubt about that. It wasn't the way Jackson would have preferred to spend their last night together, but drawing attention was what they were out to do tonight. If every tongue in the club was wagging about the new kids in town, there was no way Nicky's husband could miss them.

"He's not here," she said.

It wasn't a big surprise—there were only four or five couples active in the large room at the moment—but Jackson still felt his spirits sink. What if the man decided not to come? Not that he was in any hurry to see the sociopath who'd made Nicky's life a living hell, but after all their planning it would be beyond frustrating if Derrick didn't show. And Jackson knew Nicky would be devastated. She was so thrilled by the thought of seeing her daughter again.

Jackson was pretty thrilled himself. He couldn't wait to meet the little blond-haired, brown-eyed girl he'd seen in Nicky's pictures. Abby was the spitting image of her mom, a fact that made him love her before he'd even met her.

God, he was a hopeless case where this woman was concerned. And probably the world's sappiest dom. If Nick knew half the thoughts running through his head, his "big and bad" rep would be out the window in seconds.

"Nope, no Derrick, but I really like that bench in the corner." She ran her tongue lightly over her lips. "I mean really, *really* like it."

"It's called a Black Stallion," Jackson said, letting his hand wander down to cup Nicky's ass through the soft satin. "They're exceptionally well built, made to support a lot of weight. I could position you at one end, spank you until your pussy is dripping down your thighs, and then climb up and fuck you from behind. It would support both of us."

Nicky's breath came faster, her breasts rising and falling in a way that made Jackson ache to get her tits in his mouth. "You think the boys in the van got all that?"

"No. I have the switch to turn on the cameras and mics right here. It's a remote control built into my watch." His fingers teased under the hem of her shorts, tracing the curve of her ass, making her shiver. "I don't want any of them hearing or seeing anything but what they need to hear and see. Tonight, you're mine."

"Yes, I am." Her eyes slid closed and her lips parted, an invitation Jackson couldn't resist.

He captured her mouth with his, slipping his tongue between her lips, tasting the shot of brandy they'd each had and the sweeter, spicier taste that was pure Nicky. As his tongue tangled with hers, his fingers found their way between her legs. Pulling the scrap of fabric masquerading as her panties aside, he plunged first one finger and then a second into the molten heat of her pussy.

"You're wet already," he said, his own breath coming faster. "You little slut."

"*Dirty* little slut," she amended, contracting her inner muscles until they gripped his fingers. "Who can't wait to get fucked."

Jackson kissed her again, moaning against her lips as his cock thickened within the tight confines of his leather pants. God. Damn. How had he managed to go nearly three days without touching her? How had he resisted the overwhelming need to get his fingers, his mouth, his cock inside her sweet little pussy?

"Are you going to fuck me, Jackson?" she asked, her hands molding to his chest. "Are you going to take me in front of all these people? Show them that I'm yours?"

"We agreed no penetrative sex, Nick. I'm not going to change my mind about that. But I will make sure you're satisfied. If..." His words trailed off as he drove his fingers in and out of her pussy one last time, making her eyelids flutter and her breath rush out on a moan.

"If what?"

"If you're a good girl." He pulled his hand from between her legs and brought his fingers to his lips. Holding her eyes, he sucked the two that had been inside her into his mouth, taking the taste of her from his own skin.

Nicky's eyes grew impossibly wide and her nipples tightened until they poked through the thin fabric of her top. "I'll be good. What can I do to show you how good I can be?" She licked her lips again, bringing to mind images of Nicky on her knees, sucking his cock the way she had that first night in the cabin.

"Soon. Not just yet." With no small degree of effort, Jackson forced himself to get his mind back on business. It would be so easy to fall into a scene with Nicky, to get swept away in pleasure and forget the real reason they were here. But he couldn't let that happen. Nicky and Abby were both depending on him being man enough, dom enough, to make sure this night went according to plan.

"Let's check out the other room," he said, unable to resist running his knuckles over her nipples through the gauzy material as he spoke. "Then we'll find a place to play."

"Yes, sir." Nicky's words were perfectly submissive, but the look she cast up at him through her lashes was tinged with defiance. They let him know she wanted more out of tonight than a confrontation with her ex, that she wanted him to stake his claim and there would be hell to pay if he tried to deny her.

Jackson turned back to her, nearly encircling her narrow waist with his hands and squeezing none too gently before leaning down to whisper in her ear. "I'm going to spank you, bind you, and make you scream my name as you come while all these people watch. Don't doubt that for a minute."

Nicky's hands drifted up to cling to his biceps, but he stopped her with a word. "No. Hands at your sides. Keep your hands to yourself until I tell you otherwise. Show me you can be patient and obedient."

"Obedient, yes. Patience, however, isn't a virtue." She narrowed her eyes, clearly not thrilled with the idea of waiting much longer.

"Give me another look like that one again and you'll be punished."

"And how would you punish me?" she asked, the arousal in her voice enough to make his cock twitch in his pants. She knew just how to play him, how to dance the edge between obedience and defiance, to arouse and frustrate him at the same time—both of which ramped up his own desire to a ridiculous degree.

"I think nipple torture would be most fitting," he said, smoothing his hands up to capture her tits in his palms. He pinched her nipples between his fingers as he continued to speak in the same low, soothing whisper. "First I'll touch you like this, until you squirm and your pussy drenches those little panties you're wearing."

Nicky sucked in a ragged breath, but didn't say a word.

"Then, I'd find some real nipple clamps. Or, in a classy joint like this, they might have dual electrode attachments for breast play. Have you ever had electricity shooting across your nipples, Nicky?"

"I heard that could be dangerous. That it . . . could cause . . . a heart attack," she said, her hands fisting at her sides as she fought to hold still despite the fact that he'd only intensified his attention to her nipples. "I think we have enough electricity already."

"I agree. But above-the-waist electrical play can be completely safe. If you know how to do it the right way."

"And I bet you know just how to do it the right way, don't you?" Nicky's words ended in a gasp as he pinched her nipples—hard—one last time and then pulled away.

"Of course I do." He smiled down at her, not letting himself think about how stupid it was to keep demanding a true power exchange from Nicky.

It didn't matter that this was their last night together. They had to make their relationship look like the real thing. Besides, he couldn't seem to treat Nicky any other way. He behaved as if she was really his submissive, his girl, and they were learning how to be a pair, a dom-sub couple for life.

The thought filled him with a longing so fierce he felt like a jolt of electricity had surged into his heart. Maybe Nicky was right and they already had enough of that particular energy.

"Now why don't we check out the other room?" He took her hand in his and walked toward the hall connecting the two playrooms.

The passageway was constructed so it appeared to be carved through solid rock and took patrons behind the waterfall located in the main lounge. There were several nooks and crannies along the way, perfect for a couple looking to hide in the shadows, but he and Nicky were the only patrons in the darkened tunnel. It was only nine thirty and most of the clientele still seemed to be in the drinking, snacking, and chatting phase. If Under My Thumb was anything like other clubs he'd been to, the real action wouldn't start up until closer to midnight.

"Look, the backside of water. I always wondered what that looked like," Nicky said, then laughed softly.

"You're the dorkiest sex symbol I've ever met." Jackson smiled at her over his shoulder.

"I know." She laughed again as she turned back to look at the waterfall. "I really am such a dork, I—"

She suddenly froze, her hand going slack in his, the look on her face making his heart race.

"What's wrong?" Jack asked, twining his fingers through hers and pulling her close, as if he could protect her from whatever she'd seen. More like *whomever*. There was little doubt in his mind that it was the man who had inspired the fear and anxiety in Nicky's eyes. "It's him, isn't it?"

"Yes. He's sitting at the bar." Her voice was little more than a whisper.

She sounded so much younger and weaker than the Nicky who had sassed him in the other room or joked about that backside of water a few seconds ago. And the bastard in the other room was responsible. He was the one who had done his best to break the spirit of the woman next to him. It made Jackson wish for the hundredth time that he was going to be allowed to break the other man's face.

Instead, he moved behind Nicky, wrapping his arms around her chest as he pulled her back against his front. He dropped a soft kiss on top of her head before he spoke. "Which one?"

"The one in the long-sleeved black shirt. With the sandy blond hair."

Jackson didn't know what he'd expected, but the man seated a dozen feet away certainly wasn't it. Derrick was amazingly... average-looking. Probably around five feet nine, average weight, average build, average California tan and light brown hair, even an average-looking profile with a slight bump on the bridge of his nose. The only thing unique about the man was that he was sitting with a gorgeous, if rather artificial-looking, blonde with enormous breasts wearing a white slip so transparent it made Nicky's look positively modest.

"He's with someone. I should have known he'd be with someone," Nicky said. He could tell by the way she spoke she was nibbling her bottom lip. It was a nervous habit, and reminded him that, no matter how average-looking, this was a man capable of inspiring fear in the woman he loved. "What if this doesn't work the way we planned?"

"Don't worry about it." Jackson hugged her a little tighter. "Just because he's here with someone else doesn't mean he won't be pissed to see you here with another man. Besides, that woman has nothing on you. She's an imitation—you're the real thing."

She laughed, but it was no longer a carefree sound. "Derrick likes imitation. He's been trying to convince me to get implants and a tummy tuck ever since Abby was born."

"He's certifiable," Jackson growled. "You're perfect. Women pay thousands of dollars to try to look half as beautiful."

"Derrick didn't think so. He saw every line and stretch mark." Her hands trembled as they moved to grip his forearms, her fingers squeezing gently before abruptly dropping back to her sides. "Sorry, I forgot I wasn't supposed to—"

"Don't worry about it, babe," Jackson said, feeling like a complete ass for putting more pressure on Nicky. She didn't need to be worried about obeying dom-sub rules when she was getting ready to confront the man who had threatened their daughter's life.

"No, I *want* to worry about it." She turned in his arms and lifted her troubled eyes to his. "I need you, Jackson."

"I'm here. Anything you need. And I'll be close by when you ask him to go out—"

"No, not that." She sucked in a deep breath and nibbled her lip again for a moment before continuing. "Don't back down. Don't take it easy on me. Make me yours."

"Nicky, I—"

"Control me. Dominate me." She smiled, a sad little twist of the lips. "Even if it's just for tonight."

So she knew. She could sense that this was the end. "Are you sure?"

"I've never been more sure of anything." The eyes that met his were filled with a longing so intense, Jackson felt like he'd been sucker punched in the gut. "Make me forget he's here, and that he could be watching everything. Make me forget about everything . . . but you."

Chapter Seventeen

icky could barely breathe as she followed Jackson back to the spanking bench she'd had her eye on a few minutes earlier. Her mouth went dry and her lips buzzed. Her body felt numb except for where Jackson's hand squeezed hers, and she figured there was a better than decent chance she was going to pass out.

She couldn't do this. Not really. She'd been a fool to think anything about this night would be bearable, let alone enjoyable.

Derrick was in the other room. If he swiveled around on his bar stool, he'd be able to see her without even leaving the lounge. There was no way in hell she'd be able to concentrate on obeying Jackson, let alone enjoy what he was going to do to her. Not knowing her ex could be watching. What had seemed like such a fantastic idea in theory was proving very, very disturbing in real life.

She already felt violated by Derrick in so many ways. Now she wanted to add this to the list? Let him watch while she submitted to another man, the very thing he'd always wanted her to do when they were first together? No matter how much she'd wanted to please him back in the early days, she'd never been able to bring herself to do as he asked.

She was a one-man girl, always had been. Once she fell for a guy, her ability to find any other male sexually attractive was severely impaired. She couldn't let a man she wasn't attracted to touch her, not even to please the man she loved. The idea made her skin crawl, and reminded her of those nights back in Carson City, when Jackson and Phil's wife wouldn't be home from work until late, when she'd be alone with Phil and the younger kids.

Her foster father's "attentions" hadn't crossed the line until she was almost sixteen, and she'd always managed to escape anything worse than a few forced kisses and a little inappropriate fondling, but she'd known it was only a matter of time before his advances escalated. That's why she'd run the morning after Jackson left the house for good. It was either get out or put out, there'd been no doubt in her mind.

And there was no *way* she could have told Jackson. He would have gone crazy and gotten himself thrown in jail or worse. Besides, she'd been ashamed to tell him Phil sometimes had his hands on her only hours after she and Jack had been together. It made her feel dirty, as if she were the one who had done something wrong. Even years later, grown up and with psychology courses under her belt that should have taught her otherwise, she still felt some of that shame every time she thought of those last nights in her foster father's home.

Jesus. Nothing like thoughts of Derrick and Phil to kill every last shred of her desire. This just wasn't going to work.

"Jackson, wait." She tugged on the hand he held, but he didn't slow his stride for a moment. "Maybe I should just go talk to him and forget about this. If I tell him I'm with someone else, I'm sure he'll—"

"Quiet, don't speak again until I give you permission." The command was thrown over his shoulder, but Nicky could hear the determination in his tone loud and clear. She'd told him she was certain she wanted him to dominate her, and he'd taken her at her word.

There was no turning back now.

The knowledge awakened a thread of heat low in her body. She wasn't nearly ready to mount the bench Jackson now circled with a critical glare, but neither did she want to vomit at the very thought of sex. Jack had banished her dark thoughts with a single sentence. It just went to prove what she'd been thinking since they left the cabin—he was the only man capable of mastering her completely, for now, for always. For life.

Too bad he only wanted a one-night stand.

"Listen, I don't know—"

"Quiet," Jackson ordered in his low, silky dom voice, staring at her over the rounded leather hump of the spanking bench.

It looked almost like one of those pommel horses gymnasts vaulted over, but with a ledge on either side to support the knees. In a few minutes she could be straddling the thing, her ass presented for Jackson's disciplining pleasure. The very thought made her pussy plump inside her white thong panties, no matter how many reservations she still had.

"Don't make me ask a third time. If you defy me, this isn't going to work."

Nicky's breath rushed out through her teeth and she darted a quick look into the lounge. Derrick was still at the bar, and still had his back to them. Thank god.

"Look at me." Nicky obeyed, gazing up at Jackson, feeling her awareness of the outside world fade a bit as soon as their eyes connected. "Don't look at him, don't think about him. He's not here. There's no one else here. No one except you and me. Do you understand?"

Nicky nodded her head, feeling her nipples draw tight against the thin fabric of her shirt. Just the sound of Jackson's voice, so deep it seemed to vibrate against her skin, was enough to turn her on. The electricity that never failed to make an appearance when they were together arced between them, making her breath come faster, making her hands itch. She wanted to feel him, to run her fingers over the bulge in his leather pants, to feel his sex growing hotter, harder under her touch.

"Come here," Jackson commanded. "I want you to do something for me before we start."

Nicky circled to his side of the bench, turning her back on the lounge, which immediately helped her concentrate her attention on Jack and only Jack. From this position she could be any blond woman; Derrick would never guess her identity simply from seeing her from behind. She hadn't been to a club in years, since before she was pregnant with Abby, and he certainly wouldn't be expecting her at a VIP event.

"Kneel."

She obeyed, a thrill of desire sweeping over her skin as soon as her knees hit the floor in front of Jackson. It had been so long since she'd knelt in front of a man and meant the act of submission with every bone in her body. Derrick had demanded she meet him at the door every day on her hands and knees when he got home from work, but her heart had never been in it, especially not the last couple of years.

But with Jackson, it was like her entire being lit up from the inside. Blinding need, hot and thick, consumed her in a suffocating rush. Her skin suddenly felt too small and the aching inside her too big. Her pussy clamped down around its own emptiness as her nipples puckered so tightly they began to sting. Suddenly her mind flooded with images of what it would be like to meet *this* man at the door every night.

One night he might demand she take his cock between her lips, service him with her mouth until he jerked and pulsed, spilling cum down her throat. Another night, he might demand she strip and get on all fours. Then he'd drop to his knees behind her and shove his way into her ass and fuck her—hard—all while telling her how much he'd missed his dirty little slut while he was at work.

Call her twisted, but just imagining the moment made her breathless.

"Do you like kneeling for me?" he asked, the tone of his voice making it clear he already knew the answer.

"Yes, sir," she said, marveling at how right it felt to call him "sir." It was amazing how easily they transitioned from the easy banter of old friends to the world of the dom and his obedient sub. It made her long even more fiercely for the chance to find out if their relationship could have lasted for the long haul.

"Does it make your pussy wet?" he asked, bringing her mind back to more pleasurable things. She wasn't going to think about their inevitable separation anymore. From now on, she was going to be focused on enjoying the present.

She sucked in a deep breath and let it out, allowing her mind to clear as she did so. "Yes, sir."

"Show me. Touch yourself," he said, in a whisper so soft only she could hear.

Hand trembling with excitement, Nicky slid her fingers down the front of her shorts, inside her panties. She had only the tiniest tuft of hair left on her mound after her shaving efforts in the shower, but the feel of that coarse fuzz against her fingers was unbearably arousing. Touching those neatly trimmed hairs meant she was only a few centimeters away from slick, wet flesh, from where she was already dripping with need for Jackson.

She moaned as her fingertips eased past her clit, throwing her head back, feeling her hair brush her neck as she tipped her face toward the ceiling. Now Jackson would be able to see what it did to her, see how hot it made her to touch herself while he watched.

Nicky dipped first one finger and then two into the cream between her legs, slowly fucking herself with her hand, amazed at how close she was to orgasm. She couldn't remember ever feeling so aroused, even during the time she'd spent with Jackson in his cabin. She was hyperaware of every inch of her sensitive flesh, of Jackson standing over her, of the couple a few feet away and the noise the female sub made as her partner tied her to the Saint Andrew's cross on the wall.

"Open your eyes."

She did, meeting Jackson's with another moan. Just looking at him was nearly enough to make her come, right then. The heat in his gaze sent a shock of electricity zinging into nerve endings she hadn't even known she possessed. Her hand moved faster of its own accord, coaxing more cream from her body, until her fingers were coated with her own sticky arousal and her muscles trembled from being so near the edge of release.

But she knew he wouldn't let her tumble over. He was too good at his work.

"Stop. Show me your hand."

Without a moment's hesitation, she pulled her fingers from her pussy and held them up in the air in front of her. Jackson gripped her wrist, steadying her, then leaned down and sucked both fingers into his mouth, moaning in approval.

Nicky watched him clean every inch of her damp flesh, captivated by the profound pleasure so evident on his face. The man genuinely loved the intimate flavor of her body. It wasn't a declaration of love and she knew there were people who might even find what Jackson was doing repulsive, but it still made her throat tight with emotion to watch him taste her so thoroughly before pulling away with reluctance.

Jackson made every part of her feel beautiful, desired—inside and out. When he looked at her with such obvious adoration, she felt like she could do anything, *would* do anything he asked to make sure the light in his eyes never faded.

It might have been a frightening realization if they were planning a future together, knowing she was so eager to obey Jackson's every command. But they only had tonight, so the thought just made her feel . . . ready.

"You're ready." Jackson echoed her thoughts, his eyes darkening, letting her know he was also ready to get down to business. "Get up on the bench, hands down at the end with the cuffs."

Adrenaline dumped into Nicky's system as she climbed up on the bench, straddling the padded middle and positioning her knees on either side. The second her ass was in the air and her wrists reached down to where Jackson waited with the gold handcuffs, her mind began to soften, her awareness narrowing to the man cuffing her in place.

The familiar buzz of excitement and relaxation, anticipation and contentment, pulsed through her veins, making her feel far more intoxicated than an entire bottle of the brandy they'd sipped at the bar could have ever accomplished. By the time Jackson finished with her hands and smoothed one large, warm hand down her back, all the way to her rump, she was beyond rational thought, nothing but a bundle of nerves ready to respond.

"You may speak when asked a direct question," Jackson said as he arranged her clothing with slow, deliberate movements.

First he tugged both sides of the loose-fitting satin shorts up, exposing the cheeks of her ass to the cool air, making the fabric between her legs pull tight against her clit. It was just enough stimulation to make her gasp and tremble, wishing it was Jackson's fingers rubbing against her instead.

"Do you like having your ass bared for me?"

"Yes, sir." Nicky sighed in pure pleasure. "So much."

"What about your tits? Would you like me to see them? To touch them?"

"Yes, sir," she said, the words turning to a moan as Jackson's hands moved to her chemise, pulling at the neckline until her breasts sprang free, her hypersensitive nipples brushing against the fabric enough to send a bolt of desire surging between her legs.

"I love these tits. I love how your nipples feel in my mouth." He captured one nipple in his hand as he spoke, plucking and tugging until Nicky's breath came in little pants and needy sounds issued from the back of her throat. "I love to suck them while you ride my cock. Do you like that?"

Jackson transferred his attentions to her other breast, pinching and rolling. Frissons of excitement shot between her legs, making her voice shake when she finally managed to speak. "Yes, sir. I want you inside of me. Please."

"I'm not going to change my mind, Nick. We agreed on the terms of engagement before we left the hotel," he said, both hands busy with her nipples, making her head spin and things low in her body twist and ache.

"Please, Jackson," she begged, certain she would lose her mind if she didn't feel him filling every inch of the horrible emptiness between her legs. "Please, fuck me. I've changed my mind. Please, I—"

"No. And you should have known better than to ask." His fingers abandoned her breasts, making her moan with a mixture of disappointment and relief. She couldn't have taken much more without losing her mind from want, but she still felt the absence of his touch like a physical blow. "I'm disappointed."

"I wasn't asking, I was begging," Nicky said, doing her best to explain herself. "Jackson, please, there isn't—"

"You were only supposed to speak when answering a direct question," Jackson said as he tucked her breasts back into her shirt. Seconds later he was circling around behind her, headed toward the selection of paddles and whips on the wall. "Now, you'll have to be punished."

Excitement rushed across her skin, sharp and electric.

God. Yes. This was so perfect. This was exactly how she'd always dreamed a scene could be, each moment flowing into the next almost like they were working from a script. She should have known Jackson wasn't the kind to go straight to the paddle without any buildup. He needed a reason to spank her and he knew she needed it, too. He dominated the way he made love, with just the perfect amount of foreplay and a commitment to the business at hand that made her skin feel like it was going to melt clean off her bones.

"Tilt your hips, show me my ass." Nicky obeyed, arching her back, revealing as much of her bottom as she could while still wearing her shorts. "Beautiful. For a disobedient little slut, you have a gorgeous ass."

His hand descended on her ass a second later with a swift smack that made Nicky gasp and her entire body come alive. Just the sound of skin making sharp contact with skin was a certified aphrodisiac.

"I was going to use one of the paddles, but I think my hand is better for this job, don't you think?" he asked, punctuating his words with stinging slaps to both mounds of her ass. The pain accentuated her pleasure, intensifying the drunken feeling spinning through her head.

"Yes. Sir." Nicky's eyes slid closed and a shudder of bliss shook her body. "More, sir."

"Don't speak unless answering a question, slut." He intensified his efforts, his hand falling faster, harder, making her cry out and a wild laugh escape her lips.

She couldn't remember ever feeling so high after only a few minutes in restraints. It made her wonder what undiscovered territory she and Jack might find if they had hours to play, if they worked their way through the rooms of equipment, until they were both so unbearably aroused Jackson couldn't resist fucking her against the wall.

"This is making you wetter, isn't it?" Jackson asked, his voice caressing her sensitized flesh.

"Why don't you see for yourself, sir?"

"You want my fingers in your pussy?" He slapped her again, and again, until her already reddened ass burned. But it was a sweet heat, driving her excitement to a place where pain and pleasure fused into one all-consuming need. The need to feel *him* touching her, owning her, punished her and blessed her all at the same bliss-inducing time, until her entire body trembled with excitement.

"Yes, sir. Yes, please, I—" Her words ended in a cry as Jackson shoved aside the scrap of fabric covering her sex and shoved his fingers inside her.

He set a punishing rhythm, driving in and out with first two fingers and then three, never ceasing his work on her stinging cheeks for a moment. Low, almost guttural sounds filled the air, but it took several seconds for Nicky to realize they were coming from her own mouth. And even when she did, she couldn't bring herself to care. Jackson brought out the animal in her, the sexual creature who knew no shame when so close to complete and utter satisfaction.

"Come for me, slut. Come on my fingers. I want to feel my pussy—"

"Jackson!" Her lips remembered how to speak his name, though it certainly wasn't due to any help from her mind. Her head was nothing but a mass of swirling colors and flashing light, oblivious to anything but pure, overwhelming pleasure.

The orgasm hit hard and fast, wrenching things low in her body until it felt as if the bliss might break her. Her entire body exploded all at once, every inch of her skin on fire, every nerve ending sending messages of ecstasy rocketing up her spinal cord, overloading her brain, making her scream. She felt as if she'd been plunged into freezing water, the shock of the moment was so intense.

"Yes, god, yes." Jackson's soft words of approval were the first thing she heard as the ringing in her ears subsided and her soul reconnected with her body.

It felt as if she'd been in the grips of the fierce pleasure he'd given her for hours, like she'd lost time somewhere between when he'd told her to come and she drifted down to earth, coming to her senses enough to realize his fingers still played in and out of her slickness. It was a pleasure blackout, induced solely from the skill of the man who worked her body and mind, no controlled substances required. She'd heard about this kind of thing, but never experienced the phenomenon, never known how elated and terrified it could make her feel.

She'd truly been out of her mind, totally dependent on her dom to care for her while she explored the boundaries of how much pleasure one body could take. No matter how scary that was on one level, Nicky knew she was going to crave the experience again and again. She was hooked with one go, like a heroin addict in the making.

"Was that as good as it looked?" Jackson pulled his fingers from between her legs and repositioned her shorts before leaning down to whisper the words into her hair.

"Better," she said, shivering as he dropped kisses along her bare shoulder. A simple kiss shouldn't be able to make her entire body begin to ache once more. But it did. *He* did. "I love you, Jackson."

One large hand smoothed her hair out of her face with a tenderness that threatened to break her. "I love you, too, Nick. I always, always will."

And then he kissed her, softly, gently, making love to her lips with his. In every caress, in the languid way his tongue stroked into her mouth, she felt the truth of his words. He loved her, in the same soul-shattering way she loved him. It was going to cut him apart to leave her, make him feel like a piece of him he'd only just reclaimed was being ripped away.

But he was still going to do it. He was still going to leave. That truth was in his kiss, as well.

"I think it's just about showtime, babe," he murmured against her lips, as he typed a combination of numbers into the remote control masquerading as his watch. "Are you ready?"

It took a few seconds for Nicky to remember what Jackson was talking about. She'd been so lost in the pleasure he'd given her, she'd forgotten all about Derrick. But now she remembered, and for some reason felt stronger after submitting so completely to Jack, nearly prepared to face the man who had been the monster in her bed for longer than she should have allowed.

"I'll be ready in a second," Nicky said. "Let's get these cuffs off."

"Yes, ma'am." He squeezed her hip, a comforting gesture that sent another surge of confidence sweeping over her. That subtle touch reminded her she wasn't alone. She had major backup, at least for tonight, and she was ready to face her demons.

Good thing, too, because Jackson had just started to work on freeing her hands when a familiar voice sounded from her left. "Well, well, Nicole. What a good little slut you've become. For someone else."

Chapter Eighteen

The way Derrick said "slut" made the word sound exactly like what it was—an insult, a term used to demean a woman and make her feel small and dirty. Not surprising, really; it was more shocking that Jackson somehow made "dirty little slut" one of the sweetest, sexiest phrases she'd ever heard.

Jackson. He was here, right next to her. She wasn't alone.

She drew strength from that fact as she met Derrick's eyes. They were nearly the same brown as Jackson's, but devoid of the warmth that made Jack's so compelling. The fact that they were bloodshot didn't help things any. He must have been drinking before he arrived at the club.

"Derrick, how are you?" Nicky asked as Jackson finished loosening the cuffs from around her wrists. She climbed off the spanking bench with as much dignity as she could muster. At least all of the key areas were covered, so she didn't have to suffer the embarrassment of adjusting her clothes in front of her soon-to-be ex and his new . . . friend.

The bleached blonde with the enormous breasts was glaring

at her from slightly behind Derrick, but she was staying out of the way like a good little sub. Nicky didn't anticipate encountering any resistance from her when she asked Derrick to step outside for a talk. Assuming the cameras and mic were operational, she supposed she could make the suggestion at any time.

She'd seen Jackson do something to his watch, but were they really online? She wished she'd been able to get some sort of confirmation from the guys in the van outside beforehand, but now there wasn't time. Derrick had made the first move.

"Very well. Business is excellent, and Abby is getting so big." Derrick smiled, a nasty twist of his lips that made it clear he knew how it hurt her to hear Abby's name. "She and Jill have really hit it off." He turned to the woman behind him. "Jill, this is Nicky, the biological mother."

Nicky bit her lip, fighting the urge to fly at Derrick and tear at his face with her fingernails. *Biological* mother indeed. She was Abby's *only* mother, and there was no way in hell she was going to let another woman become a fixture in her daughter's life.

"Nice to meet you," Jill said, her voice at least an octave higher than Nicky had expected it to be. She sounded like a little girl, something she was sure Derrick enjoyed. He did love feeling like the big man, and he needed all the help he could get from the sub in his life to get the job done. Derrick only felt dominant when everyone else around him was performing at less than their potential. He'd never had what it took to master a woman like her. He wasn't strong enough.

The realization made Nicky feel at least three inches taller, and certain for the first time she was going to win this battle. Her daughter would be in her arms by the end of the night and Derrick would be well on his way to a restraining order and maybe some time in a jail cell with men who would show him what it felt like to be the slut in the relationship.

"I wish I could say the same, but I'm not in a very nice mood. Derrick has been keeping me from my daughter," Nicky said, maintaining the pleasant smile on her face even when Derrick's expression went from smug to dangerous in under six seconds. "I think it's time that ended. Don't you, Derrick?"

"I think you should watch your mouth and remember what we decided about this."

"No one tells Nicky to watch her mouth. Except me." Jackson stepped closer, until he loomed over the much shorter Derrick. "You're not in charge here anymore."

"Nicole, outside. Now. Obviously your memory needs a little refreshing." Derrick barked the order with as much authority as ever, but Nicky saw the spark of fear in his eyes. He saw there was a bigger dog in town, hence the sudden urge to get her alone.

Fine with her. He was playing right into their hands.

"May I go, Master?" Nicky turned back to Jackson, lingering on the last word.

Derrick had always wanted her to call him "Master," but she'd refused. She was a submissive, and she loved to be mastered, but for some reason the term never tasted right in her mouth. "Sir," she liked just fine, but "Master" made her feel too much like one of those male slaves who went around licking their mistress's boots. Or the hunchback guy that worked with Frankenstein.

There was a face she didn't want in her head during sex.

"She can go." Jackson put a hand at the small of her back as she faced Derrick once more. "But if you hurt her, I'll make you bleed."

Jill's eyes widened into big blue saucers, making it obvious she'd had even more work than Nicky had thought. No one's eyes were naturally that big.

"Touch me and I'll have you thrown out of here so fast your head will swim, he-man," Derrick said, his voice shaking the slightest bit.

Nicky stifled the strange urge to giggle. He-man? That was the best insult he could come up with on the spur of the moment? This was the dom she'd lived in fear of for years? He was nothing but a sad, insecure little man.

She'd been a fool to fear him, but that was ending right now. It was payback time.

"Make your threats," Jackson said, his tone still calm and even. "But make sure you listen to what Nicky has to say and know that I back her up completely. She's not a powerless woman you can get away with bullying anymore."

Truer words had never been spoken. Even without Jackson there beside her, Nicky knew what he'd said would be true. She was different, tougher, and as ready as she'd ever be to finish this thing with Derrick.

"Come with me, Nicole. Jill, wait at the bar." Derrick turned and headed for the front door.

Nicky took one last look back at Jackson, drawing strength from the confident expression on his face, and followed.

Her heart raced as she tailed Derrick back through the crowded lounge area. The bar and surrounding tables were packed and the alcohol flowing. It was only a matter of time before everyone would be loosened up enough to start heading back into the playrooms. She knew how these things worked. She used to be one of those people who needed a few glasses of wine to be in the mood to start a scene, but not anymore. Now, just a look from

Jackson, just a few well-chosen words, were enough to banish all of her inhibitions.

"I'll be coming back in," Derrick said to the bouncer at the exit before shoving past, not bothering to hold the door for her. But then, manners had never been his strong suit, and he wasn't exactly a happy camper right now. She took a deep breath, hoping that unhappiness would work in her favor.

"I'll be coming back in, too." Nicky smiled at the large man working the door, and obediently held out her hand to get it stamped for readmission.

"The door closes in thirty minutes, so be sure you're back before then," he said, then turned his attention back to the lobby.

Nicky nodded and pushed through the door, apprehension skittering across her skin for the first time. It was pretty deserted outside the club. Everyone was still going in, not coming out. What if Derrick did decide to take his frustration out on her physically? He'd never hit her before, seeming content to land his blows with harsh words and harsher emotional manipulation, but there was a first time for everything.

Don't worry. The boys in the van are watching. You're safe.

But the thought didn't give her much comfort when Derrick spun to face her, anger distorting his features. He barely resembled the man she'd known, he was so furious. It made her mouth run dry, even though she knew she shouldn't be surprised by the strength of his rage.

She'd *never* defied him. Talked back or gone against his wishes when it came to dom-sub stuff, sure, but never when it came to the big decisions. Derrick had always been the walking boss in their relationship, and he obviously didn't take well to having his authority questioned.

"What exactly do you think you're trying to pull, Nicky?"

"I'm not trying to pull anything," she said, hating the way her voice trembled. "I just want to see my daughter. I deserve to be a part of her—"

"You don't deserve shit." He stepped closer, and she had to fight the urge to back away. "You violated our contract the day you walked out the door. I don't owe you a dime."

"I'm not asking for money. I just want to be Abby's mother."

"You think you're fit to be Abby's mother? A slut like you, out getting her ass spanked at some club by a complete stranger?" Derrick moved nearer still, until she could smell the alcohol on his breath. "I saw you on the bench. You were grunting like a pig when you came. It made me sick to think my daughter came out of that diseased hole between your legs."

"I am not diseased," Nicky ground out through gritted teeth. "And if going to clubs is a problem, I'll stop. Though I have to say it seems pretty hypocritical that you get to whore yourself out with some blond chick, but I—"

Her words ended in a gasp as Derrick's hand snapped out, catching her across the face. Her right cheek burned and her ears rang from the impact, but she still refused to let herself back away. Instead she stood up even straighter, glaring into his eyes, hoping the camera was catching every second of his abuse.

"Watch your mouth," he panted, his breath coming as fast as if he'd just stepped off the track. He was weirdly out of breath for a man who worked out three times a week. But maybe he'd given up the runs along the beach. He certainly looked a lot thinner than he had just a few weeks ago. "You're the whore."

"I never touched another man while we were together, Derrick.

I know you can't say the same. You weren't faithful to me, so in my book that makes *you* the whore."

Nicky was prepared for the blow this time, but that didn't make it hurt any less. Stars danced behind her eyes and her cheekbone throbbed. The second slap was going to leave a bruise.

Good, it's just more evidence against the bastard.

The thought made her smile. "Do you hit Abby, too, Derrick? Is that the kind of father you are?"

"I treat Abby like a princess, the way I treated her mother until she broke her vows."

"Keeping her away from her mother isn't treating her like a princess," Nicky said, mind racing, trying to figure out what to say next. She had to get tape of Derrick threatening Abby, not just slapping his ex-wife around. The danger to Abby was what she needed to prove to the court so she could have sole custody of her daughter. "She needs me in her life. I was home with her every day since she was born. She must miss me. It must scare and upset her to—"

"I'm going to say this one more time—Abby is better off without you. Stay away from her, or you're going to be very, very sorry. I can promise you that."

Oh, god. This was it. This was *it*.

"Nothing could make me more sorry than missing any more of my daughter's life," she said, the tears in her voice as real as the words she spoke. It had only been three weeks since she'd seen Abby, but it felt like a lifetime.

"Your daughter won't have a life if you keep this up, Nicole." He smiled, a cold sneer that made her heart ache. This was the bastard she'd chosen as the father of her child. Abby deserved so much better. "I wasn't making idle threats when I said I'd kill her before I'd let her be raised, even part-time, by a slut like you."

"Derrick, listen to yourself. That's our baby you're talking about, an innocent child. How can you even—"

"If you don't sign the divorce decree in the next week, or if I find out you've hired a lawyer to try to get joint custody, Abby will have a horrible accident." He paused, eyes drifting to a place above her head. He sniffed and swiped the back of his hand across his nose. "I was thinking the pool out back. She's crawling so fast now. If the nanny were to leave the door open and turn her back for a few minutes . . . well, it doesn't take that long for a child to drown."

Her throat grew tight and tears stung at the back of her eyes, but Nicky didn't cry. What Derrick said wasn't going to happen, she wasn't going to *let* it happen. "You're a monster."

"Well, maybe." He shrugged, and his smile returned as his eyes met hers once more. "But I'd rather Abby be raised by a monster than a penniless whore. At least she'll have a chance at a future, to grow up to be something more than a tramp who takes her clothes off for money."

Nicky swallowed the retort on the tip of her tongue. He didn't care to make the distinction between a model and a stripper or he would have done so. Arguing with Derrick was a waste of time.

She had what she needed. Derrick's threats were now captured on tape. If all was going according to plan, Christian was already on his way to the house to get Abby. She could walk away right now and never say a word to this bastard again.

Instead she stood her ground. Until this moment, she hadn't realized how much unfinished business there was between the two of them. But now, all the questions she hadn't dared to ask in the last pain-filled two years flooded to the surface, demanding she at least speak them aloud, though she had little hope of receiving any satisfactory answers.

"Why do you hate me so much?"

His bloodshot eyes widened the slightest bit before narrowing once more. "I don't hate you. Hate is a powerful emotion. I feel nothing for you except disgust."

"Then why didn't you ask for a divorce sooner? Obviously our marriage wasn't what either of us—"

"Our marriage was fine," Derrick said, the emotion in his voice surprising her. "Everything was fine until you up and left with our daughter."

"Derrick, our marriage was not fine," Nicky said, doing her best to keep any accusations from her tone. "Nothing I did seemed to please you. Not since I got pregnant with Abby."

"That's not true."

"You didn't even want to touch me. We hadn't had sex in nearly two years by the time I left. How can you call that—"

"So you wanted to get fucked? Is that it?" he asked, taking an aggressive step forward. "Well, I'll fuck you right now if that's what you want."

"No, it isn't." This time, she took that step back her mind was screaming for. A slap or two she could handle, but if Derrick tried to touch her intimately she'd take Jackson up on the offer to make him bleed. "But when I was pregnant with Abby, and just after, I wanted to be close to you. And sex is a big part of that. Sex is part of a good marriage. Surely you can't disagree."

Derrick's eyes dropped to the pavement between them, and he ran a frustrated hand through his hair. For the first time, Nicky noticed that it was thinning on top. Derrick was twelve years older, but she'd never really thought about the age difference until now, when he suddenly looked far older than his thirty-six years.

"I just . . ." His voice trailed off, but Nicky didn't push. Pushing Derrick was a good way to make him angry, not a way to encourage him to talk.

He took a deep breath and let it out slowly. Several uncomfortable seconds passed until he finally spoke again. "I just didn't want to hurt the baby. I was . . . and you looked so different. Then, by the time she was born, it just seemed like we'd lost our place. You were so focused on the baby and . . . it hurt. I felt like you didn't need me anymore."

Of all the things she'd thought she'd hear tonight, Derrick opening up about his feelings was the very last. She was stunned.

"I needed you more than ever," Nicky said, then pushed on, refusing to let Derrick play the victim. "But it seemed like you hated me. I mean, talk about hurt. Every time you told me how unattractive you found pregnant women or women who had just had a baby, it felt like I was being cut open. It hurt. So much."

He finally lifted his head, facing her with uncertain eyes. "What if I said I didn't mean it? That I was just . . . that I'd made a mistake?"

"What?" She could safely say she'd never been more confused. What the hell was he saying?

"What if I said I didn't mean all those things I said, or the stuff about Abby?" He paused, licking his lips, the words obviously far from easy to say. "Would you think about coming back?"

"You want me back." Nicky didn't know whether to laugh or cry, or both. "But you're the one who filed for divorce."

"That's only because you left me. How could you just *leave* like that, Nicole?" he asked, his anguish clear in his voice. "I came home from work and you were just gone. I thought someone had kidnapped you at first. I was scared out of my mind."

"I was scared, too. I was afraid you'd do something to me or Abby if I told you I was leaving."

"You should have known I'd never hurt you. Ever," he said, the passion in his eyes making it clear he believed every word. He reached for her, but she stepped away again, shaking her head in disbelief.

"Derrick, you hurt me with your words for years and you just hit me—twice."

"I was just angry. You don't know what it did to me, seeing another man's fingers inside *my* wife. It made me crazy."

"Crazy enough to threaten to kill our daughter? Was that something you didn't mean, too?" Nicky held her breath, wondering if the men in the van were still recording, and how this little development would impact their case against Derrick.

If he confessed to lying about intending to kill Abby, would that make a difference to the judge who reviewed their case? Had she endangered her future with her daughter because she didn't know when to keep her big mouth shut?

"Come back to me. Come home with me right now, and you'll never have to find out."

"I can't come home with you. I—"

"Of course you can. Ditch that caveman and come home. We'll send the housekeeper over to your apartment to get your things tomorrow." He paused and a real smile stretched across his face, reminding her for a brief second of the man he'd been when they were married. The man she'd thought she'd loved. Until she'd reunited with Jackson and remembered what real love felt like. "You could be holding Abby in half an hour. Hell, you can even bring her into the bed to sleep with us if you want, the way you wanted to do when she was teething. She's missed you so much, I know she'll be—"

"No," Nicky said, hoping he heard the finality in the word. "No, Derrick. I'm never coming back to you. I don't love you anymore. I'm not sure I ever did."

His smile faded, and the terrifying Derrick returned. "Is it that man you're with? Are you *in love* with him now?"

"Yes, I am," she said, the words out of her mouth before she could think better of them. It only took a few seconds for her to realize the error of her ways, but by then it was too late. Derrick's hands were already latched around her throat.

Chapter Nineteen

Jackson was through the door the second he heard Nicky cry out, cursing himself for letting her stay outside so long. He'd gotten the call from the van five minutes ago. Everything had gone according to plan and Christian was already on his way to get Abby. There was no reason to leave Nicky alone with that waste of human flesh a second longer.

But he'd wanted to let her handle the situation, show her he believed she was strong enough to manage Derrick alone. After all, he was going to Miami in a few days. He wouldn't be here to help her anymore. She'd have to stand on her own.

But she'll have a restraining order by then, jackass.

He *was* a jackass, and now Nicky was going to have the bruises to prove it. Some dom he was, letting another man get his hands around his submissive's throat.

Jackson charged toward where Derrick had Nicky backed against the brick wall of the club with his fist raised. He'd warned the bastard he'd make him bleed if he hurt Nick. Now he was going to prove he was a man of his word.

"Jackson, wait," Nicky shouted as she shoved her ex-husband's hands from her throat. Derrick slumped forward, collapsing against her. "I think he's passed out or— Ohmygod."

Derrick suddenly began to shake, his entire body jerking like he'd stuck his hand in a light socket. He fell to the ground, still convulsing, eyes rolling back in his head.

"What's happening?" Nicky flattened herself against the wall, staring with wide eyes at the man at her feet.

Jackson reached over the twitching body and grabbed Nicky under the arms, lifting her over her ex. "Go, tell the woman at the desk to call 911."

She nodded and turned to race toward the door, but not before Jackson saw the red swelling on her left cheek. The bastard had hit her. She'd have a bruise tomorrow at the very least, if not a full-on black eye. The knowledge would have been enough to make him knock Derrick out—if he hadn't been out cold already.

"Piece of shit," Jackson muttered as he knelt by the other man, who was finally lying still. A check of his pulse revealed he was still alive—unfortunately—though his heart was racing like he'd just run a marathon, not spent a few minutes slapping around his wife. The speeding pulse didn't seem natural for a young man who looked to be in fairly good shape. Neither did the cold, clammy skin.

His suspicions were confirmed when he gently pried open Derrick's eyes and found them bloodshot and his pupils widely dilated. He'd been on something, probably cocaine if Jackson had to guess. That would certainly explain the racing heart and the out-of-control temper.

"What happened? Is he dead?" A man in a suit whom Jackson

had seen roaming the club earlier rushed out the door with Nicky close behind. "I'm Blake, the owner."

"I told him we were . . . having an argument and he just started shaking and collapsed," Nicky said, staying back a few paces as Blake came to stand just behind Jackson.

"I think he had a seizure, or maybe a stroke. Probably drug-induced. I'm a tattoo artist. By law we're not supposed to work on anyone who's been using, so I've learned to read the signs." Jackson stood. "He's still breathing and his pulse is strong, if a little accelerated. I don't think there's much we can do for him until the paramedics arrive."

"Drugs?" Nicky asked. "Derrick's been using drugs?"

"Son of a bitch. I thought he looked bad tonight, but I didn't want to say anything." Blake sighed and shook his head. "He usually keeps it at a respectable level, and he's never brought anything into the club."

"So Derrick has *been* on drugs before?"

"I've only known him a few months, but yeah, he seems to have a pretty decent coke habit," Blake said.

"A habit. While he was supposed to be taking care of an eleven-month-old." Nicky cursed, glaring at the man at her feet like she'd like to kick his prone body. "I'm going to kill him."

"You may not have to," the club owner said, as sirens sounded in the distance. "If he's had a stroke . . . well, it will just depend on how severe it was. I had a friend of mine, old college football buddy, died of combination stroke and heart attack from an overdose a few years back."

"Oh, my god," Nicky said, her voice soft as her hand flew to her mouth. "I didn't— I don't really want . . ."

"Of course you don't," Jackson said, wrapping his arms around her and pulling her close as an ambulance pulled into the parking lot. "And he might be fine. He could still live to take his beating for hitting you."

"You saw that?" Nicky asked, the face she tilted up to his washed red from the flashing lights.

"Nope, but I saw this." He brushed his knuckles softly over her cheek, feeling his guts twist when she winced slightly. "It made me want to kill him myself."

"It doesn't hurt that bad. I'll be fine." She lowered her voice even though Blake had already left to meet the EMTs as they jumped from the ambulance. "Is Christian on his way to get Abby?"

"He left over ten minutes ago. I should be getting a call soon. You'd better tell them what happened." Jackson urged her to go and then watched Nicky fill in the paramedics, his mind racing.

Derrick's unexpected collapse could either work for them or against them. If the nanny reported the baby missing the night after her employer overdosed at the same party his wife had been attending, there was a chance the police might come around, asking Nicky a bunch of unnecessary questions.

But if Christian hadn't taken Abby yet, there might still be a way for this to end even better than they'd hoped.

His cell was out of his pocket a second later. Thankfully, Christian answered on the second ring. "Hey, do you have Abby yet?"

"Not yet," he whispered, "but I'm on the property, so can this little conversation wait?"

"No, it can't. Get out and go wait in your car. I'll give you a call in a few minutes. We've had an unexpected development."

"All right, you're running this show."

Jackson snapped the phone shut and then open again. He waited until Derrick was loaded into the ambulance and the owner vanished back into the club before he put the phone in Nicky's hand. "Here, call the nanny. Tell her what happened and that you're on your way to pick up Abby."

"Christian didn't—"

"I called him and told him the plan had changed. This will work out much better."

"Right, of course." Nicky shook her head as if to clear it. "I didn't even think, but . . . this will make my case, won't it? Even without the threats, a judge isn't going to give custody to a man with a documented drug habit."

"And I'd say a hospitalization for overdose is pretty good documentation."

Nicky smiled, a weary stretch of her lips. "I wouldn't have wished this on Derrick, but I can't deny it feels good to know I'm not going to lose Abby again. God, when I think of what could have happened . . ." She sucked in a shaky breath. "What if she'd found drugs in the house? She sticks everything in her mouth, and it wouldn't take much cocaine to *kill* a twenty-four-pound baby. I just—"

"Don't think about it. Just make that call, then we'll get on the road." Jackson squeezed her hand. "You'll be holding Abby in thirty minutes or less."

This time, Nicky's smile was bright enough to light the entire parking lot. It made Jackson wish he was going to be around to see that grin a hell of a lot more. He was going to miss Nicky, more than he'd thought possible, but his leaving was for the best. The events of tonight had only proved how dangerous a failed dom-sub relationship could become. Nicky would be safer without a controlling man in her life.

He was going to do his best to convince her of that on their way to pick up her daughter. If there was ever a time to bring Nicky back to the straight side of the fence, this was it.

Jackson wished the thought didn't make him sad, but it did. Which just went to show how bad he would be for her. A man more concerned with the loss of the most complex and challenging submissive he'd ever known than with the safety of that submissive and her baby was a man with serious issues.

"Okay, we're good to go. She said she'd have Abby's things packed by the time we get there." Nicky squealed and threw her arms around his neck. "She's coming home with us, Jackson. Right now!"

"Speaking of the hotel," Jackson said, hugging Nicky for only the briefest second before pulling away, "why don't we run by and grab some more appropriate clothes on the way. I think it would be better if we didn't show up in club gear."

"Right, of course. Let's go, then." There was a hurt look in her eyes as she turned toward his truck, but Jackson did his best to ignore it. They both knew this had to end, no sense in pretending otherwise.

Tomorrow, he'd help Nicky and Abby get settled in Nicky's apartment and start the necessary legal paperwork, and by the day after tomorrow he'd be on a plane on his way to Miami. Once he was there, he'd throw himself into getting the new parlor ready to open and do his best to forget he'd ever seen Nicky, let alone lost his heart to her a second time.

It wasn't going to be easy, but he was used to living with a gaping hole in his chest. He'd been doing it for years, ever since sixteen-year-old Nicky had left Carson City.

Jackson popped the locks on the Expedition and climbed behind the wheel, tempted for a brief second to ask Nicky why she'd left all those years ago, why she'd run.

"What's wrong?" she asked, meeting his eyes with a troubled look of her own.

"Nothing. Nothing at all." He forced a smile and started the car. There was no sense digging into the past. Their past didn't matter any more than their future. It was time to grow up and move on, and finally put all those old dreams behind him.

Chapter Twenty

Two months later

The doorbell rang, shocking Nicky out of a sound sleep. A quick glance at the clock revealed it was barely six in the morning. Who in their right mind would be stopping by for a visit at this hour?

Maybe it's not someone in their right mind. Maybe it's him, maybe he was finally released from the hospital and he's not in the mood to obey the restraining order.

Nicky vaulted into a seated position. She hadn't called to check on Derrick's status in a few days, but surely he couldn't be ready to go home yet. His stroke had been massive and the doctors said he'd need months of physical therapy before he was anywhere close to his old self. They'd also promised to call her before they released him, since they knew about his history and the restraining order in place keeping him from seeing his ex-wife or child.

The bell rang again, making her heart leap into her throat. "Just a second," she called out, jumping out of bed and taking a quick peek in Abby's crib. She was still asleep, thank god. Nothing could wake her until she was ready to get up, so hopefully she'd snooze straight through whatever madness might ensue if it really was Derrick at the door.

One thing was for certain, no one was ever going to take Abby from her again. She was going to make damn sure of that.

The gun was out of its shoe box on the top shelf of her closet and in her hand in seconds. If Derrick violated the restraining order and tried to hurt her or Abby again, she'd shoot him and deal with the fallout later. Even standing trial for murder in self-defense would be better than letting him take Abby away. The past two months alone with Abby had only made her love for her daughter fiercer than it had been before, and she knew she'd do anything it took to keep her safe.

"Who is it?" Nicky asked once she was at the door, buying herself a little time as she peered through the peephole and saw the last person she'd expected.

"It's Christian," he said, the words barely out of his mouth before she threw open the door. He took in her rumpled hair and pj's with an apologetic smile. "Sorry about the early hour."

"Um, no, it's fine. Come in," Nicky said, opening the door wider, scanning the stairs behind him, a foolish part of her hoping she'd see Jackson.

But she should know better. Jackson hadn't even called to say hi since he'd left for Miami. He didn't want anything more to do with her. He'd made that abundantly clear.

"I'm on my way to Hawaii and only have a six-hour layover. I've got to jet back to the airport in just a few—Nice gun. You bring that to the door to greet all your visitors?"

"Only the ones who show up unexpectedly at insanely early hours who I think might be my ex-husband."

"That's pretty tough of you. I'm impressed."

"You do what you gotta do." Nicky shrugged and turned back to the closet to put the gun back in its hiding place. That was the good thing about a studio apartment, everything was in easy reach. "Can I get you some coffee or something?"

"No, like I said, I've got to run in a few. I just needed to talk to you. In person."

"What about?" Nicky asked, her mind immediately imagining the worst. "Is Jackson okay? He's not hurt or anything, is he? I mean, he'd probably have to be a lot worse than hurt for you to come all the way out here, but—"

"He is. A lot worse."

"Oh, god." Tears sprang to her eyes and she barely made it to the couch before her knees gave out. "What happened? Just tell me fast and get it over with."

"You happened." Christian took the armchair across from her, settling in like he'd visited a hundred times before. He certainly had a gift for making himself at home in his surroundings. "The man's a complete wreck."

Nicky didn't know whether to be relieved or pissed that Christian had scared her half to death. "What do you mean he's a wreck?"

"He's a mess. He can't concentrate on his art, he's a cranky asshole to everyone we work with, and he acts like Miami is the seventh level of hell, not one of the most happening cities on the planet." Christian sighed and pulled a pack of cigarettes from his coat pocket. "I swear to god, he's lost his mind. He's even grown a beard, if you can imagine. He looks like some sort of psycho serial killer."

"I didn't know you smoked," Nicky said.

"I don't, I just started." He flicked a cigarette from the pack and placed it between his lips. "Got some women trouble of my own."

"Sorry to hear that, but you can't smoke in here."

"That's cool, I'll just hold it. Almost as good and a lot less cancer-causing." He stared at her over the coffee table, an expectant look in his eye.

"I don't know what you want me to say."

"Say you'll take this." He reached into the inside pocket of his coat and pulled out a plane ticket, which he handed over. "And use it."

Nicky picked up the ticket and glanced at the destination. "You want me to go to Maui with you?"

"Oh, god. No." He snatched the ticket back and fished around in his other pocket. "This is your ticket. Sorry, I've been up for two days. I'm a little off my game."

"Miami," Nicky said, not even touching the ticket this time. Abby took that second to start snuffling and squirming in her crib, signaling her imminent waking. Thank. God. Saved by the baby.

"Yeah, Miami. You should go. He needs you. Believe me, I'm not the type to say that kind of thing unless it's true," Christian said, his voice absolutely sincere. "I'm really worried about him. It's like he's losing his mind or something."

Nicky opened her mouth, then closed it, then opened it again, knowing she looked like a fish out of water but unable to help herself. She had no idea what to say. A part of her wanted to take the ticket and go to Jackson, but the voice of reason wasn't buying. Jackson had made it very clear he didn't want a future with her, and he wasn't the one who had shown up on her doorstep. If he'd really changed his mind and was that miserable without her, wouldn't he be here himself?

"Mama. Maaaammmmaaa." She smiled, knowing she'd never get tired of hearing that little voice first thing in the morning.

"Just a second." Nicky vaulted off the couch and across the room to the tiny kitchenette area to start fixing Abby's bottle.

The pediatrician had suggested Nicky start buying the soy formula for toddlers, but she still couldn't bring herself to put Abby's milk in a sippy cup instead of the bottle. She wasn't ready to let those baby bottle days go just yet, especially considering Abby was probably the only child she'd ever have. She didn't want to have another baby on her own and she couldn't imagine ever getting married again . . . unless it was to Jackson.

She shoved the thought away as she picked Abby up from her crib and checked her diaper. Still dry. They'd had a diaper change at around four a.m., so she wasn't surprised.

Of course, that was just another reason not to go to Miami. Jackson hadn't expressed any interest in being a father to another man's child, especially a high-maintenance infant type of child. He'd held Abby only a few minutes before pushing her back into her mother's arms and fleeing the hotel room like he'd seen a ghost, not held a baby.

"She's beautiful. Looks just like you," Christian said, smiling as Nicky settled back in on the couch with Abby on her lap.

"Thanks." She frowned as she handed the bottle over to Abby. She liked to hold it herself now that she was an entire year old. "I have to tell you, Christian, I'm a little surprised to see you here. I didn't get the feeling you liked me that much."

"I didn't. I thought you were using Jackson to get your kid back."

"But now you've changed your mind?"

He sighed, crushing the cigarette in his hand. "I've changed my mind about a few things. Especially where matters of the heart are concerned." He paused, meeting her eyes. "You love him, don't you?"

"More than anything, except Abby," Nicky said, not seeing the sense in hiding her feelings. "But that doesn't mean—"

"It does mean. It's all you need to know, because you can be damn certain Jackson loves you more than anything in the world. He's got it in his head he's no good for you or something stupid, but I swear he's the best man I know. He's all heart under that big scary act."

Nicky felt her throat grow tight and a bubble of hope expand in her chest, making her dizzy. "I know he is. But if he doesn't want to—"

"Listen, I know you guys have got this kinky dominant and submissive thing going on, and I can respect that," Christian said, the tone in his voice making clear he did nothing of the sort. He thought they were both freaky perverts, which made Nicky smile. "But even the 'boss' needs to be told what's what sometimes. Jackson is all mixed up. So just take that ticket and go down there and tell him to quit being an ass. You three belong together, I feel it in my gut."

He pulled an envelope out of his pocket and set it on the table next to the plane ticket. "These are directions to the shop and Jackson's condo. I also took the liberty of having an extra key made to his place in case you decide to make yourself right at home. He's been working the early shift at the shop, twelve to eight."

Nicky bit her lip, trying to fight the excitement making her heart beat faster, but found it impossible. Christian wasn't a hopeless romantic, he was a practical man, even a cynical one, she would have said if judging from their first meeting. If he was here, insisting Jackson was lost without her, she had damned well better believe it.

"Let me ask you one question," she said.

"Yeah."

"Is that ticket one-way?"

He smiled. "It sure is."

She returned his grin. "Good. If I'm going to do this, I'm going to do it right."

"Fabulous." The warmth in his dark eyes finally made her see why this was a man who made women swoon. Christian really was a gorgeous human being when he let his own softer side be seen. "A woman after my own heart. Though I did get a round-trip ticket to Maui. Two, actually. I'm planning on bringing someone home with me."

"Is this the woman who inspired the change of heart?" Nicky asked, happy for the man.

"Yeah. She's got the stupidest pink-streaked hair and all these crazy feminist ideas and I was pretty sure I hated her." He frowned as he crossed the room to throw away the remnants of his cigarette. "Amazing what you learn about yourself when you hear someone's eloped with another man."

"Oh, no, I'm so sorry."

"That's all right. I'm going to get there before the ceremony, so no worries."

Nicky raised her eyebrows. "Okay. . . ."

Christian laughed. "Yeah, I'm crazy, but I heard kidnapping is the new way to prove your undying love. I figured I'd give it a try."

"Right. Assuming the woman doesn't press criminal charges."

"Of course. I've got to run in a few, but do you want me to help you pack anything before I go? The next direct flight leaves at eleven o'clock this morning. I assume you'll want to be on that one. No sense leaving that man down there to suffer any longer."

Nicky glanced around the room at the rented furnishings that came with the studio and the very few things she'd managed to bring with her and Abby when they left Derrick the first time. She wasn't going to be the slightest bit sad to leave the place that had been their home for the past two months. "No, I think I can throw our clothes in a couple of suitcases and box up the rest of the stuff before we need to catch a cab. There's not that much here."

"All right, then, I guess I'll be heading out." He crossed to the door, pausing before he left to turn and catch her eye. "You're really going, right?"

"I am."

"Thank you," he said, a vulnerability in his eyes she'd never seen before. "And don't let him tell you no."

"Thank you . . . I won't."

As she watched Christian leave, she knew she'd never meant anything more.

Chapter Twenty-one

"You want a sandwich from the Cuban bakery? They've got those hot ham and cheese ones and the pastries go half price after seven o'clock." Garret, one of the Miami studio's most talented artists, stood at the door looking like the last thing he wanted to do was bring Jackson a sandwich or a pastelito de guayaba.

He looked like he'd rather run straight into the night and keep on running until he was as far away from his boss as he could possibly get. But then, Jackson couldn't really blame the man. He hadn't been a bundle of sweetness and light the past two months.

Rabid bear with anger-management issues would be a more apt description.

Jackson sighed. He had to step up his people skills. Missing Nicky so badly it felt like his guts had spilled out all over the floor was no excuse for alienating his entire staff.

"No, thanks. I'm getting ready to head out. I've been here since noon," Jackson said, forcing a smile. "Good work today. I really dug that portrait piece you started."

"Thanks." Garret's thin face lit up, making him look even younger than his twenty-one years. He was the youngest of the three new artists they'd hired for the Miami opening, but had a gift for ink not many possessed at any age. "I'm pumped to finish it. Nice change from the average job."

"Yeah. It'll be a great addition to your portfolio. Catch you tomorrow."

"Later," Garret threw over his shoulder as he darted out the door.

There. He'd made nice. Now he could sleep sound tonight.

Riiight. He hadn't slept more than four hours straight since he left L.A. At this rate, mooning over Nicky was going to make him old before his time. He already had permanent circles under his eyes, but he wasn't too worried about them. He figured they complemented his beard and fleshed out the whole "slightly deranged" look.

"Be sure to lock up before you go, and make Tony walk you to your car so you get there safe," Jackson told Kit, the girl filling in for Delilah behind the front desk while their usual office manager was on her combination wedding-honeymoon. He never would have pegged Dee for the romantic elopement type, but she'd certainly seemed thrilled to go say "I do." He'd been happy for her. It was nice to see someone having a little success in the relationship department.

"Sure thing. See you tomorrow," Kit said.

Jackson patted his pocket, making sure his keys were still there, feeling like he was forgetting something as he headed out the back door. He wondered if he'd ever get used to not carrying a coat in the winter. It was late January, but the temperature rarely dipped below the high sixties. It was one of the things Christian loved about Miami, but Jackson hadn't been able to work up the same enthusiasm for shorts and beach time year-round.

But then, he hadn't been able to work up much enthusiasm for anything besides missing Nicky, replaying every moment they'd spent together, fantasizing about the feel of her bare skin against his, and the way she could drive him wild with just a kiss.

"Give it a rest, man," he grumbled to himself as he guided his car through the busy streets and then onto the quieter avenue leading down to his beachside condo.

He'd made his decision and he was going to stand by it. This was best for Nicky. She didn't need another volatile man in her life putting her and her daughter in danger. He was torturing himself for no reason and should concentrate on getting the hell over Nick and moving on.

Too bad that was so much easier said than done.

Maybe a stiff drink or two would help him get to sleep. He was debating scotch or whiskey as he swung the door to his condo open, but froze before he took a step inside. Someone was there. He could feel it.

"Wow, Christian was right." Her voice came from across the shadowed room, near the windows that overlooked the ocean. "Even in the dark, I can tell you look awful."

Jackson tensed, his hand gripping the door handle, shock and excitement kicking up his heart rate. It was Nicky's voice, no doubt in his mind.

Or maybe all *in* his mind. Maybe he'd finally gone crazy enough to start hearing things.

One way to find out.

He flicked on the lights, his chest and things much lower in his body tightening as he took in the woman seated in his leather easy chair. Nick was decked out in a black corset and thigh-high stockings. Her hair tumbled around her shoulders in soft curls, and her lips shone with something pink and glossy. She was a fantasy come to life, and even more beautiful than he remembered.

Too bad he had to send her on her way.

"What are you doing here? Are you in trouble? Is it Derrick?"

"No, he's still in the hospital. Besides, I've got a restraining order and the paperwork is all finished. He didn't even fight for partial custody. Now it's just a matter of waiting four more months for the divorce to be final. Some stupid California mandatory waiting period or something like—"

"Good, I'm happy for you. Now, you need to go," Jackson said, gritting his teeth as he opened the door and gestured to the hallway. "Get dressed and get out."

"No." She stood in one smooth, easy motion and stalked across the room, her high heels accentuating her long, long legs. She didn't stop until she stood less than a foot away, close enough for him to smell the addictive scent of her perfume and the spicier smell that was all Nick. "Close the door."

"I think we've established you're not the one who gives orders, Nicky, so—"

"Close the door, Jackson. I won't ask again." She pulled a mini-flogger from behind her back and held it up between them.

They both knew she couldn't do him any damage with that tiny toy or anything else, but for some reason Jackson found himself letting the door swing shut. The look in her eyes was like nothing he'd ever seen. The woman was determined, and channeling some serious dominant energy for a submissive.

"Now, I'm going to talk and you're going to listen," she said, placing one hand in the center of his chest and shoving him back against the door. Even that small touch was enough to send a shock through his body, and blood surging to his cock. "First of all, you look terrible. What have you done to yourself?"

"I grew a beard," he said, surprised to hear how penitent he sounded, as if he were a sub who knew he had displeased his mistress.

"A beard that's crawling halfway down your neck. Poorly maintained facial hair makes you look dirty." She narrowed her eyes, searching his face. "And you've got circles under your eyes. Are you drinking too much?"

"Nope, just not sleeping enough."

"And why aren't you sleeping enough?" she asked, a hint of softness in her eyes. She expected to hear something about how much he missed her, but he sure as hell wasn't going to oblige. He had to get her to leave. Her and her daughter's safety was more important than anything they felt for each other.

"I've been busy, fucking a wide array of women until the early hours of the morning," he said, keeping the words casual. "I'm actually expecting someone in an hour, so if you could get your things and be out of here by—"

"Bullshit. You're lying. You haven't slept with anyone since you left L.A."

"How would you know?"

"I don't think you'd be this hard if you'd been such a busy boy." Nicky slid her hand down over his engorged cock, drawing a groan from the back of his throat. She leaned closer, whispering her next words against his lips. "Poor Jack. This feels like it hurts, but I'm here to take the pain away."

"Stop this," Jackson said, pushing her hands away. "Listen, I understand what you're trying to do, but—"

"No, you don't understand. If you understood you'd know you should quit trying to get rid of me," she said, her dominant act faltering a bit. "Christian told me how you've been, Jackson, and I've been the same. Even with Abby back, it still feels like something's missing since you left. It's like a piece of me is gone, and I can't remember how to be happy without it."

"Nick, please. I'm not good for you and Abby, I—"

"Christian said something about that, too, that you've convinced yourself you're bad news or something stupid like that."

"Now you're calling me stupid?" Jackson laughed despite himself. "See, this wouldn't work. A big bad dominant man is not the type who puts up with his sub calling him names."

Nicky stepped closer, catching his eye with a look so intense he couldn't bring himself to look away. "Listen to me. You are not a big bad dom. You are Jackson, an amazing man who happens to enjoy power-exchange games in the bedroom. Being a dom is part of what you are, but it isn't *who* you are."

"Then who am I? If you're seeing things so clearly."

"You're the man I love," she said, her eyes glistening as she reached up to cup his face in her hand. "You're the man I've always loved, a man who would never hurt anyone."

Jackson pulled away from her soft touch and pushed past her to pace into the room. His heart felt like it was going to burst out of his chest. God, how he wanted to believe her, but he couldn't, not after what had brought them back together in the first place.

"That's what you're worried about, isn't it? That you'd hurt me somehow?" she asked. "Well, that's ridiculous. You're not that type of person. You're not Derrick. I should—"

"I kidnapped you, Nicky. Twice. Then I tied you down and

was going to permanently scar your body, and I only stopped when you started crying so hard I couldn't—"

"So what? You didn't go through with what you'd planned. You didn't hurt me."

"But I could have. And ... I might sometime in the future." He sighed as he turned back to face her. "I've never been in a long-term relationship, period, let alone a dom-sub long-term relationship. I could very well be a Derrick in training. I can't promise you I'm not, so I can't—"

"You know why I left Carson City the night after your birthday?" she asked, the abrupt change of subject enough to stun him into momentary silence. "Let me tell you."

Nicky wandered toward the kitchen, climbing up on one of the bar stools tucked under the island that separated living space from dining space. "Phil had been cornering me for months, on nights when you and Naomi worked late."

"What?" Jackson felt his stomach turn, and knew he didn't want to hear what Nicky was going to say next.

"Sometimes he'd just pin my arms and shove his tongue in my mouth, but sometimes he'd get handsy." Her eyes drifted to the ceiling. "He'd get fingers up my shirt or down my pants. Never for very long, and it never went further than that, but I knew it was only a matter of time. Especially after you moved out. Phil was afraid of you, you know. But once you were gone I knew things would be different ... worse. ..."

"Why didn't you tell me?"

"I was ashamed. I didn't know what you'd think of me and ..." She sucked in a big breath, eyes still glued to a place above his head, as if she couldn't stand to look at him. "And even if I'd told you, I knew there was nothing you could do. Aside from getting yourself thrown in jail."

"You could have gotten transferred to another home. You could have—"

"Like another home would have been so much better?" Nicky laughed. "You grew up the same way I did. You know what it's like. I had to get out. I couldn't take another two years of Phil or anyone else."

Jackson nodded, wanting to take her in his arms, but sensing she wouldn't welcome any touching right now. "I'm sorry. I hope you know now that I wouldn't have thought any less of you. It wasn't your fault. You could have come to me for help. We would have figured something out without you running off on your own."

"Yeah, I know that now. And if I could go back and do it differently, well . . ." She met his eyes again with a tight smile. "The only reason I told you is there's a point to the story."

"That the foster care system is seriously flawed?"

"Well, that." She laughed. "And that I always knew Phil was a piece of shit. I had suspicions about Derrick, too. I even tried to call off the wedding at one point because I just knew it wasn't going to work out. I didn't know how bad things would get, but I knew we weren't meant to be. But it's different with you. You may not know it, but I do. You're a good man, Jackson, and we belong together. Always have, always will."

"Nicky, I love you. You know I do, but—"

"I love you, too." She jumped off her chair, and crossed the room, taking his hands in hers. "So there's only one more question that needs to be answered. Well, maybe two questions."

"And what are those?" he asked, feeling his will to fight slipping away. He wanted to believe Nick was right, that he could be the man she needed.

Maybe, with her help, he could be.

"Do you like kids? Abby in particular? Be honest."

"That little girl is the most beautiful thing I've ever seen. I was afraid to hold her too long because I realized I wouldn't ever want to let her go. You know I always wanted kids." Jackson paused, really thinking about the possibility of being a dad and finding it even more exciting than he'd imagined. "Still do, though I'm sure a few things would have to change if there was a little one in the house. We'd have to keep the play in the bedroom, but I'm fine with that if you—"

"More than fine." Nicky smiled, tears coming into her eyes. "God, it's so good to hear you say that. I love you so much."

Jackson squeezed her hands. "And what's the second question?"

"Well, it's not so much a question as a statement." She sucked in a deep breath. "Our ticket was one-way. I brought all of our clothes and dropped the few things I had in boxes off at the UPS store on the way to the airport. Good and Trashy said I could shoot the layout I'm doing for them as easily in Miami as L.A., and I sort of told my landlord I wouldn't be coming back. I've got full physical and legal custody of Abby so . . . I hope you have room for a couple of girls around the house."

"A couple? Is Abby—"

"She's in your room. There were more pillows in there and I wanted to make sure she didn't roll off the bed if she started moving around in the night. She's a wild sleeper."

"Just like her mother." Jackson smiled, barely able to believe this was really happening. A part of him still felt like he should be fighting the overwhelming happiness coursing through his system at the thought of him and Nicky and Abby becoming a family, but the rest of him was doing a pretty good job of shutting that insanity down.

Nicky was right. They belonged together, for better or worse.

But he was going to do his damnedest to make sure it was mostly better.

"Yep, just like," Nicky said, her smile lighting up her face. "So, you want to go get comfortable in the guest room? We could snuggle up in that full bed and see how many times I kick you in my sleep."

"I think I have a better idea," Jackson said, pulling her close, letting his hands travel down to cup her ass.

"Oh? And what might that be?"

"Well, it seems a shame to waste this outfit you've put on just sleeping."

"You like it?" she asked as she wrapped her arms around his neck. "I figured you might need a visual aid as well as a good talking-to."

"An excellent idea and a truly stunning visual aid. I'm only sorry I didn't have a chance to get all prettied up for you."

"That's okay, I kind of dig the beard actually. Though I've always wondered . . ." She stood on tiptoe, closing the distance between their lips.

Their first kiss in two months was enough to make Jackson's skin threaten to melt off his bones. The feel of her tongue sneaking into his mouth, the sweet taste of her, the way she dug her fingernails into his neck as their kiss grew more frantic—all of it was even more amazing than he remembered.

"Yep, it tickles." She laughed and kissed him again.

God, there was nothing in the world like kissing this woman. Kissing Nick was like coming home and being transported to exotic places he'd never been all at the same time. She was all he'd ever dreamed of and so much more. He was one lucky bastard, especially considering how close he'd come to losing her.

"Thank you," he whispered against her lips.

"You're welcome." She sighed as she hugged him more tightly. "I hear sometimes even wise dominant men need a little reality check."

"And you should feel free to give me one anytime."

"I will. But you should feel free to give me things, too." Nicky wiggled her bottom under his hands, bringing to mind their last encounter at the club in L.A.

His cock grew even thicker at the mere thought of private spanking sessions, when there would be no reason not to end the encounter by driving inside Nicky's welcoming heat. Damn, but they were going to have some fun together. There were so many things he wanted to do to her, with her, so many boundaries to test and explore.

But tonight, he wanted to keep things simple. "No paddles tonight."

"No?" she asked, looking a little disappointed.

"No, and no nipple clamps or whips or restraints." He kissed her again, softly, thoroughly. "Tonight it's going to be just you and me."

"The real you and me?" she asked, the heat in her eyes making her real question clear.

"Of course." He released her with a smile. "So go get your ass in that bed and spread your legs. Play with your tits and your pussy, but don't touch your clit and don't come before I get there. Just get my cunt nice and wet. You understand?"

"Yes, sir." She leapt into his arms, hugging him so tight his laugh came out as a grunt, then turned and fled into the guest room.

Jackson watched her go with an ache in his chest so strong he could barely breathe. That was his girl. His love, the only woman who would ever know him, who could ever make him feel like he was the kind of man he wanted to be. And he was going to do whatever it took to show her how much she meant to him— tonight and every night for the rest of their lives.

He stopped and took a deep breath before following her, his eyes drawn down to the angel on his arm. For a moment, he would have sworn the ink looked brighter, richer than it had in years, as if the tat itself were proud of connecting him with the woman who matched him as perfectly as their identical tattoos.

Jackson smiled, resisting the urge to whisper his thanks. He might be crazy enough to kidnap the only girl he ever loved, but he wasn't quite ready to start talking to his own ink . . . at least not just yet.

Chapter Twenty-two

As she ran and jumped onto the guest bed, Nicky was laughing and crying at the same time. She'd done it, she'd really done it! And it hadn't been nearly as hard as she'd worried it would be. Her stomach had been tied in knots for the entire plane ride, not even Abby's constant squirming on her lap distracting her from her fear that Jackson's stubbornness would prove too much for her to conquer. Once he had his mind made up, he was usually impossible to sway.

But then, neither of them had ever been in love like this. What they'd felt for each other when they were kids had been wonderful and real, but nothing compared to the connection they had now.

This was what people dreamed about, wrote stories and made movies about. This was the real thing, a love she hadn't dared dream she'd find.

The thought was enough to bring fresh tears to her eyes.

"Disobeying my first order. This doesn't bode well for our future," Jackson said, the laughter in his voice making her smile.

"You're the one who said I was a pushy bottom," Nicky said, rolling over onto her back, her breath catching as she saw him standing in the door, wearing nothing but his jeans. How many times had she fantasized about that bare chest? About running her fingers over the contours of his muscles, letting her tongue trace each dip and curve?

"I was wrong. You're not pushy, just hard to handle." He stalked slowly toward the bed, making her pulse pound.

"I'll probably need a lot of discipline and punishment before I'm anywhere near where I should be." Nicky spread her legs, slowly, deliberately, and let her fingers trail up her thigh. She was already wet and aching, just seeing Jackson enough to make her body come to life. "Training me is not going to be an easy job."

Jackson watched her hand with undisguised fascination as she slid her fingers inside her thong, dipping into the well of heat between her legs. "Easy is overrated." His breath rushed out through his parted lips. "I can't believe you're here."

"I'm here and I'm never going to leave," Nicky said, the back of her throat getting tight again. "Now are you going to fuck me or not? If not, I'm probably going to start crying again and I've really had about all the—"

"Take off your panties. Leave the stockings and shoes on."

Nicky obeyed, hands shaking as she quickly shed the scrap of silk and then lay back on the bed, her nipples so hard they poked through the stiff satin of her corset. A wave of dizzying desire swept over her from head to toe, making her head spin. God, she needed this, needed Jackson to take control of her, to make her feel so safe and free and completely consumed by him.

Him. Her dom. Her master. Her love. Every name she called him made her more giddy.

"Spread your legs. Wider," Jackson ordered, working at his belt with swift, sure movements. "Show me my pussy."

Electricity shot through her entire body as she parted her thighs. She could feel her lips plump under his eyes, swelling until she felt bruised with the force of her wanting. She sure as hell hoped Jackson wasn't planning some long, drawn-out seduction, because she didn't think her mind would survive it. She needed him. Now. They could do the long, drawn-out thing at a later date, when she didn't feel so desperate for the connection she'd been denied for the past two months.

"You are so beautiful," he said, his voice catching as he shoved jeans and boxer briefs to the floor, freeing his cock. The poor man was so swollen the veins stood up along his turgid length, and his plump head dripped a single sticky tear.

Nicky licked her lips—she wanted to taste that salty drop more than she could say. "You, too. You don't know how many times I've imagined this."

"Oh, I can guess." He knelt at the edge of the bed, bringing his warm hands to the inside of her thighs and spreading her wider. "Maybe a few hundred less than I have. I swear to god, I could taste you in my sleep."

"Please, Jack." She squirmed beneath him, feeling she would shatter if he didn't shove that beautiful hardness between her legs in the next ten seconds. "I need you inside of me."

"Are you topping from the bottom again?" he asked, his voice soft as he dipped one thumb into her cunt, groaning as he slowly drove in and out of her slick heat.

"No, I just—"

"Because even if you are, I don't care. Nothing could keep me from fucking this pussy." He slid his hands from her body and positioned his cock at her entrance in one smooth movement. "Right now."

"Jackson!" She called his name as his hips surged forward, shoving his engorged length inside her.

There was a hint of resistance at first. No matter how aroused she was, he was a tight fit, his cock even thicker, harder, hotter than normal. He felt so large that a hint of delicious pain accompanied her pleasure as he filled her, driving fast and deep, not stopping until he lay buried to the hilt.

"God, Nick." His breath came in swift, shallow puffs against her lips as she wrapped her arms and legs around him, pulling him even closer to her. "I'm not going to last five minutes. You feel so fucking good."

"Five minutes should be more than enough." She rolled her hips in a slow circle, grinding her clit into his pelvic bone with a shuddering sigh. "You feel pretty fucking good yourself."

"I aim to please," he said, as his hands gripped the top of her corset and tugged, pulling at the fabric until her breasts were free. "I missed these tits."

"And I missed you calling them tits. I actually came to like the—" Oh, god, his tongue. She couldn't remember anything feeling as good as his tongue flicking across her nipples. Her hips circled faster as shocks of awareness surged between her legs.

"Nothing tastes like your skin, nothing in the world." Jackson mumbled the words against her breast before he sucked one nipple into his mouth, tugging at the aroused flesh until she cried out. "So fucking sweet."

"Please, Jackson, please," Nicky panted, tugging at his hair.

It was too much, more stimulation than her overly sensitized body could take, especially since he refused to move inside her.

He still lay buried in her pulsing sheath, pinning her to the mattress with his weight, limiting her movement to those little rolls of her hips that just weren't enough anymore. She needed him to fuck her, to slam his cock in and out of her pussy until it hurt, until that brutal penetration sent her spiraling into the bliss only Jackson could give her.

"Please!" She pulled at him with all her strength, but he simply removed her hands, pressing her wrists into the pillow above her head as he transferred his maddening attentions to her other nipple.

"Don't say another word until I'm finished with my tits." Jackson accentuated his words by dragging his teeth across her aching tip, making her scream.

Nicky bit her lip and moaned as he moved from one breast to another, slowly driving her insane, making her pussy gush liquid heat as it clutched at his thickness, so close to the edge but unable to tumble over. She couldn't come, not without his approval, not even if she'd wanted to.

Which she didn't. More than release, more than relief, she wanted to please Jackson. No matter how hard to handle she might be, that part of her was a submissive through and through. *Jackson's* submissive. Her body belonged to him, for now, for always.

The thought made her even hotter, wilder, made her legs churn on either side of Jack's.

"My pussy is so wet. I love feeling my pussy so wet," he said, before sucking one nipple deep into his mouth and letting his teeth bite down on the soft flesh of her breast. The pressure grew greater and greater, until the trapped flesh began to sting.

God, he was going to mark her. There would be an imprint of his teeth on her breast by the time he pulled away. Just imagining her pale flesh bearing the sign of his possession threatened to undo her. She wanted to scream, to beg, to cry out his name, but she bit her lip, struggling to obey his request for silence as he set about marking her other breast.

Her head tossed back and forth on the pillow and she fought Jackson's hold on her wrists until her muscles ached, but there was no relief to be found. He was in complete control, and would continue his erotic torture until he was good and ready to stop. The knowledge both thrilled and frightened her, forcing a desperate sob from her throat.

Finally, when she was certain her sanity couldn't hold a second longer, Jackson called her name, the abandon in the sound letting her know he'd reached the same razor-sharp edge. With a sound more animal than human, he drew back until only the tip of his cock was inside her and then rammed back in, setting a swift, brutal pace that was exactly what her body had been craving.

Nicky cried out as he released his hold on her wrists, wild to feel her nails digging into the muscles of his back. She wanted to mark him the same way he'd marked her, to leave behind traces of their passion that would follow him for days, so that every time he felt that slight sting, or saw that trail of red, he would think of her, of the way they were together, here where they belonged.

They were meant to be connected like this, fused so tightly it was impossible to tell where his body ended and hers began. They were a part of each other, a matched pair that would never be separated again...just like their tattoos, the things that had brought them back together in the first place.

It no longer seemed strange that she'd been so resistant to having her angel modified. The night they'd acquired their matching ink was the night she'd given Jackson her heart and he'd given her the same in return. She didn't want to lose the symbol of that momentous occasion, not now, not ever.

"God, I love you, Nicky. I love you so much."

"Me, too, so much. So much." She gasped the words into his mouth as he took her lips in a brutal kiss, mating his tongue with hers as his rhythm grew even faster, frantic, until she knew he was only seconds away from losing control. An answering wildness rose within her, tightening things low in her body, making every muscle tremble with the prelude to her own release.

She ripped her mouth from his, the room spinning as she fought to hold back the dark wave threatening to pull her under. "Please!"

"Nicky, god, Nicky." Faster and faster, until the sound of skin making contact with skin filled the room, until her every nerve cried out with the need to come, to find her pleasure around the thickness working between her thighs.

"I'm going to come. I can't help it, I'm—"

"Come, Nick. God, come for me." He groaned and his entire body shuddered as his cock began to pulse within her.

Nicky joined him a second later, her body bowing off the bed with the force of her release. Her womb contracted again and again, the orgasm so fierce it made her scream. Her nails dug into Jackson's back and her heels into the mattress as pure bliss rocketed through her body, making her sob and tears of happiness leak from behind her closed lids, making her wonder if it were possible to die from pure pleasure.

When she finally drifted back to earth, she was shocked to find she was laughing. And not just kind of laughing, but giggling so hard the tightening of her muscles had forced Jackson's softening length from her body and her sides were starting to hurt.

"You're silly," Jackson said, the rumble of his laughter underscoring her own as he rolled to lie beside her. "What kind of woman gets the giggles after sex like that?"

"I don't know." She laughed even harder, rolling on her side and clutching at her stomach. "God, that was great."

"Yes, it was," he said, gazing down at her with an amused expression.

"I love you so much," she gasped, the giggle fit showing no signs of stopping.

"Good thing I'm a confident man or this might be doing something to my self-esteem."

That was all it took to make her completely lose it. She laughed until her head hurt and her body ached, until it was hard to breathe and she contracted a serious case of the hiccups. She honestly didn't know when she would have stopped if Abby hadn't cried out from the other room.

"Oh, no, the baby's awake," she said, pressing her hands into her sore jaw muscles as she finally regained control.

"I'm guessing it was the crazy woman laughing in the other room who woke her up, what do you think?" Jackson was already out of bed, pulling pajama pants from a drawer and throwing her a T-shirt.

"Or it could have been the screaming orgasm."

"Yeah, we're going to have to invest in some soundproof walls before this kid gets any older." He smiled as he spoke, his excitement for the future—their future—clear on his face. "Do you think she'd let me pick her up and bring her in here with us?"

"I don't think she'd mind at all." Nicky smiled, fighting back the tears in her eyes. No more crazy laughing or crying. At least not tonight anyway. "I'll turn down the bed."

She shrugged on the oversize T-shirt and found her underpants on the floor. She'd dressed, used the bathroom, and put order to the bed by the time Jackson came back into the room, holding a blinking Abby. She looked confused, but not at all unhappy to be in Jackson's arms.

"She was wet, so I changed her with one of the diapers by the bed. I think I got it on right, but you might want to check," he said, the uncertainty on his face making her want to hug him.

Nicky reached out and took Abby before climbing into the bed. "I'm sure it's fine."

"Maybe, but I'm going to need practice. It took me at least three minutes. Good thing she was patient with me." Jackson took his place on the other side of the bed, smiling down at Abby as Nicky placed her on the sheets between them. The baby immediately started to nuzzle into the covers, making happy cooing noises.

"She's always loved sleeping with someone. I know I should make her sleep by herself, but I kind of dig the whole family sleeping idea."

"What if I roll over and crush her?" Jackson asked, inching as close to the edge of the bed as possible.

"You won't. Trust me," Nicky said, leaning over to press a soft kiss to his lips. "And this will just be for tonight. We'll go buy her a crib tomorrow."

"A crib sounds good." Jackson smiled against her lips. "I mean, I wouldn't mind the family sleeping thing. But it might make it hard to do certain things."

"Right. And we like those things. Sex games and babies don't really mix."

He laughed. "I wasn't even thinking about games, but yeah, I like those, too."

"Then what were you thinking about?" She sighed into her pillow, certain she couldn't feel happier than she did right now, freshly bedded by the man she loved and snuggled in with the two people she loved best in the world.

"I was thinking about maybe . . . making her a brother or sister someday soon. I mean, not too soon, but—"

"As soon as you're ready," Nicky said, breaking her vow not to get teary again. "I can't think of anything more exciting."

"Not even investing in a spanking bench of our very own?" Jackson smiled, but even in the dim light she could see the telltale shine in his eyes.

"Not even a spanking bench of my very own. Though I want one of those, too. I believe a woman can balance babies and spankings. Don't you agree?"

Jackson reached out to touch her face, careful not to disturb Abby, who was already falling back asleep. "I love you, Nick."

"I love you, too."

He was asleep a few minutes later, his deep, steady breathing lulling her into a state of profound relaxation. Still, she fought sleep as long she was able, wanting to savor these moments, the happiest of her life, and the beginning of her life with the man of her dreams.

First she sees you; then you die. . . .
Samantha Quinn lives in a world of shadows, a result of a botched demon sacrifice that left her blind. But when bounty hunter Jace Lu comes into her life, the heat between them triggers visions that awaken Sam's latent psychic power and puts them on the trail of a killer. Now Sam and Jace must stop a madman before he kills again, while dealing with an attraction that might just prove deadly.

Read on for a sneak peek of

KISSED BY DARKNESS

Coming from Signet Eclipse
in May 2010

Samantha Quinn wasn't afraid of the dark. Even when she was walking at the edge of the ruins, where demonic attacks had transformed New York City's Greenwich Village into a maze of rubble inhabited by bloodthirsty predators, the darkness could be an unexpected ally.

The scary things got cocky in the shadows. Careless. They made noise—claws on the concrete, rough skin scraping along crumbling brick—things even sighted people could hear if they were really listening. To a woman who'd been legally blind since age six, the sounds of an approaching demon were like gunshots—impossible not to notice, and easy to avoid if you had practice ducking and covering. Which she did. A girl couldn't grow up on the south end of the island without learning how to run and hide.

Or when to pay attention to the feeling that something bad was going to happen.

"I'll be there in ten, fifteen minutes, tops."

"Wonderful! We can't wait to—"

"Gotta hang up now. Bye." Sam tapped the bud clipped to her

ear, ending the phone call without waiting for Mrs. Choe to say her good-byes.

Ellen and her husband, Chang-su, had lived in the neighborhood for forty years and raised four children in the wake of the attacks twenty years before. They knew there were times when safety dictated the rude termination of a phone call. But they wouldn't be worried. Demons were easy to avoid if you stuck to the main streets and made a run for it on the rare occasions when the creatures prowled too near the edge of the ruins.

The descendants of the ancient dinosaurs weren't particularly quick. They had to rely on their prey being careless, and letting them get close enough to employ their various deadly natural weapons. Sam wouldn't let them get close. She had these streets memorized and her ability to distinguish areas of light and dark kept her from running into any large obstacles. Sure, she had her share of spills from time to time, but she felt confident in her ability to take care of herself, even on the city streets.

It's just dumb luck, Sam. Someday you're going to fall at the wrong time, and something's going to get you.

Ah, Stephen. Brother, friend, voice of doom. Why was it always *his* voice that got going in her head at night, when she was trying to pull off the whole "brave New Yorker" thing?

Because I'm right. You know I'm right. You should move back in with me and—

Sam did her best to banish her brother's voice, focusing on where she was going, not where she'd been, increasing her speed until her sandals made tiny scraping noises against the concrete as they chased the white cane tapping ahead.

The Choes hadn't been surprised to hear she'd finally gotten her own apartment. But then, they'd never treated her like an invalid or an oddity. To them, she was just another girl from the neighborhood, and the only florist they wanted to handle their daughter's wedding. Arranging flowers based solely on smell and texture created some fairly fantastic and unusual-looking combinations. Obviously Sam had never seen any of her own arrangements, but she took her clients' word for it that they were visually stunning. Old friends or not, the Choes wouldn't hire anything less than the best for their daughter. They'd finally gotten Sin Moon hooked up with a nice Korean boy and wanted her wedding to be perfect. *And* they wanted to approve every last detail months in advance.

Hence the centerpiece Sam was presently cradling with her left arm. She'd promised to bring the sample arrangement over as soon as she finished cleaning up the shop for the day, no matter what the hour.

But as the pungent smell of fresh demon waste mingled with the scent of lavender and wild roses, she began to doubt the wisdom of journeying out alone after seven o'clock. Demonic attacks had been on the rise in recent months. Attacks always increased in the spring, when the warmer temperatures brought certain breeds out of their winter hibernation, but this year it was worse than usual.

Just like her dreams. Worse than usual. More vivid, more horrific, with a heavy dose of childhood terror churned up in the mix. Unfortunately, Sam's kid fears weren't the kind that could be dismissed as pure imagination. A lot of those horrible things had really happened. And some of the things she dreamed about were *going* to happen. Stephen had never believed in her ability, no matter how much proof she presented, but she knew when a bad dream was going to come true.

She could smell it on the air. Taste it on her tongue, sharp and bitter.

Somewhere, deep in the ruins, a girl screamed, startling Sam and nearly making her drop the flowers she'd worked on all afternoon.

"Damn it." She stumbled to the side, regaining her grip on the basket, but clocking her shoulder on something big, hard, and stinky in the process.

A Dumpster, but one that had recently been emptied. The stink wasn't fresh, more the lingering sourness of ancient vegetables mixed with rotted meat and coffee grounds. Gross, but it was the best hiding place she was going to find around here.

After using her cane to check the area behind the Dumpster, Sam set the centerpiece on the ground and turned back to the ruins. She'd never ventured inside by herself, but for some reason, she knew she had to follow the cold, slippery energy oozing across her skin to its source.

Her certainty that something horrible was about to happen was stronger than ever. A woman had screamed in her dreams last night and there had been blood, so much blood. She was positive that if she didn't find the woman before whatever hunted her, blood would be spilled and an innocent person would die.

For a moment, the rational part of her mind argued that she should call for one of the many demon control patrols always a scream away in this part of Manhattan. It was their job to keep the streets safe, to make sure the thousands of tourists who came to New York to see the demonic urban habitat didn't get themselves killed trying to get a picture of some of the more fantastic species. They would take a report, get a police task force down here within a half hour, and—

The scream came again, higher and even more terrified. "And they'll be too late," Sam said, setting a swift pace toward the sound before she could second-guess herself. She tripped twice on the uneven pavement before she reached the first bend in the path, but she didn't think of turning back.

She was the only one who could save this woman. Hell, she might be the only one who could even *hear* her. Whether it was simply that her ears functioned better than an average person's because she was missing one of her other senses, or something more paranormal in nature, Sam had always heard things other people missed.

Like the sound of something breathing nearby. Something big. *Really* big.

Sam tasted the mocha she'd made just before leaving the shop and swallowed hard. God, Stephen was going to lose it when he found out she'd been wandering around here by herself, acting like some too-stupid-to-live environmentalist determined to go Jane Goodall with the demons. He'd warned her a thousand times not to go within fifty feet of the ruins. He was going to kill her for getting killed like this.

The thought was almost enough to make Sam laugh, even though the giant breathing thing was so close she could taste it. Fire and sulfur and the hint of some exotic fruit, mixed with the unmistakable smell of demon waste. It was definitely a demon, but not the one she'd followed. The scent from her dream was gone, vanished along with the cold energy that had summoned her from the safety of the street.

Whoever she'd heard, the woman was probably already dead. And now, because she was a stupid blind girl who thought she could play the hero, she was going to die too.

"But I'm going to hurt you first," she whispered to the thing in front of her as she thumbed open the secret compartment on her cane, flicking the switch that turned the red-tipped end deadly.

Switchblades were illegal in the city, so she assumed switch canes weren't something the police would approve of, but abiding by the letter of the law wasn't a priority for most Southies and Sam wasn't any different. Being blind didn't automatically mean she was a law-abiding citizen or helpless or sweet.

Or willing to wait for someone else to make the first move.

"Come and get me already," she yelled, lifting her cane and lunging forward.

An outraged squeal echoed off the bricks, but there wasn't time to celebrate her hit. Seconds later, her cane was ripped from her hands and the smell of fruit got even stronger as something whizzed by her face. Shit! She'd heard of demons that shot poison quills into their prey to immobilize them before they began to feed.

Sam ducked on instinct and felt the air stir above her head. Whirling around with her hands held out in front of her, she started to run, praying she remembered the obstacles she'd encountered on the way in well enough to avoid them. Without her cane, she had no way of "seeing" the ground in front of her before she stepped, no way of—

She cursed as she tripped over something round and hard she hadn't noticed before, and fell to the ground, the needles of the demon who hunted her pinging against the concrete near her scraped hands. Sam curled into a fetal position, her body still trying to protect itself though her mind knew this was it. She was down, and the thing behind her was coming, and this time there would be no escape.

All of sudden she was six years old again, bound and tied and waiting for the cold evil to crawl inside her body and take what her parents had invited it to take, to steal what it needed to steal. But this time, it wouldn't just be her eyes. This time, it would be her life.

If he were a different kind of man, Jace would have let the woman die. The hard core of him might still have considered it, just for a second, if it had been anyone else. Anyone other than her.

But as he watched Samantha Quinn fall to the ground, her long, silky black hair tangling around her frightened face, obscuring those big brown eyes, there was no way Jace could do anything but shoot the creature he'd been tracking for three days. Even though killing the Ju Du demon would mean forfeiting his bounty and facing a death threat or two if any of the other hunters found out he'd put the thing down.

The city wanted demons taken alive or not taken at all. They didn't pay for dead meat, and his competition wouldn't be pleased to hear he'd taken out one of the rarest species to roam the Southie ruins. But he didn't have a choice. She wasn't just a friend's kid sister or a girl he'd watched grow up in the neighborhood. Jace couldn't say exactly what she was to him—just that something inside him threatened to snap when he thought about a world without Sam Quinn. She didn't deserve to die like this; she and her brother had been through enough already.

"Don't move," Jace shouted as Sam curled into a ball on the ground.

Sam didn't scream when he fired—Jace had to give her credit for that. She lay perfectly still and quiet until the Ju Du was in pieces and the sharp reports of gunfire had faded, echoing away down the twisted corridors of the ruins. But when he crossed to her, satisfied to see she hadn't been hit by any quills, she was crying, big fat tears that streamed out of her haunting eyes.

Damn crying women. The sight sickened him. He couldn't help it. Seeing a woman cry made him want to slam his fist into a wall, or run until his lungs exploded, or kill something. Or maybe all three.

"I'm sorry. Sorry," Sam said, sucking in a deep breath and biting her bottom lip, as if she could tell how her tears affected him. "Thanks, Jace," she said, looking right into his face as he helped her up off the ground and fetched her cane from where it had fallen.

It was hard to believe she was blind when you looked into those wide, melted chocolate eyes. Sam's eyes seemed to see everything, more than the average person's. Hers were eyes that looked all the way to a man's core and took his measure. When it came to Jace, he could tell she'd never entirely approved of what she saw.

He could understand the feeling. It was one of the reasons he avoided mirrors.

"I'll walk you back to your place."

"I'm not going back to my place." She twisted her arm, pulling free from his grip on her hand.

"Oh, yes, you are." He reached for her, but she sidestepped him, almost as if she could see him coming.

"No, I'm not." Up came her chin as she half jogged toward the street, cane tapping quickly in front of her. "I have an errand to run."

"I don't give a shit if you've got an—"

"I have an appointment!" She tried to twist away from him

again, but this time Jace held firm. Still, even though he had at least six inches and fifty pounds on the woman, Sam wasn't easy to hold on to.

"You can reschedule. I don't want to see you anywhere near this area again."

"What?"

"You heard me. Stay clear of the streets near the ruins. Call Stephen to come get you, or call a car service if you need to—"

"Where do you get off?" she asked, stepping closer until he could smell the light floral scent that clung to her hair. "You're not my father or my brother or my boyfriend. Hell, I wouldn't have even said we were friends, would you?"

Jace stared down into those eerie eyes of hers, not knowing what to say, only knowing that the outraged look on Sam's face made him want to show her exactly where he "got off." And how he'd get *her* off, again and again, until she came so hard, she screamed his name and clung to him, those strong, smooth legs wrapped around his hips as—

"Would you?"

Would he what? He couldn't seem to remember the question. His thoughts were too shocking, too *wrong*.

"Honestly, I'm curious. Would you say we're friends? Is that why you feel entitled to order me around like a child? Or is it because of my brother?" she asked. "Since he's your friend, it gives you the right to play big brother when he's not around?"

She stepped even closer, her chocolate-and-coffee breath warm on his chin. If he tilted his head just the slightest bit, they'd be close enough for him to taste her. And, fuck, did he want to taste her. Bad enough that he forced himself to take a small step back, putting a safer distance between them.

"I'm old enough to take care of myself, Jace. And to know what I want."

"And what is that?" he asked, the feeling that he was crossing some forbidden line making his heart beat faster than it had in years. Demon hunting was dangerous, but not as dangerous as Samantha Quinn. And it wasn't the fact that her brother would try to kill him for touching his sister—it was Sam herself. He'd had no idea she was so . . . irresistible.

"I think it might be you," she said, standing on tiptoe, bringing her lips closer to his.

"You think. You don't know?"

"Not yet, but I will." And then she kissed him. *She* kissed *him*. He let a woman make the first move for the first time in years, and it felt inexplicably right. Everything about Sam felt right—her ass in his hands, her fingers digging into the back of his neck, her mouth hot against his, her moan as he slid his tongue between her lips, tasting the unique flavor of this woman who had totally blindsided him.

Blindsided by a blind girl.

It should have been an amusing thought, but Jace didn't feel like laughing. This wasn't funny. This was a mistake, a huge mistake. But that didn't stop him from spinning Sam in his arms and pressing her up against the wall. It didn't slow his hands as he grabbed her behind the knees and spread her legs, hitching her up around his waist. It only made him feel like the very bad man he truly was. The last kind of man Sam should even think about getting involved with.

If he were a better person, he would have cared enough to stop. But he wasn't. So he didn't. He just kissed her harder, and let his fingers trail up the silky smooth skin of her inner thigh.